To B

THE BEFANA DRAMA 2

THE BEFANA DRAMA 2

CAPRICCIA'S CONUNDRUM

BY

GIANNA HARTWRIGHT

Published by: Gianna Della Luna Publishing.

Cover Design by Damonza
Interior Design by awseomebooklayout.com

Dedication

For all the children, parents and teachers who inspired and supported me during my Befana Drama Giro-Rama tour of the UK in autumn 2013 and gave me such fabulous and uplifting feedback to use for Befana Drama 2, for my son, my family and friends, all my sources of inspiration and Gemma Goodman.

Chapter One

A juicy, globular spider tentatively stretched out its long, spindly legs and inched slowly across the shiny mahogany counter of the dimly lit café, in which pewter tankards hanging from the darkest of dark Germanic walls provided the only source of reflected light. A blonde stick insect of a woman spotted the eight-legged arachnid through her ridiculously long false skylashes, which almost resembled spiders themselves. She angrily slammed a glass down on top of it, trapping it inside, before shoving her face right up against the drinking vessel, watching her prisoner sit paralysed with fear as her squashed nose filled most of its field of vision.

Having observed the spider for a few minutes, she lifted the trap and let it go free. It scuttled for its life down the side of the counter and on to the newly mopped floor. With a swift movement, she whipped off a bright turquoise and yellow shoe with neatly tied black liquorice laces and slammed it down on top of the spider, splattering it across the floorboards.

'Ze trouble is, zat there are always two of zem,'

said a creepy voice that seemed to ooze out of the wooden walls. The blonde woman jumped with fright, observing nobody within the empty café. She peered gingerly over the counter, wondering where on earth the spooky voice with the strong German accent had originated and saw a mass of tangerine, brown and black streaked hair standing upright like a toilet brush.

'What are you talking about?' she snapped, as an asparagus green face and body emerged from the wood into which they had been blending perfectly naturally.

'Spiders,' he answered. 'There vill be another von somewhere, mark my words.'

'Couldn't care a hoot,' retorted the woman. 'I'll kill another just as quickly. What do you want to drink?'

'I am not here for a drink,' replied the strange little man. 'I am here to advise you of things most worrying. Things zat you vill not wish to hear.'

The stick insect opened her mouth extraordinarily wide and yawned, without putting her hand over her gaping mouth.

'Try me,' she said. 'I very much doubt there's anything you have to say that I want to hear.' She stopped yawning and observed the little man more closely. 'Who are you?' she asked, thinking how odd he looked and noticing for the first time that he was wearing red and white striped pyjama bottoms.

'My name is Bernhardt Bürstenfrisür,' he

replied, 'but you probably know me better as 'The Most Fearsome Feller in Folklore', which is feller as in tree feller, by ze way!'

'Never heard of you,' said the woman rather rudely.

'Zen it is a good thing zat I have heard of you,' barked the little man angrily. 'I know zat you are Capriccia Claus, formerly ze unofficial queen of Santa's village before you were despatched in a parcel for Hamburg by zat woman who now calls herself 'Bef', but who was formerly ze wrinkled and wart-ridden Befana.'

The blonde woman blushed bright red, the little man's comments having struck home, causing her a fair degree of embarrassment. She could still recall the ghastly way in which the clinging bubble wrap and sharp brown paper had wrapped tightly around her body before she'd been catapulted down the chute and roughly loaded into a sleigh. How humiliating. How disgraceful.

'Clever you,' she snapped in a highly distressed manner now. 'Why do you care about my bad fortune anyway?'

'Because I too have been a victim of zat Bef woman's tricks,' said Bernhardt, lying rather a lot, as it had been he who had tried to keep Bef prisoner when she had asked for broom enhancements from the best broom artisan in the world, whilst attempting to stop Santa taking over her Very Important Present Bringer (VIPB) patch. What annoyed him still was that he himself had not yet acquired the title of VIPB, which he longed for more than anything else. In his contorted view of events, Bef was to blame for this, even though he had discovered that it was actually Natalia Lebedev, the VIPB controlling the upper end of the Volga river, who had voted against his application.

'Thanks to that dreadful Bef woman, I got pushed out of my home,' said Capriccia angrily. 'I had to leave Capriccia Claus's Casa of Contentments, my beautiful, five-storey bright fuchsia pink apartment block right in the middle of Santa's village. I had the distress of having to abandon the longest dressing table in the world, my floor of stupendous hair pretensions and other accessories, my collection of wonderful clothes bought from the best fashion houses from around the globe, my shiny, glistening jewellery and, above all, my stunning shoe collection.' She began to sob like a baby, before stamping her feet like an angry toddler.

'I only have two pairs of skylashes to my name and just one set of Northern Highlights these days,' she continued. 'It's a crime – a huge crime that deserves a massive punishment.'

Bernhardt observed the scene, thinking to himself that he had heard that the Casa of Contentments was totally lacking in taste and full of garish, trashy nonsense, but he didn't dare contradict Capriccia, especially as she now seemed to be on his wavelength and actually listening to him!

'Vell, let me tell you,' said Bernhardt, making the most of the moment. 'Your outstanding shoe collection is being eaten away by ze moths and is getting very dusty. I have heard zat Santa's elves will be throwing all ze shoes away very soon and zat zay vill only keep ze best ones and give zem to a charity shop'.

'A charity shop!' raged Capriccia. 'A charity shop! The indignity of it!'

Bernhardt grinned. He was managing to get just the reaction he'd desired.

'Yes,' he continued. Then lying once again, he added, 'And Santa vill ask ze Bef woman to choose which shoes to send there.' He grinned to himself as he watched Capriccia turn purple in the face and screw up her nose until it resembled a walnut.

'What!' she shrieked at a pitch that sent half the dogs in the district wild. 'She hasn't got a clue about shoes! She wears those big floppy monstrosities that slap and flap and flap and slap when she walks along the pavements!'

'Do not shoot ze messenger!' said Bernhardt, smirking uncontrollably. His plan was working a treat!

Capriccia was now stomping up and down the café, building up the energy to perform one of her most notable tricks – whizzing like an out-of-control spinning top. Suddenly, she started to spin and spin and spin, before coming to an abrupt halt in front of Bernhardt and shouting, 'Pour me some bilberry juice now!' Bernhardt scurried behind the counter and did as she asked. She picked up the glass and downed the juice in one gulp.

'What's your plan?' she yelled.

Bernhardt jumped up on a bar stool to make himself bigger than his three-feet-something height minus hair. Feeling very important now, he puffed out his chest and declared.

'You are my plan, my dear lady. Revenge is also ze plan. Put ze two together and we vill have a vinning formula!'

Capriccia flicked her skylashes and looked herself up and down.

'How can I possibly attempt revenge. Look at me. I'm a scruffy waitress in a German café with no money, one pair of tatty shoes to my name and no talents of which to speak.'

Bernhardt looked at her rather sternly.

'Have you forgotten how you tricked Santa into marrying you by putting a love potion in a slice of cake that ze elves came to fetch from your patisserie in Pavlovagrad? Zat was genius. Genius it was. Do you think ze famous Bernhardt Bürstenfrisür would waste his time coming to see you, if he thought you were of no use?'

'Maybe not,' answered Capriccia, suddenly feeling quite important. 'But I am powerless against that woman's magic.'

'She's actually not zat great at magic,' replied Bernhardt rather smugly. 'Her spells are often, how do you say, wonky. She's good at spells zat involve going up and down chimneys, but not much else. Zis is all she needs when delivering presents. You vill be much better than her by ze time we have finished with you. You too, could become a VIPB once you are fully trained.'

Capriccia stood there and stretched her spine to make herself even taller than she already was. Her mouth was slightly open and, because she wasn't all that bright, she needed a few minutes to take in what Bernhardt was saying. Finally, her brain and mouth linked up.

'Who is the 'we' in that sentence?'

'Another enemy of ze Bef woman,' answered Bernhardt. 'An enemy since ze 15th century, when she was ze head of ze Florence branch of ze fairies. A fairy most foul and fabulous at ze same time. A fairy called Fiorentina by birth, but known as Fiery Tina by all who know her and her tempestuous ways!'

'Never heard of her,' said Capriccia, throwing her head back and tossing her blonde locks around.

'Yes, but you said you have never heard of me either,' replied Bernhardt. 'In zis sense, your knowledge is sadly lacking. You may not know Fiery Tina now, but you very soon vill. My broomstick is ready to take you to her very impressive castle in ze hills around Florence in Italy. She will teach you all you need to know about magic and turn you into a wonder with ze wand and … and … vell, I don't exactly know what else, but it vill be ze best training you could ever have. Meanwhile, I vill craft a marvellous broom: a broom with wicked features indeed … a broom zat vill take centre stage and be ze instrument with which we shall humiliate ze Bef woman and pay her back for her impudence!'

Capriccia looked at her one pair of grubby shoes, her stained dress and her total lack of fine jewellery and thought about all the treasured items in her fabulous Casa of Contentments. She reflected on what had been a very bumpy and bruising ride down the parcel chute and into the sleigh, after Bef had used her broom to blast her away. She could almost feel herself suffocating with bubble wrap as she thought about that terrible day when the Bef woman had sent her packing from Lapland.

'Take me to Fiery Tina NOW!' she yelled. 'I'm ready to teach that brute of a Bef woman a big lesson. How dare someone like her attempt to go into battle with Capriccia Claus.' She lifted one foot and slapped it on to the wooden floor, having seen the second spider emerge from a crack in the boards. She missed.

'Hopefully, you vill be better at magic than at spider squashing,' said Bernhardt. 'Now come come, time is of ze essence. Von thing I have not told you is zat ze Bef woman is opening her very own theme park soon. Zat is something neither of us should ever see happen and Fiery Tina agrees. It is essential zat we ruin her plans and put her in her place once and for all. Ze woman is becoming a superstar and zat cannot be tolerated. Tolerated it cannot be! '

He looked at Capriccia's face and knew he didn't have to ask her how she felt. Her Northern Highlights had turned bright green and her cheeks as red as a tomato. She was as jealous as a jealous woman could be and he knew she would throw everything she had into her magic lessons with Fiery Tina, even if she was rather lacking in the brain cell department. By working with these two wicked women, he would achieve his objective of becoming a VIPB once and for all. His plan was coming together beautifully. He danced a little jig and stared at the floor, hoping to find the spider and finish it off. Disappointingly, it was nowhere to be seen.

Chapter Two

Only a very narrow, cobbled street separated the medieval room from the impressive castle opposite – one reason why the room often seemed dreary and dark. Luigi Passarella's eyes struggled to focus on the map in front of him, so he removed his expensive gold-rimmed spectacles and carefully wiped the lenses with a pristine white handkerchief that he pulled out of his smart jacket pocket.

He half waited for dust to scatter across the floor, but then reminded himself that the plague of dust that had descended on his village had only existed in the bad days – the days when Bef had left the village, believing she was no longer wanted, and all the brooms had followed her. That had all been down to that idiot of a mayor that they had been forced to suffer back then. A man who had believed Bef had no popularity. A fool who had fallen for Capriccia Claus fluttering her skylashes at him and convincing him that Santa should take over!

Mr Passarella rubbed his spectacles again and tried to focus on the map, but his thoughts began to wander. Thank goodness he had taken it upon himself to visit the descendants of the Three Wise Men – a Dubai-based boy band called 'The Three Kings' – to try to resolve the nightmare of the dust. He had begged Gaspar, Mel and Thaz to help him find Bef and bring her home and, luckily, they did just that. The dust that had made life unbearable for men, women and children disappeared as fast as it had arrived on top of their cappuccinos once Bef returned and happy times were once again enjoyed by all.

Even better, the boys had agreed to perform at Bef's annual festival and the village had been absolutely packed to the rafters with visitors. All wanted to see both 'The Three Kings' in concert and the village's magnificent celebrations, which included men dressed as Bef descending from the ancient village buildings on ropes and wires, not to mention the world's biggest shoe, based on Bef's own massive floppy footwear, and lots of huge, colourful knitted socks hung from the medieval windows! Bef had never been so popular and he had never been so important. Naturally, after his inspired actions, the town had made him the new mayor.

His thoughts were interrupted by the sound of feet clonking up the ancient wooden stairs to his office.

'Come, come, Luigi, we haven't time to slump back in our chairs like that,' said Bef bossily, as she entered the room. 'We've a theme park to open and it won't open itself!'

Luigi sighed to himself. Much as he loved Bef, she was such an impatient witch. He stared back at the map and suddenly, as if light had descended in the room, he could see the layout of the various zones, rides and eateries that would make up Befland.

'Is that better?' asked Bef. 'I just muttered the Luce Spell, as it seemed terribly dark in here. We need to throw some light on what you are up to, after all!'

Mr Passarella had to admit that the new illumination in the room made things much easier. He straightened his back, adjusted his spectacles so they hung on the very end of his nose and began to speak as if he were the world's leading expert on theme parks!

'Bef, my dear,' he said in a very gentle tone, 'we are really well on with our plans for the park. The Candy Carousel is now fully built, as is Aniseed Alley and the Mint Ball Octopus. I have now ordered thirty Bonbon Bumper Cars and the Flying Sorcerers ride is very nearly finished. The Whirly Ball Waltzer just needs a second lick of paint and then we can progress with the Cherries Wheel, which is next door to it on the park plans. That will just leave …' He didn't get to finish the sentence, as Bef interrupted him.

'I know, I know,' she stated. 'It leaves the Candymonium feature, the Astoundabout, the Chimney Chaser and the Big Slipper. But above all, we must not forget the importance of the star ride at the park! Given my adventures in recent times, we must make sure that the Coaler Coaster is the number one feature of Befland and a ride that is talked about all over the world. It must have passenger cabs positioned between cabs of coal, so that kids have to duck and dive out of the way of flying pieces of black, messy 'carbone'. What a hoot that will be! I then want a life-size replica of Natalia Lebedev to shoot down in front of passengers halfway through their ride and scare them witless, just as she did in the coal mine in Russia. Let's hope all the families are equally taken aback! Finally, perhaps we should try to bring in that little nincompoop Bernhardt Bürstenfrisür somewhere.'

Mr Passarella looked dubious.

'We do have to remember health and safety regulations,' he said in a most serious tone, knowing that only this would stop Bef in her tracks, at least for thirty seconds. 'I am also not sure that we should replicate another VIPB – and a very angry one at that – so closely. I think we must tread carefully with this ride. We most definitely can't include that very nasty Bernhardt chap.'

'Poppycock,' shouted Bef. 'Natalia would love being made more famous than she is – and let's face it, she's not very famous at all given that she only has a very small VIPB patch at the top end of that Russian river, the name of which I forget. As for Bernhardt, it's the only bit of fame the little terror is ever likely to get! That man will never be a VIPB, so to be included in this ride should be a big honour for him. But then, thinking about it, maybe his toilet-brush hair would make children cry and we don't want that do we!'

As she spoke, a strange glint could be seen through the window. It caught her eye for a millisecond, but she thought nothing of it. It was probably just sun reflecting off a mirror in the magnificent palace opposite.

Mr Passarella sighed ever so softly. At least he'd won the point over Bernhardt, if not Natalia. Undoubtedly, the Coaler Coaster would be the coolest and most spectacular ride the world had ever seen, with all sorts of magical twists and turns added in by Bef and it would definitely cause a stir, though he was desperate to make Bef see that fake coal would be far preferable to the real variety. Parents would not want to be taking home messy, dirty children, or suffer a bump on the head caused by a piece of flying coal! Bef had sworn that her magical spells would prevent them from actually getting hit, but with so many of her spells going a little bit wonky, who knew? This preoccupied Mr Passarella for a good few minutes, as Bef rambled on.

'How's the Bef doll coming along?' she suddenly asked inquisitively. 'I just can't wait to see it! That photographer took six hours trying to get my good side, so I hope it was worth it!'

'It is in the hands of Jeremiah,' answered Mr Passarella. 'I couldn't tell you where he's up to.'

At that, Bef swung her head back 45 degrees, looked up at the room's fancy ceiling and yelled, 'Jer-e-mi-ah. Jer-e-mi-ah. Jer-e-mi-ah Needlebaum. Come here please!'

The room shook as her voice rattled around it, but faint footsteps could be heard on the ancient wooden stairs as Jeremiah made his way down from the attic and tiptoed into the room. He was wringing his hands in a most humble and apologetic way, although he had done nothing wrong. He suddenly realised this and bounded forward with a huge leap, like an over-enthusiastic kangaroo, just about managing not to dislodge any of the fifty cotton reels in his fancy chicken wire hat.

'Jeremiah Needlebaum is at your service,' he declared proudly. 'How may I assist you my dear lady?'

Bef could only smile to herself. Jeremiah was simply the sweetest person she knew, always quick to make her a cup of acorn tea without prompting and so skilled as a tailor to the VIPB world. After her last adventure, she had rescued him from a lonely life in his Siberian prison cell and convinced him that it was time he enjoyed some human company again. After all, talking to Arctic Foxes all day was all very well, but they couldn't play dominoes with the set Jeremiah had knitted!

Jeremiah had been a little sad to leave the home

that he'd made so beautiful with his knitted and sewn furnishings, but had to agree that it could be a terribly empty life living in the snows of Siberia on one's own.

So Jeremiah had quickly answered the call when Bef had said that she needed someone to design glamorous outfits for the grand opening of her theme park and also a beautiful costume for the brand new Bef doll. This was what Jeremiah was working on right now and very exciting it was too. He could hardly contain his excitement as he stood in front of Bef.

'I think you want to know, don't you?' said Jeremiah. 'Want to know, I think you do and so you shall, because there have been BIG developments overnight. My head hit the pillow and thoughts began to ping around my head like elastic bands. A shimmering gold frock with a fabulous bronze band around the hem and voluminous, bronze sleeves came to mind. It shall be finished with thousands of shimmering sequins and a hood trimmed with stitched snowflakes.'

'How on earth can you stitch snowflakes?' asked Bef.

'It's a skill I perfected in Siberia,' replied Jeremiah. 'It's quite an art and I can't reveal the trade secrets behind it.' He chuckled to himself loudly – another trait of his that always amused Bef. He was lost for a good three minutes in his own little world before saying, 'So what do you think then?'

'Is this for the doll, or for my theme park opening outfit?' enquired Bef.

'Both,' answered Jeremiah. 'Once the crowds have seen you flying above like a golden angel, they will all wish to buy the doll.'

'Favoloso,' shrieked Bef. 'You are a wizard!'

'No, technically, I am half elf, quarter gnome, one eighth Kelpie and one eighth giant dwarf,' said Jeremiah, 'so I don't wish to annoy any wizards by claiming to be what I am not.'

Bef tittered again, wondering how on earth anyone could be a giant dwarf and Mr Passarella thanked the moon and the stars for sending Jeremiah into her life to keep her in such a good mood.

At that moment the door was flung open and in burst Gaspar.

'And how are you my dear boy?' asked Bef, glad to see it was her very favourite of 'The Three Kings' visiting on this occasion … the one with whom she had shared so many adventures when seeking to protect her VIPB patch.

'Really well,' said Gaspar. 'We've just written a brand new song for the opening ceremony and it's awesome.'

'Is that good and does it have a name?' asked Bef, a little non-plussed by his modern terms.

'It's truly cool and called 'The Befland Beat',' explained Gaspar. 'It's a sort of anthem that kids and parents can both adopt and sing along to. It's got a great chorus that will get the place bouncing.'

'Oh, goodness gracious, we don't want that,' said Bef. 'The medieval buildings might collapse!'

'No, I didn't mean like that,' laughed Gaspar. 'I just meant it would be full of atmosphere.'

'Well of course it will,' said Bef. 'Atmosphere is everywhere.'

Gaspar shook his head and was about to try to explain further what he meant, but Mr Passarella had shifted his gold-rimmed spectacles an inch up his nose, which was his signal to Gaspar to give up and change the subject.

'We're also writing a big number for the finale,' explained Gaspar. 'It will be really show-stopping, gob-smackingly good and dynamite.'

Bef looked puzzled, wondering where this 'number' was going to be written and whether it would have more than six noughts in it. She didn't like to say anything, but did hope Gaspar wasn't going to blow up her lovely village with his sticks of dynamite. Maybe they would only be for show.

She looked around the room. Jeremiah was pretending to measure out material, waving his arms around dramatically. Gaspar was strumming his guitar. Mr Passarella was pouring over the plans for Befland and measuring distances between rides with a ruler. All was just perfect.

A glint hit the room again, but she ignored it completely and did not see that, across the narrow street, a green-faced little man with hair like a toilet brush was watching what was going on through a pair of binoculars and had instruments in his ears that were allowing him to pick up on conversations in her room, listening through the wood intently, as only the best broom artisan in the world could.

'So, I vill never be a VIPB vill I not!' he muttered under his very bad breath. 'We think we vill have a grand finale zat vill thrill ze vorld do we? Vell we vill attract ze attention of ze world, I can tell you, but for all ze wrong reasons. I vill make you a laughing stock in your own Befland and I promise you sincerely, oh yes, I promise you with all my venom, that it vill truly be dynamite! Dynamite it vill vell and truly be!'

With that, he pulled a thick, velvet curtain across the window and began to run his fingers through his toilet brush hair in an insane manner, thinking to himself of all the terrible tricks he could stage and all the nasty stunts he could pull to get revenge on the Bef woman.

CHAPTER THREE

Capriccia kicked out her long stick insect legs hard and made the rope swing fly a little higher off the ground. The weather was unbearably hot and sticky and the higher she rose, the cooler she became and the more she could look down on the red rooftops of the Italian city of Florence as the rays of the sun beat down upon her trailing blonde locks.

A short distance in front of her, a tall, skinny woman jumped around erratically, causing the long auburn hair, piled high on her head in a most messy fashion, to become even more unkempt. She was dressed in a black tutu and wore jet-black ballerina shoes with charcoal-coloured butterfly wings that shimmered constantly as the incredible Italian light hit the hundreds of tiny diamonds sewn into them. On closer inspection, she was seen to be leaping between different numbered squares chalked upon the ground, as she pursued her favourite pastime of all – playing hopscotch!

Capriccia yawned as she watched the fairy's antics, finding no fascination in this silly game, but her hostess, in whose fairy playground she found herself, seemed to find it truly addictive.

'Woe is me!' shrieked Fiery Tina. 'I've just landed on a line and then I wobbled and fell into the wong square. I'm sure the Wo-man soldiers never did that while playing this game. Why do I keep doing it?'

Capriccia sighed. She was finding Fiery Tina's inability to pronounce her letter r properly very irritating, or iwwitating, as Fiery Tina would say. Every r became a w and Capriccia was particularly infuriated at being called Capwiccia a hundred or more times a day! The woman clearly had no balance, either physical or mental, and that was why she couldn't play her childish game.

Fiery Tina glared at her.

'I can infiltwate your thoughts you know,' she said, again pronouncing a w in the place of what should have been an r. She hopped around again and suddenly burst into giggles and started to clap, praising herself for not having wobbled or landed on a line for once.

Bernhardt had transported Capriccia here on his broom and promptly left her with a quick wave of his little green hand, so that Fiery Tina could train her in magic. Unfortunately, every day started like this, with Fiery Tina spending at least two hours each morning playing hopscotch.

The trouble was that Fiery Tina actually found the game very difficult, as her head was slightly set at an angle to her neck, all thanks to one of her selfie spells that had once gone very wrong indeed. She was supposed to be an expert at statuefication, but having turned herself into a statue back in the 1600s, the second half of the selfie spell failed. Instead of being returned to her normal state, she found her head now permanently tilted at 30 degrees from the vertical, which was the pose she had adopted as a statue. This meant that she saw everything slightly askew and it led to her having to squint at an awful lot of people.

For centuries and centuries, Fiery Tina (Fiorentina by birth and her name until her reputation for having a foul temper had spread) had longed to be a VIPB, but had found herself living in a country in which the whole VIPB patch was controlled by Bef – the woman formerly known as The Befana. Back in 1412 she had tried to break away and set up her own VIPB patch around Florence, attempting to cast a spell that prevented The Befana from getting down chimneys. This hadn't worked at all well and Bef had got wind of it and stormed into Florence firing pieces of coal from her broomstick, hitting Fiery Tina square in the face with one torrent of coal and knocking her out.

While Fiery Tina was unconscious, Bef undid the spell and managed to deliver her gifts as normal, reminding all the fairies in the Florence branch, who were under Fiery Tina's control as their head fairy, that rebellion was not an option and she and only she was the VIPB in Italy. When Fiery Tina awoke, she found that her plan had failed and she was to be punished by the chief of the VIPB world – a person of unknown name, but of terrifying reputation. This unknown person's instructions were spelled out in the clouds and Fiery Tina's punishment, once revealed in the skies above Florence, was to become an unpaid servant for three years, running up and down stairs all day and fetching and carrying for various ungrateful lords and barons.

But worse than this, when she had regained consciousness following the coal attack, she found her lovely white tutu had been permanently stained black and also ripped by an alley cat that had found her asleep in the street. She had never got over this horrific incident and blamed Bef for it all. In the end, she had stopped trying to get the stubborn stains out of her dress and decided to make a new black tutu, which suited her personality as a very nasty, full-of-hatred fairy, who could never forgive an enemy, no matter how many hundreds of years skipped by.

Fiery Tina walked over to Capriccia with very jerky movements.

'Today,' she said decisively, 'I will teach you the art of statuefication.'

Capriccia shuddered a little. She hoped this wouldn't involve any selfie spells, as she did not want her head to be permanently tilted at an angle from her neck like Fiery Tina's. What an embarrassment that would be!

'I cweated most of the statues here in the city,' boasted Fiery Tina. 'People claim that Michelangelo sculpted the statue of David, but that is absolute woobarb! I did it! The man wasn't called David at all, but Paolo and he'd messed up my hopscotch pitch by dwipping water all over it after a morning swim, so I turned him into a statue to pay him back. He'd got no clothes on at the time, so it was SO funny!' With that, she burst into giggles. 'Oops,' I said to him, 'don't mess with anyone's hopscotch game again and put some clothes on young man! The thing was, he couldn't do that, as I'd turned him into a statue. How funny. How very hilarious it all was!'

Fiery Tina continued to giggle hysterically for a good five minutes, as Capriccia sat and waited for her to calm down. When she had stopped waving her legs around uncontrollably, Fiery Tina composed herself and jumped on to a pink stepping stone within her fairy playground, making herself even taller than she already was. With her neck askew, she tried to look Capriccia in the eye.

'Wight,' she said firmly. 'Here we go!' She reached into her tutu and fetched out a miniscule wand, which suddenly grew and grew. She waved it around her head in three big loops and a huge, well-thumbed book suddenly appeared out of thin air, floating around in front of Capriccia's dumbstruck face. It was entitled, 'A Beginner's Guide To Statuefication', by Fiery Tina. As Fiery Tina moved her wand, the pages turned over automatically, leaving Capriccia completely mesmerised.

'Oops,' shrieked Tina as she moved the pages on too far, to a chapter entitled 'How To Maintain the Statues Quo.' 'We must start at the very beginning,' she insisted as she furiously turned the pages back. 'Now concentwate Capwiccia, because we're off!'

Capriccia's eyes followed the seemingly endless pages as Fiery Tina thrust a silver wand into her hand and began to demonstrate various ridiculous and over-the-top poses that had to be adopted before statuefication spells could work. Very dramatically, Fiery Tina acted out every spell and stage of each spell, even going back and back over every move at least fifty times, to try to get it lodged in Capriccia's head.

Capriccia's silly little brain soon began to hurt rather a lot, studying not being her strong point. She had left school at the tender age of fourteen, to work in a patisserie in Pavlovagrad and had very little intelligence or common sense. She kept rubbing her eyes very hard as pages turned in front of her and yet more instructions appeared. Every so often, Fiery Tina, would point out a fat frog or a lounging lizard in the garden and demand that Capriccia try a statuefication spell. They all failed miserably and the creature just hopped or slithered away. Every single time, Fiery Tina shouted, 'Oops ... that one didn't work, did it!' which annoyed Capriccia intensely, as it made her feel even more stupid than she already knew that she was.

And so the day – and the many days beyond – featured Capriccia's feeble attempts at statuefication, as Fiery Tina enjoyed her incessant games of hopscotch and sang 'That Old Black Magic' in a truly crazy manner at the top of her fairy voice – something that she claimed kept the rest of her former fairy ring away. She said that this was absolutely essential, as she did not want any challenges to her fairy powers. Capriccia couldn't help thinking, however, that it could be that all the other fairies were better at hopscotch – something she was certain that Fiery Tina could not have taken with good grace.

Then, one day – 33.3 days after arriving at Fiery Tina's fairy camp – something clicked. Capriccia had waved her new wand in a completely new fashion, with more purpose and better movement, resulting in an innocent passing butterfly being turned into a statue, which suddenly sprung up next to Fiery Tina's ornate garden fountain.

'Goodness me, I've managed it,' said Capriccia triumphantly, as she viewed the arrival of the new statue in the garden with massive pride.

'It's actually we-ally beautiful,' replied Fiery Tina, suddenly stopping her latest game of hopscotch to come and inspect the new statue structure. She poked it with a finger and prodded it all over, to check that each part of the butterfly was now turned to stone. All sections of the statue passed the test, leading to Fiery Tina declaring, '10 out of 10, Capwiccia! How clever of you to use statuefication on a flying cweature, which is much harder than a fwog or lizard. You must have studied hard in the last few days and I suppose it's a case of better late than never, although I would have expected statuefication lessons to end some time ago.'

Capriccia rolled her eyes, partly because her name had again been pronounced wrongly, but also because she was thinking that there had been precious little tuition. She had largely been left to teach herself, with the use of text books suspended in the air in front of her, while Fiery Tina had carried on playing and landing in the wrong square and shouting 'Oops' each time she did so.

'I know what you're thinking,' snapped her irritating magic teacher, 'but, believe me, there was no more I could do to help you once I'd taught you the basics. It's pwactice that makes perfect with this one and you were just exceptionally slow – slower than a slug, in fact! As you seem to think I've not taught you very much, we shall now move on at pace, if you can keep up and not be left behind. I am the best fairy that ever lived when it comes to another bwanch of magic and spell casting,' she declared pompously. 'I shall teach you all about this area and you can then combine it with statuefication as you get your we-venge on the Bef woman.'

Capriccia arched her back, with Fiery Tina having hit a nerve by implying that she wasn't very intelligent.

'So what is this marvellous new skill that will help me get revenge?' she asked with a touch of sarcasm in her voice.

'Conundwums,' answered Fiery Tina. 'How I love conundwums ... such powerful magic can be cast with a good conundwum at its heart.'

'Do you mean conundrums?' asked Capriccia, wanting to get to the bottom of what she was expected to do next.

'That's what I said, isn't it,' barked Fiery Tina, annoyed that Capriccia had drawn attention to her inability to pronounce the letter r.

Capriccia didn't want to argue with the bad-tempered fairy, who was now stomping around and looking increasingly flushed in the cheeks, as if she was about to erupt like a volcano at any moment.

'Conundwums will be our main focus fwom now on,' stated Fiery Tina very firmly and with a hint of anger in her voice. 'I hope you love a good widdle, Capwiccia, because they can be your best friends at times.'

'Surely you mean riddle,' answered Capriccia, looking Fiery Tina in the eye and realising that she had again offended her rather moody hostess. 'If so, I can assure you that I love riddles,' she said, backtracking as fast she could to try to prevent further annoyance. 'Yes, indeed, riddles make my day,' she added, trying to do all she could to stop Fiery Tina's stony glare, as she had a strong sense that she herself might be turned into a statue at any moment. As it so happened, she wouldn't have minded having a Capriccia statue, but only one erected in her honour and given pride of place in Lapland, not one made from her own body and stuck permanently in Fiery Tina's front garden!

Fiery Tina wasn't listening. She was singing, 'That old black magic's got me in its spell: that old black magic that you weave so well,' whilst re-chalking hopscotch figures on the floor.

Capriccia could only speculate that Bernhardt had left her here with a real fruitcake, who was undoubtedly one fairy wing short of a full set! How she longed to get all her spells and magic challenges right, so that she would never have to listen to another 'Oops' from Fiery Tina's pert little mouth again! How she longed to move on, to start work on a wicked plan of revenge that would allow her to regain control of her precious Casa of Contentments. The thought of vile moths eating her beloved shoe collection was keeping her awake every single night and no woman could have wanted revenge any more than she did. When she regained control of the Casa, she would turn each and every moth into a statue ... in fact, maybe it was that thought that had made her statuefication spell suddenly work, as a poor, unfortunate butterfly had fluttered by at just the wrong time and become her very first victim.

CHAPTER FOUR

The odd-looking man with the long pointed elf ears flagged down the slightly battered car that had appeared round a bend in the road. The car squealed to a halt just after passing him and the elf-eared man sidled up to it.

'Where do you want to go?' asked the moustached driver.

'To the place where Befland is being built,' answered the hitch-hiker in a most matter of fact way. 'I am a stranger to Italy. I have no idea which direction to take. Could you possibly be so kind as to take me at least part of the way?'

The driver looked at the man and thought how strange he seemed. The length of his ears was not the only unusual thing about him. He was also wearing bright red trousers and a very thick navy jumper with the number 81 knitted into the pattern across the front in big, bold white numbers. He carried a little rucksack and had what the driver could only describe as sly eyes.

'What's your name?' asked the driver.

'81st,' replied the hitch-hiker.

The owner of the car was Italian and didn't quite understand that his would-be passenger had given him a very unusual name indeed. He gestured to the man to jump in.

'Do you know where the Befland park is?' asked the rather eccentric passenger. 'I've been walking right across Europe, so I hope I'm close now. It's far too warm for me here, so the sooner I reach Befland the better.'

The driver raised his eyebrows and wondered why the man was wearing such a thick jumper if he was so hot.

'Sì,' replied the driver. 'It will be a fabulous place, full of fantastic rides and amusements and a star attraction called the Coaler Coaster, if gossip is to be believed. But why do you want to go there now? It's not open yet!'

The man with the sly eyes was thinking to himself, 'No, and I hope it never will be,' but kept schtum. Some things were better left unspoken.

'I know The Befana,' he explained. 'We met a few months ago and there's something I need to return to her.' He went paler in the cheeks, but the driver didn't know that this happened when his particular type of elf told a lie.

'You mean Bef,' said the driver. 'We don't call her The Befana any more. She doesn't like it and we don't wish to upset her.'

The 81st elf stared out of the window thinking how very peculiar this was. What could have possessed her to re-name herself Bef? He thought she was proud of being The Befana. Why would she change her name?

As if reading his thoughts, the driver spoke.

'She says she thinks Bef is a cooler name that will appeal to more children. I think she's right judging by how popular our little town has become, especially after last year's festival. It was magnificent!'

The 81st elf scowled. He was casting his mind back to his encounter with the Bef woman in Lapland. She'd got the better of him then and had forced his darling Capriccia Claus out of her amazing pink palace. Some had said he was the only person in Lapland who had liked Capriccia and had told him to open his eyes, as she had cared nothing for him, but he hadn't listened. He had tried to protect her possessions in the Casa, but even he couldn't keep the moths out of her clothing collection, or away from her precious shoes and the infernal dust just kept falling incessantly upon her perfume bottles until he had no energy to keep on dusting. There was no way he could prevent the jewellery turning black and tarnished through lack of cleaning and care. He had to find Capriccia and communicate all of this to her, but he just couldn't find her.

The 81st elf had managed to get himself as far as Hamburg, by stowing away on board a small plane that was heading there from Lapland. But to his great disappointment, he had arrived too late.

People remembered the tall blonde woman who had served in the bar, but hadn't got a clue where she had gone. She had just vanished overnight and left no address or trail behind her. But he had scoured the room for hours and eventually found a screwed up piece of paper with the word 'Befland' written on it. It was wedged into a gap in the floor-boards, right next to a squashed spider. It was too much of a coincidence and this was what had led him to travel to this Befland place. He just prayed that he would find Capriccia. She would have one of the hissy fits that he found so amusing once she knew what was happening in her stupendous Casa of Contentments.

'Befland is just over the hills that way,' said the man, gesturing to the left. 'Where do you wish me to take you? Into the village? To a hotel?'

The 81st elf was actually planning to sleep in a hedgerow, as he had done halfway across Europe, but didn't want to tell the man this.

'Yes, if you just take me to the village, I will sort myself out from there.'

'I could walk you right to Bef's operations room,' said the driver. 'She'll be working there with Mr Passarella, the mayor.'

'No, no, I wish to surprise her and need to buy a few things first,' said the 81st elf, panicking slightly. He needed time to snoop and spy on Bef when he found her – one of the things he did best, if the truth be told.

The driver didn't think anything of this, so did as instructed and dropped his passenger outside the city walls.

'No cars are allowed in there,' he explained. 'You'll have to walk in.'

The 81st elf waved him goodbye and darted up a dark side street, lingering in the shadows to get his bearings. Gradually, he made his way further into the town, turning away from people heading in his direction and keeping in the shady parts of the streets wherever possible. Eventually, he found himself outside a building with a sign reading 'Ufficio di Befland', which he worked out meant Befland Office. The windows of the building were wide open and he could hear voices above. As he stood there in the shadows, he looked up and saw something glinting in the sun. He squinted hard and adjusted his eyes as he stared towards the sky. It was someone with binoculars – someone else was spying on the Bef woman.

The door by which he was standing was suddenly flung open and he had to quickly turn his face to the wall. A very colourful chap in a hat made from chicken wire emerged. He was carrying several rolls of material piled up high on his arms to a height that almost came up to his nose.

'Jeremiah, please remember that I like the purple and maroon material for the park uniforms,' shouted a voice he instantly recognised as belonging to Bef.

He kept his face to the wall, watching what was happening behind him by staring into the glass window of the neighbouring shop. In this way, he could see what this chap Jeremiah was doing. To his alarm, he saw that he was resting the rolls of material on the edge of a drinking fountain, taking a breather after carrying them down the stairs. Even worse, Jeremiah was looking straight at him!

'Very unusual choice of daywear,' said Jeremiah, talking directly to him. 'Wool is actually a good choice in hot weather. Not many people realise that. I have to say that your jumper is beautifully knitted. Very nice stitching indeed.'

'Thanks,' said the 81st elf, hoping to end the conversation very quickly. It worked. Jeremiah picked up his material and walked off.

At that moment, a woman came hurrying down the stairs and out of the door, accompanied by a grey-haired man wearing gold-rimmed spectacles.

'But it is a really big problem,' whispered the woman to the man. The 81st elf's long pointed ears pricked up and he tuned in to the whispering tones of this woman in a hurry. 'I can't believe the sign maker has called the park Befanaland. What a disaster it would have been if I hadn't noticed. You know that Bef can never again call herself The Befana. If she did, the promise she gave to Old Father Time would be broken.'

'Yes,' agreed the man. 'The last thing she would want would be to become centuries old again. She loves being Bef. She must never call herself The Befana again.'

The 81st elf was grinning broadly to himself. Suddenly the choice of the name 'Bef' made perfect sense. This was powerful knowledge indeed – knowledge that would be like gold dust to Capriccia.

He remembered the glint of the binoculars and his heart skipped a beat. His wonderful Capriccia was probably spying on the bossy Bef. All he had to do was get into the building and find her. He looked up and reckoned the glint was coming from the fifth floor. He scurried across the street like a little mouse and tried a door. It didn't open. A hefty woman waddled past.

'The entrance to the palace is around the corner,' she said.

The 81st elf mumbled his thanks and scarpered. He found the entrance and noticed a guard on duty. The moment the guard turned his back, he slipped in and stealthily walked up a flight of stairs. He began to count – 30, 60, 90, 120, 150. He stopped at that level and looked around a dark landing. There was a shaft of sunlight coming from under one of the doors. He headed towards it and listened carefully, trying to spy through the keyhole at the same time. Someone was moving around in the room. His heart skipped a beat. He was sure it was Capriccia. He imagined he could smell the scent of her favourite perfume and, if he closed his eyes tight, could almost hear her shrieks and screams running through his head.

He turned the door handle and boldly went in, fully expecting to see a tall woman with long blonde hair, who would yawn when she saw him and maybe not even remember who he was. But as he entered the room, he was totally unprepared for what he actually found. As he focused his eyes, he found not Capriccia, but a funny little man with tall hair like a toilet brush: a little man wearing red and white striped pyjama bottoms.

'Who on earth are you?' the 81st elf demanded.

'And I may vell ask ze same of you!' replied the man. 'Why are you bursting in here and disturbing my bird watching?'

The 81st elf took his time.

'I am a friend of Capriccia Claus,' he declared boldly. 'I am here to find her and take her back to Lapland.'

'Vell, I am a friend of Capriccia Claus too!' answered the angry little man, 'but I have done something far more positive to help her,' he declared, 'whereas you … what possible use to her can you be?'

The 81st elf felt deeply offended and rather jealous. Who was this man declaring that he was of more use to Capriccia than he was? Was he not aware of his own total devotion to Capriccia?

'I happen to think I can be of great use to her,' said the 81st elf defensively. 'I have a real pearl of knowledge to present to her – one which will brighten her day no end and one that will give her lots of possibilities on the revenge front, to get back at the woman who is planning to mock her by opening a theme park so soon after Capriccia has lost her own palace of amusements.'

'Revenge you say,' said Bernhardt. 'That's a word I love. I vill give you a chance and take you to Capriccia, though I am not convinced zat you vill have anything zat can be of more benefit to her than ze skills I am making sure she develops. Nevertheless, I know a creepy, untrustworthy elf when I see von and I can see zat you are ze perfect example of an untrustworthy elf. What is your name?'

The 81st elf suddenly realised that being called the 81st elf only worked if he had a job in Santa's Post Office, where that number meant something. Sadly, he had been sacked. Just like Bef, he now needed a new name, a trendy name that suited his own personality. He therefore answered the question very slowly.

'Sly', he declared. Just call me Sly.'

CHAPTER FIVE

'Oops,' yelled Fiery Tina as a broom whooshed just inches above her head causing her to fall over on her precious hopscotch court. 'What on earth made me do that?'

She lifted her head at its tilted angle and stared across her fairy playground. The broom with its two passengers had landed rather abruptly over by her glittery see-saw, which was pink at one end and black and silver at the other. She liked to sit at the dark end and put guests at the other. Capriccia had already been forced to sit on the pretty pink seat several times during her stay.

Fiery Tina stood up angrily, straightening her spine and opening her mouth widely.

'You made me topple over,' she yelled. My game is woo-inned!'

'Ruined,' said Capriccia, correcting her. 'But never mind that ... who is that with Bernhardt?' She blinked her eyes in the bright sunlight, but couldn't get the answer she sought. The body was just a silhouette in the sun.

The two figures began to walk across the fairy

playground, but Fiery Tina stopped them in their tracks and pointed her wand straight at them as they advanced.

'You woo-inned my game, so now you can amuse me.' She waved her wand and lifted Bernhardt on to one end of the seesaw and the 81st elf to the other. 'Now, off you go, up and down and up and down.' The pair of them started to rise and fall at an incredible speed as Fiery Tina rolled around on the grass laughing loudly.

Capriccia began to slowly walk over to the seesaw, still wondering who the second arrivee could be.

'Stop, I beg you woman,' yelled Bernhard. 'I am feeling incredibly sick.'

Fiery Tina continued to laugh like a little child.

'Oops', she giggled. 'I can't remember how to undo the spell.'

Capriccia glared at her.

'Stop it now,' she demanded forcefully. 'I can't see who the new visitor is. They're travelling too fast for me to work it out. It could be an enemy.'

Fiery Tina scowled, but lifted her wand and stopped the seesaw so that both men were suspended in mid-air at once. From one seat dangled legs covered by a pair of stripy red and white pyjama bottoms. From the other, legs belonging to an elf.

Capriccia walked up to the contraption and stared at the 81st elf.

'Don't I know you?' she asked, in a slightly dim and wholly disinterested kind of way now she realised it wasn't Bef.

'Yes, of course you do,' said the 81st elf, delighted to see his beloved Capriccia again. 'It's me, your faithful and trusty servant, the 81st elf.'

Capriccia yawned without putting her hand over her mouth.

'Don't you mean the 66th elf?' she said sarcastically. 'I seem to remember that you were demoted.'

The 81st elf felt a pang of hurt run through his entire body.

'Well, no matter,' he said. 'I'm called Sly now, so numbers and positions no longer matter.'

'Unattractive name,' replied Capriccia, 'but I have to admit that it suits you to a tee. What are you doing here?'

She wasn't in the mood for much social chit-chat and was slightly creeped out by seeing the devious little elf, who had annoyed her daily once upon a time, but who had been slightly useful now and again. She found him rather slimy and annoying, so was not particularly interested in his answer, but had nothing better to do right now than listen.

'Good question,' said Bernhardt, regaining his sense of balance having jumped off the seesaw and walked a few paces. 'He says he has a pearl of knowledge to give to you … oh, and he also has news of your Casa of Contentments.'

'What news?' asked Capriccia, grabbing the 81st

elf by the neck and picking him up off the ground. 'Tell me what's happening, NOW!'

'Well Mistress,' said the newly-named Sly, 'I tried so hard to keep everything tidy and did as much dusting and cleaning as I could after your departure, but the moths just arrived in their hundreds and took over, eating into your clothes and shoes. The rest of your possessions started to gather an extraordinary amount of dust that seemed to suddenly arrive on the wind. Some said it came from the Bef woman's village, but I don't know if that was true.' He took a deep breath and then continued.

'I believe that Santa is to sell off your collection soon, or parcel up new items to give as presents next year. Elves in the Post Office were asked if they wanted any outfits or shoes, but nobody was interested.'

'Not interested?' snapped Capriccia. 'Not interested? What's wrong with my clothes and shoes?'

'Elves have no taste,' replied Sly quickly. 'So the upshot is that Santa is going to send a lot of items back to the stores that you forced into giving you goods for free. It's rather embarrassing for him that you demanded things because you were Santa's wife and refused to pay for them.'

Capriccia had steam coming out of her ears.

'Sending items back! No takers! Moths! Dust! This is an outrage. Something MUST be done very quickly! Things are far worse than I imagined! How long is it since you were last in the Casa?'

'Maybe two months now,' said Sly. 'But then it all became so grave that I knew I had to find you, so started to journey across Europe. I arrived in Hamburg just after your departure, so have had to walk or hitch a ride from there to get to Italy. I discovered Bernhardt, but also uncovered another very useful fact – a real gem in my view!'

'Let me guess,' said Capriccia sarcastically. 'You found out that the Italians like to eat a lot of pizza!'

'No,' said Sly, 'I already knew that!'

'So, you discovered that Italian tailors make the best clothes then?' added Capriccia.

'No, and I'm not sure that they do,' said Sly in a slight huff by now. 'I've encountered the VIPB world's best tailor lately and he may be better than Italian tailors.' Capriccia looked vaguely impressed.

'Where did you encounter him?' she demanded.

'In the street outside Bef's office,' he replied, 'while Bernhardt was spying on her from the palace opposite. I saw the glint of the binoculars and headed towards it, thinking it was you. By then, I already had the gem of wisdom that I have mentioned.'

'Really,' said Capriccia, 'and what on earth do you think could interest me so much?'

'Perhaps knowing why the Bef woman no longer calls herself The Befana,' said Sly boldly, waiting for an intake of breath from Capriccia, who had started to walk away from him.

On hearing his words, she suddenly spun back around to face him. Bernhardt, on the other hand, took three paces towards him and stood with legs akimbo waiting for more words on this subject. Fiery Tina stopped rolling in the grass and stood up right in front of him.

'And why pray does she call herself that?' asked Capriccia, as all waited with baited breath for the answer.

'Yes, why choose a name that can be used in mocking sentences by those who hate her and wish to laugh at her by saying she's 'Bef as a post', 'must have a Bef wish' and has 'two Bef feet?' giggled Fiery Tina.

Sly suddenly liked the attention he was getting.

'Sit down and I will tell you all,' he said, trying to build up his own sense of importance. He plonked his bottom down on the grass and sat cross-legged waiting for the other three to join him. 'Come come,' he continued, patting the ground and feeling as regal as a king.

Fiery Tina slumped to the ground. Bernhardt crouched. Capriccia huffed and puffed about not wanting to get grass strains on her dress, but eventually sat down.

'Good, bend in towards me and I will reveal everything' said Sly. All three members of his audience leaned in, desperate to hear the reason for Bef choosing her name. Sly began to talk abnormally slowly.

'The Befana must never again call herself The Befana, or she will no longer be a young and pretty-in-a-certain-light witch. She will be turned back to her original state – a wart-ridden, wizened old woman who is centuries old. Gone will be the lipstick. Gone will be the appeal for children across the world. Gone will be her popularity. Gone will be her festival and gone will be her theme park. She will no longer be able to have adventures and no longer be able to fight against us and our combined powers.' The elf finished his speech in a highly dramatic tone, as all three of those listening to him sat there with their mouths open wide.

Fiery Tina was the first to speak. 'How do you know this?' she demanded.

'I heard the mayor and a woman talking about it,' explained Sly. 'They were whispering, but I have keen ears.'

Bernhardt was looking ever so peeved. After all, he'd be listening in on conversations in Bef's office for weeks, but hadn't heard anything about this. It was certainly a gem, just as the annoying elf had said.

'And who told her about ze name rule?' asked Bernhardt inquisitively.

'A man called Old Father Time apparently,' said Sly.

'That makes sense,' said Fiery Tina. 'Makes a lot

of sense. Just the sort of thing that old coot would do.'

'So what!' shouted Capriccia, trying to remove a fly which had flown into her open mouth. 'It's of no use to me, or my plans to rescue my Casa. Who cares about this rule? It's in place now and she's not going to break it, is she! It's meaningless!'

'You are so wong,' snapped Fiery Tina. 'You we-ally are extremely dim at times. This is indeed a pearl of wisdom, a gem of knowledge, a diamond for those with devilish intentions. We can do so much more than we imagined now! We can use magic to not just humiliate the Bef woman, but also woo-in her life and make her theme park a disaster. You are a twuly perceptive elf,' she declared, beaming at Sly.

The former 81st elf looked vaguely pleased, but had no interest in Fiery Tina's praise. What he wanted was the attention of Capriccia, her admiration and her love. He got none of this.

'Well, I don't get it,' said Capriccia in a bored sort of tone. 'How can this possibly save my glorious Casa?'

'Conundwums,' shouted a very exasperated fairy. 'I told you we would work on conundwums and now we can cweate a conundwum with venom, a conundwum with bite, a conundwum full of evil intentions! A plan is al-weady forming in my head! I haven't been this excited since 1412, when I thought I would become the VIPB contwolling Flo-wence.

By the time our conundwum is complete, I shall achieve that aim all these years later.'

'She means conundrums,' Capriccia explained to Bernhardt and Sly. 'She can't pronounce the letter r properly. Even so, I still don't get it or see what difference being called Bef makes at all. She's still standing in my way and we're just sitting around making up stupid 'widdles', or riddles to anyone who can pronounce an r!'

Fiery Tina looked highly displeased with her pupil and was deeply offended and ready to blow up like a volcano until Bernhardt stepped in.

'If Fiery Tina sees ze forward path, none of us should argue with her,' he insisted. 'She clearly has a plan in mind and we need to listen to her.' He looked Capriccia in the eye to communicate that she needed to behave.

Fiery Tina seemed delighted by this support from the world's best broom artisan.

'Indeed you should,' she said, 'because we will cweate a conundwum that will woo-in the Italian witch ... a conundwum that will steal from her what she values most, just as she stole away your husband's heart, your Casa and your self-we-spect: a conundwum that will twap her and leave her with only one possible course of action. It will be a conundwum that all who find VIPBs highly iwwitating will applaud!'

Bernhardt, Sly and Capriccia all stared at her, wondering what on earth she was talking about, but realising that it had to be good, as she found it more appealing than hopscotch for once.

'Oops, did I just make a speech?' asked Tina. She began to giggle uncontrollably. 'What a pearl you have bwought to me today!' she said to Sly, slapping him on the back. 'What a gift fwom the heavens you are. I have a feeling that you and I will get on we-ally well.' Within ten seconds, she'd forgotten all about him and was playing hopscotch.

Bernhardt's face had clouded over. Why should this newcomer get all the limelight when he had been spying on Bef for months? Capriccia's face had lit up as she started to think about wearing her garish clothes and gross shoes once again. A terrified lizard scampered across the fairy playground believing that no good could come of this news.

And in Lapland, many many miles away, the Northern Lights turned from green to red.

'That's not good. That's really not good at all,' said the best reindeer whisperer the world has ever seen. 'Trouble's brewing, or my name is not Lars Llangfjord.'

Chapter Six

Bef woke up with a start. Her nose was twitching violently and that was never a good thing, especially when accompanied by tingling toes. She jumped out of bed, throwing back the sheets and rushed to the mirror. There it was again: uncontrollable twitching of the nose.

'This is a worrying sign,' she declared as she looked at her nose movements for several minutes. 'Something, somewhere is affecting me. This only usually occurs when a vicious enemy is up to no good. And when my toes are tingling, it means even bigger plots are afoot. Let's see if the other signs are there.'

She rushed down the stairs of her ancient little house and found her trusty broom tapping on the floorboards in a frantic manner, as if seeking help. It lifted itself a little off the floor each time and then seemed to tap around twenty times per second.

'So you sense something too,' she said, addressing her best friend in the world. 'But what can be going on? Who would be wishing us ill?'

The broom spun on its bristles.

'What did you say?' asked Bef. 'Capriccia? Don't be silly! She's far too dim to be of any danger to us. She couldn't put a strategy together to attack us, even if she tried!'

The broom swung from side to side in a frantic manner, almost knocking half the pots off the draining board.

'Well, yes,' said Bef, 'I have to agree that Bernhardt Bürstenfrisür is a different kettle of fish entirely. But he knows that it was Natalia Lebedev who prevented him becoming a VIPB and that it had nothing to do with me. That's his bone of contention.'

The broom continued to rock from side to side.

'So, you really do think it's Bernhardt, do you?' asked Bef, now very worried by her broom's behaviour indeed. 'Well you were crafted by him, so in a way he was your original master, even if you didn't like him one little bit!'

Bef looked very thoughtful. She hitched up her nightdress and stepped up on to an old wooden stool. She reached as high as she could and pulled down a document wedged between books on the very top of her ancient dresser. She began to flick through the pages of 'A Second User's Guide To Broom Ownership' until she found the page she was seeking. The words at the top of the page read, 'How to instruct your broom to warn of the presence of its original owner in cases of dispute, fear or revenge.'

'Hardly a snappy headline!' tutted Bef. 'I wish people would write these things in a more user-friendly way!' She scoured the page and focused hard on the text. 'Va bene,' she said, 'I think I know what to do now. It's lucky that I have a big bucket and all the right ingredients.'

She brought a huge metal bucket out of a cupboard and filled it with lukewarm water from the tap. She deftly pulled three petals off a rose drinking in water from a vase on her windowsill and crushed these in a bowl before adding them to the bucket of water. She then reached inside a crammed cupboard, to pull out a tiny bottle of delicate rosehip oil. She pressed its dropper and added six drops to the liquid. Finally, she pulled some lavender off another plant growing in her kitchen and dropped that into the bucket too, uttering a few magical words as she stirred the mixture.

'Over you come now broom,' she said. 'This should be very soothing for you and give us both some answers.'

She carried the broom over very carefully and lowered it into the bucket. As she did so, she began to chant, 'Mostra maestro', over and over again. Her broom began to quiver and Bef checked its broom pulse, in a way that only an experienced broom owner can do, using the back of a spoon as a stethoscope placed on its handle.

'My, your heart is really racing,' she said. 'Let me consult the manual to see what that means.'

She shifted her spectacles up her nose a little and referred back to the page she had read previously. She didn't find the answer, so impatiently turned the page and then the next page. Finally, she found the information she sought.

'So your first master is actually very close at hand,' she exclaimed. 'In fact, according to this, he's within a couple of miles, if your heart reading is correct. What can he possibly want from us?'

At that moment, Jeremiah breezed through the door.

'I went out early to pick some fresh mushrooms to make us a delicious soup for lunch,' he explained. 'It's a little damp outside, but marvellous weather for mushrooms!' He stopped in his tracks, noticing Bef slumped at the table and the broom stuck inside a bucket. 'What on earth does this little scene mean?' he enquired. 'Have plans for Befland gone a little off track?'

'No, far worse than that,' explained Bef. 'My nose has been twitching and my toes tingling. Then my broom was tapping and it has now revealed that the dreadful Bernhardt Bürstenfrisür is close at hand. This can not be anything but bad news.'

Jeremiah stroked his stubbly beard and pondered.

'Well, there are more of us in Team Bef than there are of him, so I'm sure we can take whatever he tries to throw at us. You've outwitted him before, so I'm sure we can all pull together and see him off again. Maybe he just wants an invitation to the opening of Befland!'

'You are always so optimistic,' said Bef. 'The man is, however, totally unpredictable and the warning signs are clear to see. We must be very much on our guard. I must call a meeting very quickly.'

'I will go and knock on doors right now,' volunteered the truly kind-hearted Jeremiah. 'I will round up 'The Three Kings', Mr Passarella and Marianna too and we shall all meet you at the theme park in an hour. After all, it's test day for some of the rides, so we should all try them out. I'm so excited by that, by the way! I didn't get much opportunity to ride roller coasters and spin around in teacups when in Siberia.' With that, he hopped out of the door and began to spring down the street.

Bef began to feel beads of perspiration on her forehead. She took her broom out of the bucket and stroked it gently.

'I will make sure he doesn't get his hands on you again,' she said. 'I promise you that. I will guard you with my life.' Broom leaned in to her cheek and she gave it a gentle kiss. 'Now enough of this soppiness,' she declared. 'Let's head to the park and get those rides tested. We can't live in fear of what Bernhardt may or may not do ... we have a theme park to open!'

As Bef hurried down the cobbled alleyways of her small town, she noticed an eerie shadow fall across her path. Looking up to the sky, there was only clear blue for as far as the eye could see. 'Odd,' she thought, as she could swear that something had to be blocking the sun for such a shadow to be cast.

There was also a strange whistling on the breeze – the sort of noise that might suggest a flock of birds was flying in formation across the golden fields beyond the town, but she could see nothing.

She knew she had somewhere to go before arriving at the theme park … somewhere very important indeed. She arrived at a fancy door with a huge golden knocker carved in the shape of a lion. She rapped the knocker three times, waited ten seconds and then rapped another four. After counting ten seconds out to herself again, she rapped five times. The door swung open a couple of inches and a pair of dark, beady eyes looked at her from inside the building.

'What do you want?' asked a man with long, grey curly locks that tumbled past his shoulders. His tone was not exactly welcoming: in fact, rather grumpy. At the same time, however, he seemed secretly pleased to see his visitor.

He turned his back and shuffled inside, allowing Bef to enter the house. His red robe swept the floor and caused a rustling sound as he walked along with a slight stoop that made him tilt to one side as he carried on along a long dark corridor. He fixed a monocle into one eye.

'Make sure you bolt the door,' he demanded.

'We don't want any of the town's folk snooping around, or any of your strange friends tagging along. You seem to have acquired some very odd followers of late, sister. I keep track of what you are up to, you know!'

'What's the matter with you?' asked Bef, slightly peeved that her brother should think 'The Three Kings' or Jeremiah Needlebaum odd. 'I think you are just peeved that I've been rejuvenated while you are in the same old state. I had no choice, you know. It wasn't vanity that led me to seek Old Father Time's help.'

Her brother looked at her quizzically, as if not quite believing what she'd said.

'So why are you here?' he asked.

'I need to go through my documents,' she answered. 'There's one I need to check, which has been in your keeping for quite a few centuries now.'

'You could have given me some warning,' snapped her brother, as he continued to walk through the maze of a house, which just seemed to get bigger and bigger every time they turned a corner, or passed through a doorway.

'You are my brother, Lorenzo,' replied Bef. 'I don't expect to have to give you any notice and, as it happens, there has been a dramatic turn of events that has forced me to come here. I haven't been to visit you for a good fifteen years, so the least you could now do is help me to find my records. Remember that I pay you very well for being their guardian.' She brushed cobwebs out of her way as she made her way through to another part of the slightly dank and dimly lit house, trying to ignore the tutting from her brother, who now shuffled along behind her in his thick leather boots.

As she passed several smaller rooms, full of finely carved furniture and luxurious cushions and table decorations, she headed down a narrow corridor and glanced at the walls, realising that they were full of photographs – photographs of her and her brother as a child, with another person in the background. The sight of that person made her shiver and it seemed as if her eyes followed Bef up the corridor and through the house, as yet another and another photograph appeared. The strange thing was that there had been no cameras all those thousands of years ago when she and her brother had been children. How on earth were these photographs here, decorating his walls?

Lorenzo grabbed her shoulder and pulled her back.

'I must go first,' he dictated. 'Your documents are down in the cellar as always, but the steps are crumbling. I will guide you down. I'll warn you now though, there are a few rats down there, but they won't have nibbled your papers. Nothing could bite through the Casket of Confirmations. '

Bef nodded, realising that this was probably the safest place she could ever have chosen to house her important papers.

'Let's go down quickly,' she urged, putting her hand on Lorenzo's shoulder. 'Time may be of the essence.'

Lorenzo pushed her away, seemingly annoyed by her touch.

'Don't hurry me, sister,' he said in a stern voice. 'I will find your documents in my own good time. I've looked after them for centuries. I won't be rushed now.'

Bef raised her eyebrows in a way that signalled displeasure with her brother. He'd always been difficult, even as a child. He'd grown even more cantankerous since 1705, when he'd lost the tip of his little finger on his right hand in a sword fight. He was a few years older than her, which made him think he could boss her around. She'd always suspected that he resented the fact that she had become The Befana, loved by children all over the world, while he had no role other than keeper of her casket.

While she was pondering this thought, Lorenzo came to a halt in front of a massive, oak-carved door. He pulled out a golden key from his robes and fitted it into the lock. He had to force the stiff key to turn, making Bef fear that it would snap in the lock. Eventually, they heard a click and the door opened a few inches. Lorenzo gave it a huge shove and then grabbed Bef's hand and brought her through the doorway quickly.

'Don't dilly-dally,' he demanded. 'We must lock the door behind us as quickly as possible.'

As he fiddled with the lock once more, Bef tried to adjust her eyes to suit the total darkness into which they had been submerged. The silence was broken by a dripping of water coming from somewhere to the left, while the rustling of rats could clearly be heard from down below.

'Which document do you need?' asked Lorenzo.

'My Broom Registration Document', replied Bef, 'or to give it its full title, 'The Treaty of Trento Signifying the Transference of Broom Ownership Rights'. I lodged it with you for safe keeping around 1044 or 1045, shortly after my trusty broom fell into my hands.'

'Indeed, indeed,' agreed Lorenzo. 'It will be filed with the 11th century documents and then in alphabetical order within the Casket of Confirmations. Come over here. It is behind an invisibility shield in this corner.'

He headed towards the right and moved his hand through the air in circular movements a few times, while muttering something under his breath. A huge, golden casket appeared before them, decorated with glorious turquoise peacocks and shining red rubies. Lorenzo fiddled underneath his grey curly hair and pulled out a small key from behind his ear. A whole number of locks suddenly appeared on the casket, dancing away, inviting the key holder to guess which lock they needed to open.

This did not confuse Lorenzo. He went straight to a lock about eighteen inches down and three feet across. He put the key into the lock and turned it slowly. A golden drawer shot out, almost hitting him on the nose, but Lorenzo just rummaged inside and instantly found what he was looking for.

'Here it is,' he declared. 'I'll fetch some light so that you can view it.'

'No need,' said Bef. 'I'll cast the Luce Spell.'

The dark cellar suddenly received a shaft of light from above, which fell on Bef and the important document she held in her trembling hand. Lorenzo noticed, for the first time, that Bef was shaking in fear. He watched her continue to quiver as she turned the pages of the document and scoured every word on their ancient parchment pages.

'Just as I suspected,' she said.

'What?' replied Lorenzo. 'Is there a problem?'

'Yes,' replied Bef. 'After 1020 years, the maker of my broom has the right and power to demand its return to him, to carry out all of his wishes. Unfortunately, that time is now and my broom is already in a panic. It must sense that its days with me are numbered. Knowing who made my broom, I am not surprised that it is suffering traumatic episodes. Alternatively, this may be because the maker is causing panic tremors, which are reaching my broom, because he is close at hand.'

'Who is the maker?' said Lorenzo, looking slightly unnerved. 'Pray tell, sister.'

'Bernhardt Bürstenfrisür, the Most Fearsome Feller in Folklore,' answered Bef, 'a nasty, spiteful little man, who wants to become a VIPB. He is an enemy of mine now, but also the best broom artisan in the world. How could he not be, having made such a beautiful broom as mine?'

'What can you do?' asked Lorenzo, fingering the folds of his robe in an agitated fashion. 'Without your broom, you are finished!'

'You are so right,' said Bef, turning very white. 'I must find a way of changing the rules, amending the document, or protecting my broom through magic. I cannot let Bernhardt take it back. Without it, I would be a lost soul. It is like a child to me. Put the document back and do not let anyone – and I mean anyone – near my documents or into this cellar. Nobody must know about this. We have kept these documents safe for hundreds of years and must continue to do so.'

'Do you take me for an idiot?' said Lorenzo, looking offended.

'Not at all,' replied Bef. 'But there is far more powerful magic out there than I can perform and I sense that my enemies are gathering. You must keep your wits about you at all times, Lorenzo, and we must keep our family ties secret.'

'Very well,' replied her now concerned brother. 'Take yourself out the back way and I will secure all locks and bolts and make sure nobody enters. Nothing and nobody will get past me.'

Bef patted him on the shoulder.

'I will not forget this, brother,' she said, as she swept up her skirt and headed up the stairs. She had to hurry now. She was due to meet the others at Befland in less than twenty minutes, but more importantly, she had to get back to her broom.

Chapter Seven

Pastel pink trails painted across the azure sky were the only sign that Bernhardt Bürstenfrisür had just flown across the valley in which Bef lived. The trails would only last for seconds and to most people just seemed like pretty patterns in the sky caused by the sun. Only a broom owner would know what they meant. Unfortunately, Bef was fetching her own beloved broom and didn't glance up at the sky.

Bernhardt was not alone. Capriccia had flown with him from Fiery Tina's home and was desperate to see the much talked about 'Befland', which she was sure would be a complete flop, as, in her opinion, the Bef woman didn't have a clue about designing anything, let alone a theme park! 'The woman can't even dress herself properly,' she had exclaimed at least ten times during the short broom flight from Florence, as Bernhardt had simply nodded and shut his ears to the rest of her very blonde babble.

Jealousy was actually eating Capriccia up. If there was one thing she desired, it was her own theme park. Capriccia Claus's Casa of Contentments was the nearest she had come to it and now she'd even been deprived of life in that bright fuchsia pink, five-storey pleasure palazzo. She would make sure that there was no way Bef had something she couldn't have herself. If it was the last thing she did, she would destroy these plans for the ridiculously named Befland!

The two of them landed on the hillside overlooking Befland and took up position behind a large, craggy rock. Bernhardt reached for the binoculars in his broom-sack and handed a pair to Capriccia.

'What on earth are those round things?' she asked, fiddling with the binoculars to bring them into focus.

'I believe zay are ze Acorn Teacups,' replied Bernhardt. 'It seems zat ze boys called ze 'Three Kings' are sitting in zem right now?'

Capriccia fiddled with her binoculars. 'Who are 'The Three Kings'?' she demanded.

'Zay are what is called a boy band,' answered Bernhardt, observing a delighted look on Capriccia's face.

'They are very good looking,' replied Capriccia, totally distracted for a moment. She then moved the binoculars. 'What the devil is that big stack thing and what is the huge rollercoaster. It's absolutely incredible. I've never seen anything like it!'

'Vell,' said Bernhardt. 'Ze first is ze Chimney Chaser, according to ze plans that I've managed to overhear in ze office. Ze other is ze Coaler Coaster, ze main attraction at Befland. Apparently, coal vill fly in all directions. It was suggested zat a replica of me be used in ze ride. Naturally, zat would have made it more successful, but I vill not stand for it, not to help zat Bef woman and not if I cannot be a VIPB!' He was shaking in anger from head to toe as Capriccia eyed him up and down.

'You?' she asked in amazement. 'Who would want you in Befland? That would be simply ridiculous! If anyone should be in there as a replica, it's me. I can see myself now as the star attraction. I'm amazed the Bef woman hasn't thought of it, but maybe she doesn't want anyone as attractive and fashionable as me in her little park.'

Bernhardt began to smoulder, with steam almost coming out of his ears.

'Perhaps you could be in Aniseed Alley,' he replied. 'I believe zat aniseed balls ping at all angles as ze visitor travels down it. I can certainly see you being a target in there!'

Capriccia scowled at him. She secretly hated this silly little man, but knew that she had no choice but to put up with him. She would do absolutely anything to get her hands back on her Casa of Contentments and it seemed Bernhardt was essential to that plan. She picked up her binoculars again.

'The Bef woman has entered the park,' she said, noting Bef's arrival by broom right next to what she took to be the Cherries Wheel, the sight of enormous great cherry-shaped pods being enough of a clue even for someone as dense as Capriccia.

Capriccia was absolutely right. Bef had landed by the Cherries Wheel knowing Mr Passarella and the boys would be somewhere close at hand. Thaz was the first to spot her, waving to her from his Acorn Teacup as it spun around on its circular route. Jeremiah soon came bustling over.

'I've just had the most amazing time testing the Big Slipper,' he enthused. 'It's favoloso, as you would say. There you are, riding in a nice comfy slipper one minute and then down you slip at such a rapid speed, it's almost as if your feet are in your mouth.' He began to dance around in a most excited fashion. 'Next up for me is the Astoundabout,' he shouted, as he darted off. 'Mr Passarella wishes to test all the rides today, except the Coaler Coaster, of course, as we don't yet have the coal!'

Bef began to flush red with anxiety.

'What do you mean we don't have the coal?' she shouted, as Jeremiah disappeared around the bend of the Flying Sorcerers, leaving her standing alone. She looked around. Luigi Passarella could be seen making notes by Candymonium. The boys were giddily going round and round on the Acorn Teacups. Jeremiah was probably now jumping aboard the Astoundabout and Marianna … where was Marianna?

Bef looked around. She desperately needed to find the super-efficient Marianna. Marianna was in charge of sourcing the coal for the star attraction, The Coaler Coaster. Marianna always dealt with the coal order for Bef's normal coal and candy deliveries at Epiphany. Marianna was the queen of coal in Bef's eyes. When the mine at Torino closed, it was Marianna who directed Bef to Russia, where she had travelled with Gaspar to visit the mine at which both Natalia Lebedev and Bernhardt Bürstenfrisür had so unexpectedly arrived. Bef had to head towards Mr Passarella. He would know where Marianna was. Perhaps she was testing a Bonbon Bumper Car ... but how could she be, as they hadn't arrived yet? Maybe she was on the Mint Ball Octopus ... that would be it. Bef would simply have to ask Luigi and then no doubt find her there.

Sitting up on the hill, Capriccia was giggling to herself.

'Just look at the Bef woman,' she said. 'Something's wrong. She's in a panic about something or other, but goodness knows what. She's standing there like a fish stranded in a river without water. She doesn't have a clue what's going on. Her mouth is just dropping open and she's got a ridiculous puzzled look on her face. How hilarious! I love this binocular watching. It's the best fun ever!'

As Capriccia revelled in Bef's deep confusion, a shrill whizzing sound pierced her eardrums. She put her hands over her ears and hid behind the rock. It was as if rockets were being fired at her, but nothing had cascaded down on her and Bernhardt. What on earth was it?

Suddenly, Fiery Tina popped out of the sky and tumbling down after her came Sly.

'Oops,' said Fiery Tina, almost predictably. 'I'm not too good at this bwoom flying and I'm sure the bwoom you left us was second-class! Never mind, here we are now. Just in time for the fun, I hope. Have you marked out a hopscotch court yet?'

Capriccia rolled her eyes. She'd hoped she'd escaped Fiery Tina for a while, even if it had meant spending time with Bernhardt. Fiery Tina was so high maintenance. If she wasn't demanding games of hopscotch, she was bleating on about her blessed 'conundwums' and that was something that made Capriccia's brain hurt.

Sure enough, it was the first thing Fiery Tina wanted to talk about.

'So have you come up with a twuly special conundwum yet?' she asked. 'It's the best magic you can use against the Bef woman. In fact, I can't wait. It will make her look widiculous and give us lots of fun while we watch her tear about twying to solve it, but it can also we-ally hurt her. That's what we all want isn't it?' She looked at the other three and demanded instant support.

'Ja!' shouted Bernhardt.

'It's what she deserves,' agreed Sly.

'But why do I have to decide on the conundrum,' asked Capriccia, sighing even more heavily than usual. 'Why can't you create the conundrum and help me carry it out?'

'We've been th-woo this.' snapped Fiery Tina, being as fiery as her name suggested. 'The magic will be a hundwed times more powerful if you cwe-ate the conundwum and you will only get what you most desire if you do that. Now tell me again, what it is that you most desire, Capwiccia?'

'To have my Casa of Contentments back,' answered Capriccia as she scowled at Fiery Tina for once again calling her Capwiccia and not Capriccia. 'I want to make my Casa bigger and better than ever before. I want to hurt the Bef woman. I want to feel like a queen again. I want my shoe collection to be saved from the moths and I want all my wonderful clothes back. I want to be able to spray every single one of my perfumes and smell the wonderful fragrance floating on the air. I want to put all my Northern Highlights in my hair and put on every single shade of skylashes that I possess – well, maybe not all at once, but I want it all back. I WANT MY CASA BACK!'

Fiery Tina, Bernhardt and Sly had all covered their ears as Capriccia gave one of her infamous screams. A swarm of wasps left their nest in a rock close to where her three fellow plotters sat and all swiftly ducked as the insects flew angrily over their heads. Down in the valley, Bef lifted her head as she heard a weird noise on the wind. A cloud of wasps whizzed past her and she wondered what had disturbed them. What was that noise? It had sounded almost like a scream. She surveyed and scanned the hillside above and thought, for one split second, that she had seen a glint in the sun, but it had now gone. Her imagination was playing tricks on her.

Fiery Tina had got to her feet and stood with her hands on her hips.

'Well, if that's what you want, Capwiccia, you had better stop being lazy and get your conundwum sorted out. As I've told you, at least thirty times, you need to work out who or what the Bef woman loves most in the world. Then, we can build the conundwum and twick her into falling into our twap. Now concentwate Capwiccia. I want you to devise the conundwum within the next fifteen minutes and I will not be a happy fair-wee until you've done it.'

Fiery Tina waved her wand around wildly and a hopscotch court appeared in the dust of the hillside. She began to lose herself in her very favourite pastime, leaping from square to square with her head tilted at its usual very odd angle.

'Bernhardt,' whispered Capriccia. 'You must help me with this. How am I supposed to know what Bef loves most? You must know. Please help me. Pretty please.' She batted her eyelashes at the best broom artisan in the world and he looked decidedly pleased with himself. Sly, on the other hand, was fuming. His ears were twitching in anger and he felt a jealousy he had never experienced before. It was he who had gone to Capriccia with the gem of information that she would use in her conundrum. It was he who had done everything she had ever asked of him in Lapland. It was he who worshipped her, who thought her the most wonderful woman who had ever lived and yet here she was asking for help from a tiny little German who she hardly knew. His anger was simply spilling over, but he couldn't work out who he was most angry with … Capriccia, Bernhardt or both!

Bernhardt was thinking deeply.

'Vell,' he said, after a while. 'Look through ze binoculars and you vill probably see it all.'

Capriccia focused on the scene down below in Befland.

'OK,' she said slowly. 'She loves those three boys … whatever they are called. Then, she loves that funny man in the bright coloured clothes, so that's four things. After that, she seems to like that man with the gold-rimmed spectacles.' She paused, suddenly hitting a bit of a block. She looked through the binoculars again.

'Got it,' she shouted. 'She absolutely loves those appallingly big shoes that flap and slap and slap and flap. She never takes them off her feet. Now, that's six things, isn't it? So, I think I need two more.' Her face reddened. 'She may love my husband,' she yelled, 'but I don't know if that's what she loves most.' She again looked through her binoculars.

Marianna was explaining to Bef that there was a

big issue with the coal supply for the Coaler Coaster, as an unexpected incident had occurred at the Russian mine that they'd been relying on. The miners were claiming they'd seen a fairy flying through the mine, who told them that bad luck would befall them if they mined for any more coal. The boss of the mine felt they'd all turned barking mad overnight and that it would pass, but nevertheless had no men to mine for the coal that Befland needed. Bef was looking terribly pensive, but put her hand on Marianna's shoulder in a kind sort of fashion.

'OK,' said Capriccia. The seventh thing she loves is that woman down there, whoever she is.'

'And so what is the eighth?' demanded Fiery Tina, suddenly stopping her hopping around to give Capriccia her full attention.

Capriccia's forehead was furrowed as she screwed up her face trying to think very hard. It was clear that no matter how much she grimaced, she wasn't going to get the answer. Bernhardt leaned towards her and began jerking his head towards his broom. Capriccia stared at him in amazement, clearly not getting the clue. Sly noticed this and leapt up, heading towards Bernhardt's broom.

As if not realising what was going on, Sly declared, 'How I would love a broom, if I had one. How I would cherish it and treat it like a pet, or maybe even a child. How lovely life would be, if I had a broom.'

Suddenly, the penny dropped with Capriccia. She looked Fiery Tina in the eye.

'The eighth thing is her broom. She absolutely loves her broom,' she said confidently.

Fiery Tina scowled back, annoyed that Capriccia had managed to find the eight things that she also believed Bef loved most.

'Are you sure your husband isn't one of the eight things,' she asked spitefully.

Capriccia glared at her.

'No, she would be living with him in Lapland by now if that were the case.'

'What about the Reindeer Whisperer,' asked Sly, out of the blue. The eyes of Bernhardt, Fiery Tina and Capriccia all turned on him.

'Oh yes, the Reindeer Whisperer,' said Capriccia. 'I'd almost forgotten about him. The man who controlled the mind of the Head Elf. The man who speaks Lynx. The man who helped her, that Bef woman, push me out of my Casa of Contentments!' She shouted the last bit of the sentence very loudly indeed, getting angrier and angrier as the memories came back.

Fiery Tina jerked herself forward and came within two inches of Sly's nose, looking up at him with her tilted head.

'Do you think she loves this man, whoever he is?' she demanded, putting an emphasis on the 'you'.

'I have no idea,' said Sly. 'I was just suggesting she might.

Fiery Tina jumped back.

'If we get this wong,' she said, 'the conundwum might not work. Does she, or does she not love the weindeer whisperwer?'

Capriccia looked blank and Bernhardt seemed very annoyed by Sly's interference. He himself didn't know much about the Reindeer Whisperer and couldn't answer the question.

'Oh goodness,' yelled Fiery Tina. 'You are all as useless as each other.' She picked up a massive handful of dust and angrily threw it at her hopscotch court. A pile landed in each of the first eight squares. 'I think that means we've got it wight,' she said, not sounding too convinced. 'Does anyone think diffewently?'

'No,' said Capriccia. 'He's not here planning Befland with her, after all.'

'No,' said Bernhardt. 'I think he was simply useful to her.'

'Not sure,' said Sly. 'Without him, she wouldn't have regained her VIPB patch.'

His three companions looked at him in disgust.

'What makes you think you know better than we do,' said Capriccia, making him wince with the harshness of her voice. 'I am sure I am right. You just like to argue with everything other people say.'

Sly shrank back behind a tree stump, feeling wounded by her words. He watched her giggle with Bernhardt and felt extremely angry inside. He would still have a job if it weren't for Capriccia. He would still be in Lapland working in Santa's Post Office. She hadn't shown him one bit of thanks for the help he had given her recently and had never been very nice to him before that either. He looked at her for the very first time and thought what a vain, shallow and very rude woman she was.

Fiery Tina didn't seem to notice anything other than the success of the dust landing on her hop-scotch court.

'Now then,' she shouted. 'Which of the things that she loves most are we going to take away from her first?' She hopped over to Capriccia and plonked her bottom down next to her. 'Whisper in my ear, so nobody else hears,' she demanded, in a typically bossy tone.

Capriccia, started playing with her bottom lip as she considered this point. Once again, she looked completely clueless. She picked up her binoculars again and looked at the scene below in Befland. Jeremiah and 'The Three Kings' were all running down Aniseed Alley, seemingly having great fun as they dodged the flying aniseed balls. Mr Passarella was sitting on a seat by Candymonium still making notes. Bef's shoes were on her feet and her broom was in her hand. Capriccia still seemed baffled.

'You must come up with a stwategy by 8am,' dictated Fiery Tina, extremely disappointed by the flaky, second-rate performance of her pupil. 'I want you to decide who or what you will take away first and then tell me what fate you have decided they will suffer, using the magic I have taught you. The better your stwategy, the more chance you have of getting your Casa back. If your magic is weak and doesn't work pwoperly, you will fail, as the conundwum will be useless. Get thinking, get your silly little blonde head sorted out and for goodness sake we-member all I have taught you. The future of your Casa is in your hands now and if you want it back, you had better do some hard work tonight! Get your homework done Capwiccia. Get your homework done!'

Capriccia thought how much she actually detested Fiery Tina, but said nothing. If putting up with this insane fairy and her ridiculous obsession with hopscotch meant getting her Casa back, she would do it. She would even spend the entire evening working out lots of evil things to do to everyone and everything that the Bef woman loved. If being evil was all it took to be reinstalled in her five-storey pink paradise, it was an easy challenge for someone who was naturally nasty at the best of times. She would also prove to the insane fairy that she wasn't the only one who could concoct a decent conundrum. She would one day turn the tables on Fiery Tina and pay her back for the way she was treating her like a dunce. She just needed to perfect her magic skills first and tonight would be just the start of her campaign of nastiness.

CHAPTER EIGHT

Bef sat at the office table anxiously running her fingers through her hair in great distress.

'Mamma Mia!' she cried, 'The Coaler Coaster is supposed to be the star attraction at Befland. What on earth am I going to do? If there's no coal, the ride will be like a damp squib. What's going to happen if there's no coal in the Coaler part of the Coaler Coaster? I will be a laughing stock and children will then think that, if I can't get coal for the ride, I won't be able to find any to pop in their stockings. The number of naughty children will rocket and they will be acting up in the street, at school, on the buses … it will be a nightmare!'

Marianna sat in silence, looking down at her feet, wondering what on earth she could do. She had tried all the usual mines that had supplied Bef with coal in the past, but all had closed down. The only other one was that which Bef had visited during her great adventure to save her VIPB patch. And something very strange had happened there.

'Tell me once again what the Russian mine manager said to you,' said Bef. 'He seemed a decent enough chap when I met him last. He appeared very obliging in fact and delighted with all the gold I paid him. He could have a similar amount of gold this time, so I don't understand the problem. Something must have spooked him.'

'Yes,' said Marianna, 'it has. As I told you, the miners were all chipping away when they saw what they say was a fairy.'

'A fairy!' exclaimed Bef. 'As if a flimsy little fairy would head into a filthy coal mine!'

'Indeed,' exclaimed Marianna. 'And, as if she would be wearing a black tutu and cursing the miners for producing a nasty substance that stained her beautiful white tutu! The men must have been driven mad by working underground for so long!'

Bef leaned forward over the desk and grabbed Marianna by both arms. She pulled Marianna towards her.

'What did you just say?' she asked in a very panicky voice.

'I said that it was crazy for them to imagine they'd seen a fairy in a black tutu, who claimed that nasty coal had stained her white tutu,' replied Marianna.

'Why did you not mention this before?' cried Bef. 'This changes everything!'

'What do you mean?' said Marianna. 'I didn't think it was important. I thought it was just a case of miners having over vivid imaginations.'

'No, far from it,' answered Bef slowly. 'I would

say they simply described what they saw … an insane fairy who's never forgiven me for firing lumps of coal at her and ruining her little white dress. Apparently, the black one suits her personality much more anyway, so I actually did her a favour, but she won't let it drop, even though she started the whole row by trying to rob me of part of my VIPB patch. I fear what the men saw was a deranged fairy called Fiery Tina.'

Marianna looked extremely nervous and her bottom lip started to quiver.

'What does this mean?' she asked.

'I will explain what I think is happening when the others arrive,' said Bef. 'They all need to hear what I have to say and decide what they wish to do about it. Let's hope they've stopped playing in Aniseed Alley and get here soon.'

Bef put her hand down to the floor and checked that her beloved broom was still under the table, where she had hidden it that morning. It was not leaving her sight at the present time. Thankfully, she felt the unmistakable texture of its wood and knew that it was still safe. The broom responded by lifting itself a couple of inches, like a cat arching its back in pleasure at being stroked. Bef breathed a sigh of relief.

'We had better make sure we have cups and cups of acorn tea for Jeremiah,' she said, trying to take the strain off Marianna's shoulders for a minute or two. 'He's a sensitive little soul at the best of times, so goodness knows how he will respond when I tell him what I think is happening.'

'I'll go and check that we have enough in the cupboard,' replied Marianna, 'and I will get the kettle and Bialetti on in preparation for everyone's arrival, so we can have lots of lovely tea and coffee to calm ourselves down and think rationally.' She got to her feet and gently placed a hand on Bef's shoulder. 'Whatever it is,' she said, 'you know we are all behind you and will do whatever it takes to get Befland opened.'

As Marianna disappeared down the stairs, Bef breathed in deeply and shut her eyes. She realised that she needed to rapidly do some spell swotting, as she hadn't looked at most of the spells in her Grandissimo Libro di Scongiuri for many years. She just didn't need much magic these days and her last adventure had shown just how rusty her skills were and how wonky most of her witchcraft was. She wasn't even sure where her willow wand was stored, as she hadn't required its assistance since the 18th century. Her broom had been all she'd really needed. She was going to have to do a lot of homework, if her worst fears were actually a reality.

She started to thump her head, as she always did when trying to think hard, wondering where on earth she had last spotted that wand of hers. Was it even in one piece? Maybe it was riddled with woodworm! Even worse, maybe she'd sat on it and snapped it in half. Her massive book of spells was sometimes used as a doorstop, so she knew where that was, but it was an awfully long time since she'd tried to perform most of the spells in it. She'd only been a young witch when her mother had taught most of them to herself and Lorenzo ... and the third person in the pictures on Lorenzo's wall, of course. She tried to dismiss those images from her mind. They certainly wouldn't help.

Faint footsteps could be heard, which soon turned into the sound of a herd of elephants thumping up the stairs. Within seconds, in burst Thaz, followed by Mel, then Jeremiah in a particularly snazzy outfit that he'd made the night before and then Mr Passarella. Gaspar was bringing up the rear before Marianna appeared to join the rest of them in the office.

'Here we are, all present and correct my dear lady,' said Jeremiah. 'We have had an absolute hoot on all the rides! The Chimney Chaser is just incredible. How you manage to get up and down chimneys so easily is beyond me, if that little treasure of a ride is anything to go by, but I absolutely love it! Children are going to have so much fun in Befland!'

Gaspar looked at Bef expecting to see her beaming from ear to ear, but she was not. Instead, she looked very upset, almost on the verge of tears – something Gaspar had thought impossible for such a feisty witch. He drew his chair closer to hers.

'What on earth is the matter?' he asked.

Mr Passarella adjusted his spectacles. Thaz and

Mel hopped on to the floor to sit closer to Bef and Jeremiah jumped up to sit on the edge of the desk.

'Yes, what is the matter?' asked Mr Passarella.

'We have what we might call a 'problem', explained Bef. 'You might call it a problem of great proportions. You could call it a problem of enormous proportions. In fact, it's a problem beyond all probable problems. It's a big problem.'

All six people in the room had turned an ash grey colour.

'Would you like to explain the problem?' asked Mr Passarella, in his usual efficient way. In his heart, he was fearing a return of that dreadful dust and started to move his mouth around in a funny manner, remembering how it had tasted on top of his cappuccino every morning.

'The problem first became apparent to me when I awoke to find my nose twitching and my toes tingling. That is typically a sign that trouble's on the cards. When I then found my broom tapping the floor, I knew there was something afoot. To clarify what was happening, I found my big bucket and stood my broom in water, with a few little additions to keep it calm. From there, I deduced that my trusty broom believes its maker is close at hand. I told Jeremiah this early on today, but there have been further developments since then.'

Jeremiah began to wobble, almost falling off the desk and on to the floor.

'What on earth, do you mean further

developments?' he asked, in a most frightened voice like a little mouse trapped in a corner.

'And also,' asked Mel, 'can I just check if the broom maker we're talking about here is that little devil, Bernhardt Bürstenfrisür?'

'I am afraid so,' said Bef, 'and the further developments are equally distressing. For a start, I have discovered that Bernhardt has the right to take my broom back, as it has been 1020 years since he first made it and he can demand its return now, at any point, so it can carry out his wishes. That is tearing my heart apart, as you can imagine. However, there is a further twist to the tale. My broom seemed to believe someone else was close at hand assisting Bernhardt and seemed to suggest that this was Capriccia Claus. Now that I could not believe, as she is an airhead of a woman, whose head has unfortunately lost its brain somewhere along its journey through life. She could never do anything that would seriously harm me and I think my broom must have got a little confused.'

Bef's words were interrupted as her broom jumped up a little in indignation from under the table. She looked at it curiously, wondering why on earth it felt it was right and she was wrong. She sought to explain things not just to her friends, but to her broom as well.

'The reason I think my broom was confused,' she said, in a gentle tone that would not further annoy her wooden friend, 'is that it is a woman who is probably assisting Bernhardt. I think they have planned to ruin the opening of Befland by cutting off our coal supplies in Russia. The mine workers, at the mine that Gaspar and I both visited, report seeing a fairy in a black tutu, who blamed coal for ruining her white tutu. In fairness, she probably said woo-inning, as she can't pronounce the letter r, but I expect they didn't realise that, being Russian … in fact, it's a wonder that any of them understood her at all, unless she'd cast a spell.'

The eyes of everyone in the room were fixed on her.

'What does this mean?' asked Gaspar slowly, as if acting as a spokesperson for the group.

'It means,' said Bef, 'that I must guard my broom with my life. We must also be on our guard, as Bernhardt and the fairy in the black tutu, who goes by the name of Fiery Tina, may plan to disrupt other rides at Befland. Before we know it, we could have a case of exploding aniseed balls, or a pile up of Bonbon Bumper Cars. We must be very vigilant and stay together as much as possible. There is safety in numbers and that must be our number one rule.'

'Oh dear, oh dear,' fretted Marianna, getting into a terrible state. 'I think I had better go and fetch us all a cup of acorn tea.' She sprang to her feet and headed out of the door and down the stairs.

'What will Bernhardt get out of these pranks?' asked Thaz intelligently.

'Revenge, I suppose,' answered Bef. 'Although he knows it was not I who voted against him and prevented him becoming a Very Important Present Bringer, he still hasn't acquired VIPB status. The same is true of Fiery Tina, who wanted to be the VIPB for Florence back in the 15th century. I had to stop her doing that by firing coal at her, which is when she unfortunately got knocked out by a stray piece and covered in soot. I hadn't intended that to happen, but sometimes one's spells and equipment go a little awry.'

Mel was almost giggling to himself at this point, until Mr Passarella gave him the sternest of looks.

Mr Passarella straightened his tie, adjusted his spectacles, took his handkerchief out of his waistcoat pocket and blew his nose violently, so that it sounded like a trumpeting elephant.

'Befland is at great risk, by the sound of it,' he declared. 'We must alert the town's folk and ask them to help stand guard over it. If we organise a rota, we should be able to keep these dreadful fiends away. It is in everyone's interest that Befland opens, as it will bring so many visitors to the town and where there are visitors, there is money to be spent in our shops and cafés. Befland MUST go ahead.'

'There is no harm in trying,' said Bef, 'but it is I who must be on my guard. It is like our last adventure all over again,' she said to Gaspar, trying to raise a smile as she did so.

'You know I'll be there to help you,' replied

Gaspar. 'I will work up some more of our potions. They knocked out Bernhardt last time, so we can do it again. As for this Fiery Tina woman, we shall have to wait and see.'

Bef beamed. She had such a soft spot for Gaspar and knew how loyal he was. He had more than proved himself last time and he was right, he had knocked out Bernhardt twice. Whether this meant that Bernhardt was also seeking revenge on him, however, was something she did not dare consider.

'We must get that tea,' she said, realising that all were in a state of shock. 'Marianna,' she called, 'is the tea ready yet?'

No reply came from downstairs.

'Marianna,' screeched Bef. 'Do you need some help down there?'

Again, there was no reply.

'I'll go and chivvy her along,' offered Jeremiah, jumping off the desk and bounding out of the room. Within minutes, he was rushing back through the door in an absolute panic, his green and white spotted waistcoat flapping wildly and his chicken wire hat wobbling madly on his head, causing the cotton reels to almost topple out.

'She's not there,' he gasped, out-of-breath and shaking from head to foot. 'There's no sign of her.'

'Perhaps she's gone to fetch some milk?' suggested Thaz.

'No, we have plenty,' replied Jeremiah. 'The strange thing is that Marianna is not there, but

I found this piece of rolled up parchment.' He whipped a roll of yellow coloured paper out of his pocket and handed it to Bef, who undid a red ribbon that was holding it together. She unfurled the paper and started to read a riddle.

'Marianna was all in a flurry,

Making her tea in a hurry.

Now there's no more of that:

She hangs like a bat …

To find her, you really must scurry.'

'What in heaven's name does this mean?' asked Mr Passarella.

'I have no idea,' replied Jeremiah.

'It's a kind of riddle,' replied Bef. 'Fiery Tina loves her little games. This has her hallmark all over it. Marianna is somewhere suspended like a bat. We need to think where she could possibly be. Where in Fiery Tina's contorted head would she have taken dear, sweet Marianna? Where would be the logical place?'

'The attic!' declared Mel, at which the three boys all darted up the stairs, thumping heavily on the floorboards above Bef's head. Within minutes, they were back again, with a gloomy look painted on each of their faces.

'I take it she's not there?' said Bef in a dejected

tone. 'We must think harder. Where would Marianna logically be? Where does she typically spend her time? This is where we will find her. Fiery Tina wants us to locate her for some reason, or she wouldn't have left the riddle.'

An inspired look fell across Mr Passarella's face.

'In the church tower,' he declared triumphantly. 'She spends so much time in the church, it's the logical place for her to be.'

At that moment a peal of bells came from the church's bell tower, ringing out all over the town. This was not normal for this time of day and many of the townsfolk rushed out into the main square, to find out what was going on. Bef, 'The Three Kings', Mr Passarella and Jeremiah, flew down the stairs and joined them. As they reached the piazza and looked up at the bell tower, they could see Marianna hanging upside down in bat mode.

'Why is she not moving?' asked Gaspar in a true panic. All looked up and saw that he was right. There was not a single movement from poor Marianna's body.

'Because she has been turned to stone,' said Bef. 'Statuefication is one of Fiery Tina's best tricks.'

At that moment, something came fluttering down from the sky and landed on Bef's head. She grabbed it quickly and turned a piece of blank card over to reveal a letter B.

'We must go and help her,' shrieked Jeremiah.

'We can't,' said Bef, in a most depressed tone.

'This letter tells me that this is not just a simple riddle, but part of a complex conundrum … another thing for which Fiery Tina is famous. Until we receive more letters, Marianna will be stuck up there like a bat.'

Tears began to roll down her face and on to the stones below her feet. In that split second, Gaspar knew they were in serious trouble.

CHAPTER NINE

Capriccia was beside herself with excitement. At the precise moment when Fiery Tina had deposited the screaming Marianna at her feet, she had sweated herself into a total panic and completely forgotten everything Fiery Tina has taught her. Luckily, the mad fairy had been as nutty and annoying as normal, dancing around the ruins of the castle in which they had taken up residence singing, 'Dim, blonde Cap-wi-ccia: dim, blonde Cap-wi-ccia.' In a moment of anger induced by Fiery Tina's taunting, Capriccia had performed not only statuefication to perfection, but also carried out a Muoversi Manoeuvre, which involved concentrating on a suitable place to which to move her victim and then devising a clever riddle for those who needed to be taunted and upset. Marianna had suddenly been transported to the church bell tower, hanging like a bat, but one cast in stone.

If the truth be known, once Capriccia had performed the statuefication and Muoversi Manoeuvre, Fiery Tina had lost interest and had gone back to her favourite pastime of playing hopscotch. This gave Capriccia the opportunity to get into a huddle with Bernhardt and devise the riddle to send to Bef, with his much-needed help. All that then remained was for Bernhardt to fly over the piazza, taking care not to leave telltale pink trails in the sky, to drop the letter B down on to Bef's head.

Sly was feeling bitter. While Fiery Tina played hopscotch and was lost in her own crazy world, he was being treated like an outsider, excluded by both Capriccia and Bernhardt, even though, without him, there would have been on conundrum, no riddle, no statuefication and no Muoversi Manoeuvre. Without him, they would all still be scratching their heads in Florence, wondering how on earth to hurt Bef. How easily they had forgotten that. How quickly they had left him out of their plans. How foolish they had been to forget how his name 'Sly' was SO appropriate!

As the hours continued like this, he sat and festered, feeling lonely and unloved, detesting the woman, who he had trekked across Europe to help, more and more with each passing day. The longer he sat there, the more he thought that he would make all three of them pay for treating him like this. At least in Fiery Tina's case he could put it down to her insanity! Capriccia and Bernhardt had no excuse.

Capriccia was unbearable now. Every few seconds she kept declaring how clever she now was, what a great and wicked fairy she had become, how her skills knew no bounds. Every time an insect or a reptile appeared in the undergrowth, she turned it to stone in the blink of an eye, becoming increasingly evil as she went along, until she began to turn on stray cats wandering through the crumbling castle and beautiful, helpless birds. A vile laugh cackled and echoed around the castle every time she performed a trick. She was hardly recognisable as the woman Sly had known, apart from when she yawned widely in his face whenever he spoke to her.

Down in the village, Bef was in a panic. She had turned every page in the Grandissimo Libro di Scongiuri at least twenty times and found nothing to undo a statuefication spell. This was the reason why Fiery Tina's stone victims still lay scattered across Florence all these hundreds of years later. Nobody could free them, even the best of witches … and Bef definitely wasn't that. She could only perform the pietrifisico spell and keep people in a semi-permanent stony state for a few minutes. In truth, she should have studied harder when younger.

Bef turned the letter B over in her hands again and again. What did this mean? Was it a B for Bernhardt? Was he simply trying to tell her that he was behind this, as if she didn't already know that? Was he that bigheaded? The answer to this was undoubtedly 'yes', but somehow she felt there was more to this than one triumphant letter. She was sure it was a conundrum, but until she received more information from those suspending Marianna in stone, she was completely powerless.

'Could this be a B from the title of VIPB?' asked Jeremiah, trying to be helpful as always, but becoming ever so irritating as Bef sat there feeling helpless.

'Forse,' she said, forgetting that he couldn't speak Italian. 'Perhaps,' she explained in English, rather wearily.

The boys tried to keep everyone's spirits up, but none of them could stop their eyes moving up towards the church tower whenever they left the building. There, the sight of Marianna in her bat mode made all of them shudder and feel absolutely useless. Who in their right mind would do such a thing, however annoyed they felt?

Bef's broom was also behaving weirdly. It kept insisting on jumping on to its bristles, spinning around and trying to communicate that Capriccia was behind this. Bef wasn't listening. She had convinced herself that Capriccia wasn't capable and that her broom was confusing her with Fiery Tina, who certainly was likely to do such a nasty, vile thing as to turn a poor, innocent woman into a stone bat.

'She probably chose to put a bat in the belfry, because she has enough bats in her own belfry,' explained Bef at least ten times a day as they sat there and tried to get on with the planning for Befland with very heavy hearts.

In Lapland, there were other things happening.

Lars could not ignore the fact that the Northern Lights had turned red and not just red for a short while … they had been red now for at least four days, maybe longer. This was not normal and it was not just a myth spread by the Lapps that the sign of red lights in the sky spelt terrible troubles. Whenever red lights had appeared for a long period of time, it had always meant disaster for someone, somewhere. No matter how much he tried to forget about the colour of the sky, he could not. He simply had to know who was in trouble, as his very sharp senses were telling him that the red skies were intended to be a message for him – the best reindeer whisperer the world had ever seen.

Lars knew what needed to be done. Like most Lapps, he knew that the Northern Lights were actually created by an Arctic Fox dragging its tail across the snow and causing sparks to fly into the sky. When times were good, the fox always seemed to manage to send up only green, yellow and blue sparks. Why should it now be deciding to create red sparks?

Lars decided to do something decisive. He cupped his hands together and made a distinctive call that the reindeer in the grazing grounds around Santa's village instantly recognised. One by one they started to make their way to the fence by which Lars was standing. Lars greeted them by rubbing their noses and stroking them gently. He then took the decision to share his concerns.

'My friends,' he said. 'Look at the skies. See how red the lights are and how fiery and angry they seem. Something is amiss, but I know not what. I must speak with the Arctic Fox and discover why he feels he must send the red sparks skywards. In the meantime, we must be ready to fly and assist those who are in danger, as I see this as a personal sign, though that is just a gut feeling that I have, rather than one based on fact. Something or someone seems to be calling to me and I must be ready to respond. I know that I always insist that you rest and prepare for Christmas, but just this once, will you do as I ask and fly with me, should the need arise?'

The reindeer grouped together, before the leader approached Lars and nuzzled his hand gently.

'Lars the Reindeer Whisperer,' he said, 'You saved us from the terrible strains placed on our herd by that dreadful woman, Capriccia Claus, and we shall be eternally grateful. Before you came back to us, she was flying us to Milan and Paris and New York two or three times a week: now our life is content and restful again. To fly to assist you would be an honour and a journey that we could not refuse to make.'

Lars bowed his head in thanks.

'Do you have any idea where to find the Arctic Fox?' he asked, speaking in perfect reindeer.

'He will run past the top perimeter fence at approximately fifteen minutes past midnight,' said the leader of the herd. I will wait there with you and we will ask him to tarry a while, although he travels at a great pace and is not easy to stop in his tracks.'

'Thank you,' said Lars. 'Perhaps we can gain some clues as to what is happening.'

The pair of them made their way to the fence at the appropriate time and sat in the snow, comforted by the warmth of a small fire that Lars managed to light to provide heat and protected by a small shelter that fended off the cold winds. Sure enough, a crunching noise could be heard gathering pace in the snow as 12.15am approached and the head of the herd nudged Lars, to tell him to get to his feet. Together, they straddled the path, stopping the Arctic Fox in his tracks. He skidded to a halt at the feet of the herd's leader.

'What do you think you are doing?' snapped the short-tempered fox, as Lars looked skywards and saw no red sparks flying from his tail. Mystified, he attempted to talk to the fox in his language, though he was by no means a master of it.

'What is making the sky so red and fiery?' he asked. 'We need your help to tell us why you are sending red sparks skywards.'

'I am not,' said the Arctic Fox rather indignantly. 'I myself have been fretting about the colour of the sky, but have no answers. You will need to talk to the Siberian Jay. I think that meddlesome bird must be responsible. I am simply carrying on running, to try to turn the skies back to their normal colour. It's wearing me out, but I don't know what else to do.'

'Then let me not detain you any longer,' said Lars. 'Off you go and, if you see the Siberian Jay, please send him my way.'

'Are you not Lars the Reindeer Whisperer?' asked the fox. 'If so, your friend the Arctic Warbler is the best one to talk to, if you wish to speak with the Siberian Jay. They are in regular communication, or so I believe.'

The Arctic Fox carried on with its journey, leaving Lars pondering what to do. He cupped his hands together again and murmured, with a bubbling sound. Nothing happened, so he tried again, this time seemingly louder and more urgent in tone. Suddenly, a fluttering noise could be heard in the stillness and the Arctic Warbler flew down on to Lars' arm.

'My friend,' said Lars, speaking in perfect Arctic Warbler. 'What is the meaning of the red, fiery skies? I have asked the Arctic Fox and he knows nothing. He tells me the Siberian Jay may know and that you speak to him regularly.'

The bird began to twitter to Lars in words the reindeer could not understand, but Lars was nodding and seemingly taking a whole tale on board.

Lars turned to the head of the herd.

'My friend here tells me that the Siberian Jay has indeed been lighting the sky, as he was warned by a snow goose that there were troubles brewing many thousands of miles away. The snow goose apparently heard this from a grebe in Germany, who had news of the dreadful Capriccia Claus. Apparently, she was living in Hamburg, but was whisked off to Italy by a man who caused a great disturbance in the sky, causing flocks of birds to scatter. A passing buzzard informed the grebe that this was a man named Bernhardt Bürstenfrisür, known as the 'Most Fearsome Feller in Folklore'. They tracked his progress as far as the Italian border, but then his trail disappeared without trace.

'Capriccia is nowhere to be seen in Germany, much to the relief of all the creatures there. The Siberian Jay is apparently trying to warn wildlife that a woman with a love of furs, feathers and ridiculous and distasteful fashion items is re-emerging and becoming more powerful, day by day, if recent reports are to be believed.'

'From where do the recent reports come?' asked the reindeer.

'From a little town in Italy. A town in which pigeons have reported that a woman has been turned to stone and is hanging like a bat in the bell tower.'

'Do you know what this means?' enquired the reindeer gently.

'I am not sure,' said Lars, 'but our friend Bef is the only person of my acquaintance in Italy and she, of course, knows both Capriccia and Bernhardt. Putting all of this together, I can only wonder whether she is in great danger. For all I know, she could even be the woman in the bell tower, heaven forbid.'

'What are you going to do?' asked the head of the herd.

'I need more guidance,' replied Lars. 'I must do the sensible thing and consult the Rock of Erik the Enraged. It has never failed a soul in need before and it will guide my thinking now. There is no point us charging off without better knowledge of what may be happening, or what we may face on arrival. The last thing I would do is put any of your herd in danger. We must be calm and cool and make sure we know exactly what our plan of action is. The Rock of Erik the Enraged should be able to show us a clearer path, though it will take me several days to trek into the hills and reach it and several more days before I can return to talk to you. I cannot ask you to fly the route to the rock, as it can only be reached on foot and only by those with a real need to consult with it and listen to its wisdom. I just hope that I have the time to do this and that it will not be too late for Bef by the time I return.'

The reindeer nodded and, without speaking further, the two of them packed up their belongings and began to walk back to the rest of the herd.

As Lars turned to leave the reindeer, to return to his hut, the wise old leader called after him.

'Do not forget the power of amethyst, my friend,' he urged. 'Remember that Santa's village has a ready supply of amethyst drawn from the mines around these parts. It may be that you need this to help you in your ultimate mission.'

Lars took this on board, stroking his long beard and looking thoughtful.

'Indeed,' he said. 'Your words are extremely intelligent and I must build this into my planning. It will take a little extra time to collect a supply, but amethyst has powerful qualities and it will do me no harm to have some on board. Who knows whether I may need to call upon it to come to my assistance? After all, I am no magician or wizard, merely a reindeer whisperer.'

With that, the pair of them parted, both shivering slightly at the prospect of Capriccia Claus being back on her horrendously decorated feet. As Lars walked back towards his hut, he looked up and saw the monstrosity that was Capriccia Claus's Casa of Contentments, towering above Santa's village, with its bright fuchsia paint standing out like a dreadful gaudy beacon, a tasteless, garish eyesore, still all lit up, as if she had never left.

'At least the moths are doing a good job of destroying that dreadful shoe collection,' muttered Lars. 'The sooner Santa gets rid of it all, the sooner our recollections of that awful woman can fade.'

Back in Italy, Bef stared up at the church tower and shuddered for the umpteenth time that day at the sight of poor Marianna still hanging in her bat-like state. Just across the street, in the palace, Capriccia and Bernhardt had their binoculars trained on the same bell tower and were in fits of giggles as they stared at their first victim.

'Who shall we go for next, Capriccia?' asked Bernhardt, highly amused to be part of this wicked game.

'I haven't yet decided,' said Capriccia rather vacantly. 'Fiery Tina says the conundrum should gain in strength, starting with the weakest victims and then moving on to those who have more power and strength.'

'So who do you have in mind?' shrieked Bernhardt, enjoying the very thought of the plot ahead.

'Well goodness me,' exclaimed Capriccia, 'I haven't worked out who the weakest are, yet!'

She treated Bernhardt's question as if it was the most ridiculous she had ever heard, leaving him shaking his head in bewilderment, while she was enjoying the view through the binoculars once more. He did worry that the fate of his VIPB future and the whole of this plan lay in the hands of someone who wasn't terribly bright and who could actually be described as downright dumb. He could only hope that Fiery Tina, for all her faults, managed to keep Capriccia on track ... if she could tear herself away from her games of hopscotch for long enough!

CHAPTER TEN

The mood was highly subdued in the Befland planning office. Mel, Thaz and Gaspar had tried to lift everyone's spirits with some lively music, but nobody was interested in being cheerful and upbeat – not while Marianna was still in the bell tower. Jeremiah was doing his best to chivvy everyone along and keep things lively, but Bef was on edge every minute of the day, drumming her fingers up and down on the desk and desperately trying to rack her brains as to what to do.

'Surely they've had their fun now,' she declared in an exasperated tone. 'If Bernhardt wants to order my broom to return, I wish he would just make his intentions known, rather than playing this silly and hurtful game. Why make poor Marianna suffer if he just wants to rob me of my broom? It makes no sense. No sense at all.'

'We must get on with our preparations, no matter how hard it is,' urged Mr Passarella, as everyone else just sat there looking glum. 'Befland is supposed to be a happy and exuberant place and we must remember that. We must put all our plans into action. Marianna would want us to do that. If we don't keep things on track, there won't be an opening and the whole town will suffer.'

'What's the next thing to be done?' asked Bef, in a less than enthusiastic tone. While she knew Mr Passarella was right, she was finding it difficult to feel energetic.

'The Bonbon Bumper Cars are due to be delivered today,' explained Mr Passarella. 'We'll have thirty cars in ten different, vibrant colours and ten different flavours. We'll have to test them out later today, to check that they work and provide the fun we hoped for. I am sure children will love these, not to mention their parents. It's going to be quite something to dodge other cars, while experiencing the sweet taste of bonbons smacking the taste buds at the same time. I think we've ordered Stupendous Strawberry, Ridiculous Raspberry, Luscious Lemon Fizz, Amazing Almond, Brilliant Banana, Magic Mandarin, Riveting Rhubarb, Bonza Blackcurrant, Lickable Lime and Barmy Butterscotch. What a treat it will be!'

'Sounds crazy,' agreed Gaspar. 'We'll help test them, won't we guys!'

'Sure thing,' said Mel. 'Should be cool.'

Thaz nodded in agreement. 'Love driving fairground cars,' he enthused. 'Best fun ever.'

Bef looked thoughtful. Mr Passarella read her thoughts.

'You're worrying about the Coaler Coaster again

... I can see it in your eyes. We will get on the phone this afternoon and see if we can contact other mines around the world. The evil fairy can't possibly stop every mine around the globe from supplying us with coal. We just need to get some phone numbers and start talking to the right people. We will sort it out one way or another.'

Jeremiah jumped to his feet.

'Happy to help, in whatever way I can!' he declared boldly. Even if I have to knit and sew bundles that look like lumps of coal, we will have something to put in the trucks when the park opens.'

'Not a bad idea,' said Mr Passarella. 'It would certainly resolve the health and safety issues. Nobody would be hurt and none of the children would get dirty. That would make all my dreams come true.'

Bef scowled. The last thing she wanted was for people to leave the park without having had the thrill of getting coal dust on their face. She loved the feel of coal on her skin. There was nothing quite like it, but maybe she'd just been up and down too many chimneys during her exceedingly long lifetime.

'What time do the Bonbon Bumper Cars arrive?' asked Mel, getting terribly excited about the day ahead.

'Around 2pm,' explained Mr Passarella. 'I've to get down there a little earlier, as there's also going to be a delivery of more aniseed balls for Aniseed Alley. I hadn't realised they would bounce away quite as much as they did. In fact, we may need to put some nets up to make sure they don't escape so easily!'

The boys nodded in unison, while Jeremiah was lost in his own thoughts, doodling sketches of the coal he could knit and sew and thinking deeply about which material would be best suited to the pressures of having to be flung around quite so much.

Bef was still deep in thought.

'What are you thinking about now?' asked Mr Passarella gently, hoping that she would snap out of her mood enough to contribute to the planning for Befland.

'Wondering if someone else I know has any idea how to undo a statuefication spell,' replied Bef. 'Just because I didn't listen when I was younger doesn't mean everyone did the same. Perhaps I need to go out and ponder this back in my house, or see if I can find any notes that relate to statuefication. Surely Fiery Tina can't be the only one who can perform this spell! Maybe it's a thought worth exploring.'

She got to her feet.

'Where are you going?' asked Gaspar, worried by the sight of her looking older than he'd seen her look since Old Father Time had turned her back into a witch aged 30-something.

'Home, just home,' she replied, in a tone that didn't sound too convincing at all, as she slipped on her massive floppy shoes and began to shuffle out of the room, with her broom firmly in her hand.

'We could look after him,' said Gaspar helpfully.

'I can't run the risk, or put you in danger, with Bernhardt on the loose,' explained Bef. 'If anyone is to defend my broom, it has to be me. I won't be long. Go to the park and I will meet you all down there at 2pm.'

Bef left the room, leaving the others sitting in total silence. Jeremiah began to sketch again and 'The Three Kings' looked at each other helplessly. Mr Passarella moved behind a computer, which sat on the desk normally reserved for Marianna.

'Does anyone know how to turn this on?' he asked helplessly. 'I need to try to find some mines that we can contact to get that dratted supply of coal that wc need so much.'

Bef shuffled down the street feeling as though eyes were watching her from every crack and crevice in the wall. It was as if the village cats were staying away from her, in case they too were turned into stone. She didn't even dare look up at the bell tower. She just could not bear the sight of Marianna suspended up there.

Surprisingly, she didn't head towards her house. Instead, she followed a path that took her back to the door with the grand, golden knocker. She hadn't called on her brother for years, but here she was now seeing him twice in two days.

She knocked quite quietly, nervously wondering

if she was being watched. She looked over her shoulder and all around her, but saw nothing. She pretended to be picking something up from the ground, as if she had just stopped because she had dropped a coin or a note. A spyhole opened up in the door.

'Come round to the back,' said the gruff voice of her brother. 'I've been expecting another visit.'

She picked up her broom and pretended to be shuffling back up the street, before darting down an alleyway and through a tiny gate that led to the back of Lorenzo's house. A creaking noise preceded the opening of a cellar door, just a smidgen and just enough for Lorenzo to check that only his sister was waiting to enter. He opened the door wider and ushered her and her broom into the building.

'Why did you think I would call again?' asked Bef, in some surprise that her brother should be so wise.

'Because that woman who assists you with your VIPB present runs is currently suspended in the bell tower like a bat,' replied Lorenzo. 'It doesn't take a genius. You've come here to see if I can help you. You wonder whether I paid more attention to certain spells when I was a boy. You're even wondering whether you concentrated far too much on spells that got you up and down chimneys and not enough on those that were of more general use. Am I right?'

Bef looked slightly peeved, but had to admit that he was spot on.

'It's statuefication,' she said. 'It has to be Fiery Tina. If you recall, I told you about her just after our little tiff a few centuries ago. It would seem that her bitterness knows no bounds. I know of nobody else who can perform statuefication in that way, but worse still, I know of nobody who can undo it.'

Lorenzo looked her in the eye.

'You inherited the Grandissimo Libro di Scongiuri,' he said, as if a little hurt by that fact. 'Have you not studied it, to see if there is a spell you can use?'

'I have tried,' explained Bef, 'but I have so little time and there are so many pages in the book.' She paused for a few seconds. 'That is why I have brought it to you,' she continued. 'You have so much time on your hands, I thought you could maybe look through it and see if there's anything in it – anything at all – that would help Marianna.'

Bef reached inside her cloak and pulled out the Grandissimo Libro.

'Please, Lorenzo. Not for me, but for Marianna.'

Lorenzo took the book from her.

'Sometimes, you seem to regard me as some sort of ogre. Someone who scares you. Why that is, I do not know. I never meant you any harm.'

'I know,' replied Bef, 'but seemingly there are enemies who do wish to seek revenge. I am on edge and have no idea who I can trust and who I cannot trust. I do, however, know that you are my brother and you will do what you can to assist me, even if we do rarely see each other these days.'

She turned to head back to the door.

'I must not stay,' she said. 'I must not alert anyone to your presence here, or make our relationship known. We must tread carefully and you must watch your back too. Who knows what is happening out there at the moment! We must all be on our guard.'

She was almost halfway back up the cellar steps when Lorenzo called her back.

'Sister,' he said sternly. 'I do not know why, but I am seeing amethyst in my mind. Make sure you refresh your knowledge of amethyst and make use of it should it fall into your hands. This is strange, I know, but I have been dreaming of it at night and awaking in a sweat that is so severe that I cannot drowse off again afterwards.'

'Are you seeing anything else,' she asked, remembering the power of his brother's dreams and how they had assisted her in the past.

'Curiously,' he said, 'I am seeing letters. An array of letters.'

'Not just one?' asked Bef.

'No, several,' he replied. 'But I am also seeing clocks, the fingers of clocks, the mechanism of clocks and much more. I even hear the ticking of clocks in my sleep.'

'I don't know why this is,' replied Bef, 'unless

it is because Marianna is hanging underneath the church clock. I will remember it though, in case it starts to make sense.'

'More importantly, sister,' warned her brother, 'remember the amethyst.'

'I will,' promised Bef. 'I most certainly will. Please just do as I ask in return and read the Grandissimo Libro, page by page, until you find something.'

'Consider it done,' replied Lorenzo. 'Godspeed.'

Luckily for Bef, Capriccia and Bernhardt were far too occupied gazing at the goings on at Befland to have noticed her visit to Lorenzo. Situated on the hill above, they were watching delivery trucks arriving.

'What do you think is in those trucks?' asked Capriccia.

'We vill soon find out,' replied Bernhardt, pointing out the arrival of Mr Passarella. 'And over here, we have those singing boys and zat little pipsqueak Jeremiah with his fancy clothes and ridiculous chicken wire hat. Look how zay all run around, like overgrown children playing with new toys. It is simply ridiculous!'

Capriccia was staring at the scene below.

'Which of them would make the best statue?' she asked. 'Which one shall I choose? Which one deserves my attention?' Her eyes moved from man to man as she changed her mind over and over again.

'She'll be here soon,' urged Bernhardt. 'The minute she steps on a hopscotch line, she'll be flying in to find you and she'll want an answer from you. You don't want to upset her. She's in a bad enough mood as it is today.'

Capriccia muttered something rude under her breath. She wished she could be rid of Fiery Tina once and for all. Only the thought of getting her Casa back was making her bite her lip and not go into one of her famous screaming fits with her. She looked back at the scene below and made her decision. That was just in the nick of time. A fluttering on the breeze was followed by a graceful fairy landing by Fiery Tina.

'So who is your next victim, Capwiccia?' she asked in her usual irritating way. 'Whisper in my ear and tell me where you would like me to put them!'

Capriccia leaned over, brushing Fiery Tina's tutu, much to her teacher's annoyance. After she'd smoothed the black net down again, Fiery Tina began to simper.

'Seems a good choice to me,' she said, almost giving Capriccia praise for once.

Down below, there was great excitement. The Bonbon Bumper Cars were being unloaded and put into position within the ride area that had been built for them. 'The Three Kings' were lovingly eyeing up each car, jumping in to test the seating and going into raptures about all the Bonbon smells that were filling their nostrils. Jeremiah was leaping around like a flea, jumping from in front of one car to the other, helping the boys take pictures of themselves behind the steering wheels. For a few minutes, it seemed they had forgotten all about Marianna.

The sight of all this frivolity made Capriccia's hackles rise. Why should they be having such fun while she was being deprived of her wonderful Casa of Contentments? She began to turn red in the face and clenched her fingers into her hands so tight that her fingernails dug deep into her skin.

'I want to do it now!' she shouted.

At that moment, Bef arrived at the park, flying in on her broom and immediately placing it under its invisibility shield, in an attempt to try to keep it safe. She noticed the boys messing around in the cars and was spotted by Jeremiah, who ran up to greet her and take her over to the Bonbon Bumper Cars.

'They're absolutely super!' he enthused. 'The smells are so wonderful they are making my tummy rumble. I must get to a sweet shop as soon as possible, as it's just like the real thing. Children will love these!'

He bounded around like an excited hare, making Bef feel ever so dizzy and distracted. Her mind was full of thoughts of amethyst and clocks, of ticking and letters, of her brother reading her book of spells and of coal supplies and mines around the world. As that last thought entered her head, she looked around.

'Jeremiah,' she said, getting no response from her excited friend at all. 'Jeremiah,' she repeated, still getting no reaction. 'Jeremiah Needlebaum, please calm down and tell me where Mr Passarella is,' she shouted at the top of her voice.

Jeremiah stopped jumping and strained his eyes in the sun.

'He was over there just now,' he replied. 'He was talking to the delivery men and there was one Bonbon Bumper Car missing, so they went back to the van to check where it was. I expect he's still at the van.'

Bef shuffled over to the truck, her massive, floppy shoes looking very odd when matched with her quite stylish dress. There was no way she would be parted from her shoes, however. She spotted a delivery man and called to him.

'I am looking for Mr Passarella. Is he there with you?'

The man shook his head and suggested he might have gone to the Coaler Coaster. Bef hurried that way, wondering if a supply of coal had suddenly been found. The boys watched her scurry past and decided to follow. She walked all around the Coaler Coaster, but could find nobody. She turned back, with a distressed look on her face.

'Everyone shout out at once,' she demanded. 'After three.'

She counted to three and all five of them shouted out Mr Passarella's name, but not a sound was heard around the park. We must dash back to the office and see if he has gone back there,' she urged.

'Jump in the car and grab the broom,' demanded Mel. 'It will be quicker that way.'

They drove off at speed, with the tyres squealing on the hot, sticky surface of the road. They roared up towards the town walls and jumped out, to walk the last part of the journey on foot. Up the hill they struggled, all walking as fast as their legs could carry them, to get to the office as soon as possible and try to locate Mr Passarella.

They began to stride past the town's grand fountain and the statues of former Dukes who had ruled the town centuries before. As they continued on their way, something struck Bef. There were too many statues in the square. She swung around and almost toppled over. As she regained her balance, she looked up to the sky and straight into the face of a brand new statue – not any of the Dukes and not part of the fountain. She came face to face with a statue of Mr Passarella, still holding the clipboard that he had been using down at the park.

Everything about him was turned to stone, from his gold-rimmed spectacles to his lovely white handkerchief. His expression looked strained and his brow was furrowed, as if he had been deep in concentration when the statuefication spell had been cast.

The others, who had carried on walking, were a few feet on when Bef shouted, 'Mr Passarella is not in the office.'

'How do you know?' yelled Gaspar, as her four remaining companions turned round.

'Because he is here,' answered Bef weeping. 'He is here, right here in the piazza.'

Mouths fell open as the others looked at the statue and realised that she wasn't joking. As every one of them pulled their clothing a little tighter around their bodies in fear, a pigeon swooped down and dropped something at Bef's feet. She made to shoo it away, but then realised that it had left her a gift ... a gift of a letter N.

'What does this mean?' asked Gaspar aghast at what had happened.

'It's the second letter of the conundrum,' replied Bef slowly, knowing that this statement would cause fear and horror among her friends.

'Second?' shrieked Thaz like a girl. 'Do you mean there are more?'

'Seemingly so,' answered Bef dejectedly. 'B and N mean nothing on their own. The game has hardly begun.' She met Mr Passarella's stony stare once more and repeated, 'The game has hardly begun.'

Chapter Eleven

Lars pulled up the woolly collar of his warm overcoat and wrapped a wide scarf around his mouth. He placed goggles over his eyes and a woven hat on his head. The wind was beginning to whip across the mountainside and he could not quite recall where to find the Rock of Erik the Enraged. He had sworn on it in the past, when he had been determined to seek revenge for having been sacked as Santa's reindeer keeper. In a way, he had settled the score when Bef had taken him back to Lapland and, having made his point, had now made his peace with Santa. He had certainly shown his worth in recent months, keeping the reindeer happy after all the trouble caused by the dreadful Capriccia.

Lars had to wonder where Capriccia was. Could she have made her way to Italy, as the birds suspected? He had thought she would have reappeared in Lapland by now, not to see her husband, but to take up residence once again in her terrible Casa. Lars had suggested demolishing the garish building, but Santa just seemed to want to let sleeping dogs lie. Somehow, Lars didn't believe Capriccia could stay quiet and out of the limelight for long. He often awoke with a jolt in the night, fearing she had returned. He knew the reindeer still dreaded the sound of the siren that Capriccia had used to summon them whenever she wanted to satisfy her shopaholic needs and have them fly her to Milan, Paris or New York.

These thoughts filled his head as he trudged through the snowy uplands surrounding Santa's village. There was no life up here, not even the Arctic Warbler would venture this far. All he could see for miles and miles was snow, white snow that was turning black as the very little light that they enjoyed here at this time of year began to disappear fast behind the mountains.

He stopped and lit a lantern, which swung in the wind and cast strange shadows across the snow, first a leaf shape: next a silhouette of a stooped figure. He held a compass in the other hand, trying to steer himself to where he thought the Rock of Erik the Enraged could be found. His legs were aching – walking in thick snow being no easy task. It was slow progress and the weather was getting worse. Although he wanted to help Bef as soon as possible, he had to stop. He was too weary. He had to build himself a snow shelter before it got too dark and nestle down, out of the wind. His journey would have to start again tomorrow.

Capriccia was not feeling tired in the slightest.

Her joy at having performed another perfect statuefication spell was immense. She and Bernhardt had taken up a viewing position in the palace, from where they could see the piazza. Her binoculars kept resting on Mr Passarella's statue and filling her heart with glee.

'I SO need a bilberry juice to celebrate,' she declared. 'What a perfect statuefication that was. Just note the look on his face ... absolutely flabbergasted by what was happening to him! He turned from human to stone in no more than ten seconds, from top to bottom. The Marianna woman took longer than that, so I reckon I'm getting better at magic by the day.'

Bernhardt sighed to himself. She had said all of this at least twenty times already and he had informed her that they didn't have any bilberry juice in this village. He found her extremely tiresome, but knew that if he wanted to be a VIPB, he would need someone like Capriccia – someone cunning, devious and self-centred – as an ally. He didn't have the capacity to get the better of Bef himself. He could put up with Capriccia for a few weeks more and then, once she'd ruined Bef, he would take charge and demand VIPB status. Capriccia would be so powerful by that point, she would probably control several VIPB areas, perhaps even Santa's. It would be so easy to convince her that he should be given one of them.

Across the street, in Bef's office, there was

total silence. 'The Three Kings', Bef and Jeremiah had arrived back, after having seen Mr Passarella in the piazza, and Bef had written on a piece of paper the words, 'Say nothing: write everything down.' Somehow, she suspected that her enemies had bugged the room and were listening in on their conversations. She was right. Just yards away, Bernhardt was fiddling with his listening equipment and picking up nothing. That was frustrating him hugely. Why was nobody saying anything?

Pieces of paper were passed around the office, starting with Bef writing, 'None of us must ever be alone.'

Thaz had written, 'We must find a way of tracking our enemies down.'

Mel wrote, 'Befland must open on time. We owe that to Marianna and Mr Passarella.'

Jeremiah then scribbled, 'Anyone for a cup of acorn tea?' The other four all held up a piece of paper saying 'No'. Jeremiah shook his head in despair. Things had come to a pretty pass if nobody wanted a calming cup of his favourite refreshment.

Gaspar held up another note. It read, 'Who do you think will be next?' All had just shrugged their shoulders, so he added his own suggestion, which was, 'I reckon the three of us will all be taken at once.' Bef looked mortified by that thought, so he put his arm around her and squeezed her tightly.

Mel then instructed them all to write a list of what needed to be done for the opening of Befland.

They flicked through files on Mr Passarella's desk, found his notebook, looked at documents on the computer and eventually came up with a list. It was just days to the opening date that they had set nearly a year before. How could things have gone so badly wrong at pretty much the last minute?

Jeremiah opened his mouth, about to gush about something or other, judging by the expression on his face. Bef, Thaz, Mel and Gaspar all glared at him, making him put his hand across his mouth very quickly. All he gave was a little squeak.

'What is going on?' said Bernhardt, listening in across the street. 'All I am picking up now are ze squeaks of mice!'

Jeremiah wrote down what it was he had been about to say. His note read, 'I think we all need to go home and get some rest.' The others all nodded their heads in agreement. They packed up their belongings, which in Bef's case meant just picking up her broom. The boys signalled that they would head back to the apartment they were renting, while Bef linked arms with Jeremiah and indicated that they would return to her house. All gave each other a good luck sign, without uttering a word.

Bernhardt didn't even realise they'd left the building, as not a single word had been picked up. They all managed to slip out into the street without him knowing. Had they realised that he would be sitting uncomfortably for at least another two hours without appreciating that the building was empty, they'd have laughed loudly. As it was, they had no idea he was even there.

Up in the Lapland mountains, Lars was having a hard time. He was losing some feeling in his feet, so undid his backpack and found more blankets to wrap around himself. The wind was now howling and he was glad he'd made the decision to build a camp. He started a small fire, which added some warmth and then opened a can of food, which he warmed on the flames. It tasted incredibly good and heated him from the inside. If he could just manage to get some sleep, he was sure he could find the Rock of Erik the Enraged in the morning.

Bef and Jeremiah were also praying for a good night's sleep. They bolted all doors and put shutters across all windows, not sure how Fiery Tina would enter buildings, or whether she even could. A big gap could be seen on Bef's bookcase, marking the place where her massive book of spells would normally be found. She wondered whether the diligent Lorenzo had found anything that could be of help to Marianna and Mr Passarella. She continued to rack her brains to think of any other magic that could assist, but she had done that a hundred times already.

'Can we speak in here?' asked Jeremiah, breaking the silence.

'Well, you just have,' replied Bef, a little tetchily. 'I suppose we can't not talk. We just need to talk about everyday things and not the big things.'

'Do you mean that we can't talk about things like the table and chairs?' asked Jeremiah, not getting her meaning at all.

'No, of course not!' tutted Bef. 'You can talk about tables and chairs as much as you like. We just can't talk about the big things that are going on, or what our plans are under the current very difficult circumstances.'

'Oh, I'm so glad,' replied Jeremiah, 'because I wanted to tell you that the table has a wonky leg. It's about 3mm shorter than all the others, which is why it rocks a lot.'

Bef burst out laughing for the first time in days.

'Only you, Jeremiah, could bring something like that up at this disastrous point in time,' she laughed.

Jeremiah didn't quite understand what she meant, so carried on talking.

'Well, having worked that out,' he said, 'I've made a little felt patch that's exactly the right width to fit under the table leg and stop it from tippling from side to side.'

'Eccellente!' declared Bef, still highly amused by Jeremiah's antics. 'Pop it under there then and I shall be happy for you to make some acorn tea.'

Jeremiah got on to all fours and slipped his bright orange felt pouch under the table leg. Sure enough, he had got the measurements just right and it no longer rocked.

Bef clapped her hands to give him a round of applause.

'What next?' she asked.

'Probably better to ask 'who next?' replied Jeremiah. 'If it's you, what do you want me to do? I'm not sure I could manage to open Befland on my own and I don't think I would have the heart to, if you weren't around my dear lady.' A tear began to roll down his cheek. Bef wiped it away with her thumb.

'Don't cry,' she said. 'I will be just fine and I will make sure we find a way to undo all the damage that our enemies are causing. I just don't know how, right now.'

Jeremiah tried to stop sobbing. 'I will just go and plump up the pillows,' he said, hoping to compose himself again while doing something very domesticated.

'Good idea,' said Bef. 'We need to be as comfortable as possible tonight.'

'Then I think I will turn in,' explained Jeremiah. 'It's been an exhausting and emotional day and I'm a very emotional fellow at the best of times.'

'Yes, indeed,' replied Bef. 'I shall head to bed too, taking my broom with me, of course. Maybe things will look a little better in the morning.'

She began to tidy up a few things while Jeremiah flitted around upstairs.

'Night,' she heard him shout, a few minutes later.

'Sleep tight,' she replied. She cast her eyes

around the room and double-checked that all the doors and shutters were locked.

'Come on broom,' she said, as she picked up her best friend. 'You can sleep at the foot of my bed tonight.'

As Jeremiah had said, the events of the day had been truly exhausting. Her eyes felt heavy even before she rested her head on the pillow. Within minutes she had dropped off into a lovely, calming slumber, which was punctuated just by a strange snuffling sound, which she knew was the noise of Jeremiah snoring.

A few hours later, she shot up like a bolt.

'What was that?' she asked her broom, praying it was still at the foot of the bed. Her broom appeared to be quivering, which sent Bef into a terrible panic. She suddenly realised she couldn't hear any snoring coming through the wall and jumped out of bed as fast as she could, nearly tripping over her long nightdress as she dashed into Jeremiah's room as quickly as humanly possible. Her worst fears were realised, as she focused her eyes on an empty bed with the sheets all thrown back in a terribly messy way.

'NO' she shouted at the top of her voice. 'How could they take him from here?' She rushed down the stairs to check the locks and bolts and ran slap bang into Jeremiah, who was walking around in a very bizarre manner.

'What are you doing, giving me the shock of my

life like that?' she yelled, in an almost angry manner, which was actually down to her being so upset at what she thought had happened to him. Instead of answering back, Jeremiah just kept on walking, right up the stairs and into his bedroom, without uttering a word. He seemed to be in a trance and though she wanted to shake him out of it and tell him off, she knew she couldn't.

'Goodness me, broom,' she declared. 'If we haven't got problems enough, Jeremiah is now sleepwalking! I thought for one moment that Fiery Tina had claimed her third victim.'

Normally, her broom would have responded with a 'no', or something that signified that he agreed with his mistress, but it did nothing, seeming to be even more subdued than ever.

'Perhaps Marianna and Mr Passarella are the only two victims and Bernhardt will now demand your return,' suggested Bef. Again, her broom did nothing to respond.

At that moment, there was a loud rapping on the back door. She leapt in fright and gripped her broom tighter.

'Who would call on us at this time of night?' she asked. She moved slowly to the door and moved the spyhole cover so that she could see who was outside.

'Let us in quickly,' shouted two voices, as they continued to rap on the door. 'It's Gaspar and Mel. Open the door, Bef. Please open the door.'

Bef immediately pulled the bolts back and swung the door open. In piled two of 'The Three Kings', landing in a heap on Bef's hand-woven rug.

'Disaster has struck,' they panted, almost in unison. 'Thaz has disappeared. Just vanished, without a trace, while spending some time outside on the balcony getting some fresh air. We didn't check for a while but then he didn't come back and, when we went out, he wasn't there. He's just gone and he wouldn't run out and leave us. There's only one explanation.'

Bef was wringing her hands in anguish.

'Did you hear any noise? Any voices? Any whirring noise like a flutter of wings? Anything at all?'

'No, not really,' Gaspar explained.

'What do you mean, not really?' asked Bef, now beyond upset.

'Well, when he first went out, he was talking incessantly to a woman down below in the street. He then bobbed back inside to get a notepad, as she wanted his autograph passed down to her from the balcony.'

'Did he describe this woman to you?' asked Bef, trying to process all this information in her mind.

'Well, I seem to remember him saying he needed to give a pretty blonde an autograph,' said Mel. 'Yes, and he also said that she was so tall she could almost reach the balcony.'

Bef's broom suddenly started to spin on its

bristles again. Bef watched it with a look of amazement on her face.

'He's been telling me all along,' she said. 'My broom has been telling me that Capriccia was behind this, but I refused to believe it … I mean, how could I even contemplate that she could be capable of doing all this? Now, I think he's right. I think she's the pretty, tall, blonde woman that Thaz was talking to. Incredible as it seems for a woman whose brain is as dense as a soggy doughnut in a glass of milk, I think Capriccia has been taught some magic. This alters everything, because maybe we're not fighting just two enemies. Perhaps there are three of them.'

'Or more,' speculated Gaspar. 'Remember that odd elf who you said used to rush over to her Casa the minute she clicked her fingers? Perhaps he's also helping her. He seemed to be her only fan back then.'

Bef reached for her sugar bowl and suddenly scattered sugar cubes across the table as she yelled, 'Nemici!' Three of eleven cubes grouped together, leaving seven some inches away and one on its own, exactly halfway between the two groups of sugar cubes. Bef scooped them all back into the bowl and threw them out again. Once more, three grouped together, one sat alone and the rest were all in a pile. For a third time, she repeated the process, again ending up with the same pattern.

'Well,' she said, 'I think you're right.'

'What does Nemici mean?' asked Gaspar, staring at her in amazement.

'It means 'enemies',' explained Bef and you can see here that we seem to have three, not two. But the interesting thing is this one stuck here between the two groups. This is someone who's not quite sure if they are an enemy or not ... someone excluded by the other three. A bit of a loner.'

Gaspar and Mel looked bemused, but went along with the witch's logic. She actually suddenly seemed more animated, even though the number of enemies they thought they were facing had now increased.

'What we must do,' she said decisively, 'is discover who this sugar lump is.' She pointed at the one on its own in the middle of the table. 'If we can win them over, we can maybe find out more about enemies 1, 2 and 3!'

'There's just one slight problem with that,' suggested Mel.

'What's that?' snapped Bef. 'How can it be a problem and not an opportunity?'

'Well, because,' said Mel, a little scared of Bef's fiery temper, 'all we have to go on is a sugar lump!'

Gaspar couldn't help grinning and even Bef was tempted to break into a smile. Instead, she chose to become very solemn-faced and looked at the pair of them disapprovingly.

'I don't know why you are laughing,' she said. 'Your band mate is missing and we have no idea where to find him! We don't even have a clue this time, let alone a letter.'

She slumped into a chair and placed her head in her hands, staring at the coals burning in the grate.

'What's that sticking out of the bottom of the chimney?' she asked, as something caught her eye. Gaspar went over to inspect.

'You're right,' he said. There's a bit of card stuck in here.' He pulled it gently and a heap of dust came down, spilling on to the floor and pushing the card out and on to the rug. Bef picked it up, tutting at the mess caused to her home. She turned the card over and revealed a letter F. Before she could say anything, another piece of paper fluttered down. Gaspar grabbed it.

'It's another riddle,' he explained. It goes like this:

'Thaz really did like to drum,

He preferred it to having a strum.

Now he's hidden away,

But drumming all day,

Where you want so many children to come.'

'He's at Befland,' shouted the three of them within milliseconds of each other.

A door at the top of the stairs opened with a creak and Gaspar, Mel and Bef huddled together in fear. A figure in a cloak-like garment stepped out and cast a shadow down the stairs.

'No, I'm not. I'm here, you funny old sillies,' chuckled Jeremiah. 'What on earth makes you think I'm at Befland? ' He looked at their blank faces and shrank a little inside. 'What have I said?' he asked, in his usual very innocent way.

CHAPTER TWELVE

Thaz was already quite an attraction at Befland. He had been cast in stone in a pose that saw him sitting at his drum kit, with sticks in his hand, as if in the middle of his drumming practice.

'I categorically can't bear to look at it,' said Gaspar, as a group of dusty-faced workmen gathered round to laugh at the new exhibit and hang scarves around his stony neck and hats on his well-cemented head.

'He would be mortified by this,' agreed Mel. 'He always thought himself so cool and trendy.'

'Fiddlesticks,' said Bef, 'I don't like the way we are talking in the past tense. We will find an answer to this. We will NOT let them win, or my name's not The …'

'Stop!' yelled Gaspar. 'You nearly said it then and you know what will happen if you do!'

'Mamma mia!' cried Bef. 'You're right, I nearly did! It's so hard to break the habits of a lifetime.'

The two remaining band mates took one last look at Thaz. Bef had called a planning meeting, to try to find ways of keeping the rest of them safe. Everyone had agreed that was a very good idea.

Bef kept turning over the three cards she had received. She had a B an N and an F. The word she had to form couldn't possibly be VIPB, as Jeremiah had suggested. Before the F had arrived, she had wondered whether the word was Bernhardt. But there was no F in that. She now feared it might be Bürstenfrisür. If that were the case, another ten people would be turned to stone. She was beside herself with worry about this possibility.

All gathered around her as they held their planning meeting at the Bonbon Bumper Cars. Every one of her friends was sitting in a car and had formed a circle around her, as she sat in her favourite, bright yellow Luscious Lemon Fizz car.

'They won't be able to overhear us here, I'm sure of that,' she explained. 'They've now taken away three of our friends, who were so important to the opening of Befland. We now have to question whether their aim is to ruin the park, rather than to steal away my broom, as I had originally thought. We could still open Befland and I think perhaps we should. If we can all stay close, I do not think they will strike. It seems to be that they only snatch one of us when we are alone, even if that is just for a few minutes. Perhaps we should all move in together and have one of us keep watch all the time. If we are alert to the danger, perhaps the danger cannot harm us.'

All pondered this point for a few minutes.

'What is it they really want?' asked Gaspar. 'Even if they stop the park from opening this month, they must know that we will open it later. They cannot ultimately win, as every one of the townspeople would help us to open Befland, if we asked them to. They must have a bigger wish. What could that be?'

'For Bernhardt, it would be to become a VIPB,' said Bef. 'I have no doubt about that, given his ego, which is very big for such a little, pyjama-wearing man! For Capriccia, I would imagine it would be to return to her absolutely tasteless Casa, with her shocking shoe collection, which I once had the misfortune to have to clean! For Fiery Tina, I can only think that the aim is to inflict deep pain on me. This is the real problem. Fiery Tina has to be our number one enemy: she must be driving everything. If we can get to Fiery Tina, I am sure our other enemies would crawl back into their holes.'

'So who is the sugar lump?' asked Mel very bluntly.

'I don't know,' said Bef. 'It could be anyone, but we really need to discover who this is, as the sugar lump could be worked upon.'

'Don't you mean that they could be dissolved?' chuckled Jeremiah. 'In a warm cup of my acorn tea, perhaps!'

Bef rolled her eyes. Sometimes, Jeremiah seemed incapable of taking anything seriously.

Sometimes, though she hated to think it, he could be very annoying.

'How are the costumes coming along, Jeremiah?' she asked. 'Have you managed to do anything with them since all this trouble started?'

'Things are very bright,' explained Jeremiah. 'I just need to test some of my little gems out, so I have placed an advertisement that asks the towns-folk to come forward and volunteer to be stand-in models for our dress rehearsal, or as I described it, our 'Bef Rehearsal', which I thought exceedingly clever of me.'

'Have you had many volunteers?' asked Gaspar, a little surprised by this revelation.

'About a dozen so far,' explained Jeremiah. 'Of those, I have three who are going to step in to the role of Bef and test drive her costume.'

'When is this?' asked Mel.

'First rehearsal is this afternoon,' explained Jeremiah. 'I have arranged to hold it in the entrance area to the Candymonium ride.'

'Great, we'll help you with that,' offered Gaspar. 'If we can get Befland launched before they strike again, perhaps they'll give up and give us our friends back.'

Bef played with her hair and adjusted her spec-tacles to sit further up her nose.

'Gaspar, we need to create those potions that you mentioned, which each of us can have on our person. Perhaps, if we can hit them before they hit us, we can prevent a snatch ... and even maybe capture one of them. If we did, we might have better bargaining power to get Marianna, Mr Passarella and Thaz back.'

'OK,' said Gaspar. 'I'll go back and work on something now.'

'With Mel,' instructed Bef in a most strict tone. 'You must not go back alone.'

Gaspar nodded his head, understanding the need for extreme caution.

'We'll go back together and then return to help Jeremiah. If you stay here with him, we'll nip back to your house and play around with potions.'

'Agreed,' said Bef, 'but let none of us forget about the sugar lump and the need to find them.'

This was greeted with furious nodding as Gaspar and Mel departed, slapping their stone band mate on the back as they swore to him that they would get him back to normal as soon as possible.

'What now?' asked Jeremiah in a typically sweet manner.

'I need to practise my Befland opening routine,' explained Bef. 'Mr Passarella thought that I should do an aerial display above the park, performing plenty of my famous 'broomies', creating many of my renowned mouth shapes in the sky, thrilling people with my flair-o-batics and then performing musical dumps, where at set points within the music, I dump a bag of coal on top of someone in the audience! Mr Passarella didn't seem too convinced by this, but I think it will be a hoot! The routine is all worked out, but I've had no time to run through it and see how it fits together. Broom and I need some quality time together so that we can perfect it and make sure it's as stunning as Mr Passarella and I imagined.'

'Super-doopah,' said Jeremiah. 'You and I will be in view of each other all the time and, if you are flying, you'll be able to spot any nasty enemies approaching in the sky, while I keep my eyes peeled on the ground. I can go about my business and put the finishing touches to all the glorious costumes that I've designed, before all the volunteers arrive. All shall work out fine, you'll see, or my name's not Jeremiah Needle-eye.'

'But your name's not Jeremiah Needle-eye,' snapped Bef, rather exasperated by Jeremiah's flippant attitude.

'Oh no, you're right,' said Jeremiah. 'I don't know why I said it was. How stupid of me.'

Bef looked at him very oddly.

'Are you feeling alright, Jeremiah?' asked Bef, with great concern.

'Oh yes, just as well as Thaz over there,' explained Jeremiah.

'But he's been turned to stone, Jeremiah,' she said, tutting at his insensitivity.

'Just as well, as he was getting a little too plump for the costume I'd made for him,' answered

Jeremiah. 'We wouldn't want him splitting his pants mid-performance. Perhaps it's a blessing he can't shift … after all, he really didn't have the moves that Gaspar and Mel have.'

Bef was now getting very annoyed with Jeremiah. 'That's an awful thing to say, Jeremiah,' she said, 'and I thought much better of you. What is wrong with you today?'

'Just a little tired of being told how to behave by a witch,' replied Jeremiah, looking at her in quite an evil way.

Bef shrank back and began to wonder what on earth was happening. A thought crossed her mind … maybe Jeremiah was the sugar lump, working with Bef and her team, but secretly being on the side of Fiery Tina and her crew.

'Jeremiah Needlebaum,' she stated in a very matter-of-fact way. 'I am going to ask you a question and, because I am a witch, you must answer it honestly. Are you, or are you not, the sugar lump?'

Jeremiah looked her in the eye for a good ten seconds and then burst out laughing, collapsing to the ground, holding his ribs and giggling like a girl.

'Oh, my dear lady,' he cried. 'Of course I'm not a sugar lump! I'm the best tailor within the VIPB world and you've known me for centuries. I may be very sweet, but I'm definitely not a lump … in fact, I've become very trim since I left Siberia and stopped making seedie biscuits!'

Bef breathed a sigh of relief, but was still

worried about him. He was never nasty to anyone, but his comments had been rather hurtful and insensitive. She resolved to keep an eye on him. His sleepwalking incident had also been very odd and unexpected.

'If you're sure that you're OK,' she stressed, 'broom and I will start to practise our routine.'

'Go, go. Shoo, shoo,' Jeremiah urged. 'I have costumes to attend to.'

Bef took herself to the top of the park and up on the hill, not letting Jeremiah out of her sight once, walking backwards for most of the way, to keep her eyes fixed on him. She positioned herself at a take-off point that Mr Passarella had built into the hillside. It was a perfect spot and the music was lined up already, on equipment housed within a little hut. She started the soundtrack playing and then whooshed up into the sky, with her voluminous skirt trailing behind her and her long black hair flying wildly in the stiff breeze.

Her first manoeuvre was a series of broomies, which saw her tilting the broom almost upright and sailing through the air in that position, whooping loudly as she went. She then performed a series of dramatic loops, noting Jeremiah below her as she did so. Next came incredible mouth shapes, as she created images of the mighty Colosseum in Rome, Big Ben, the White House and the breathtaking Taj Mahal, before going into a series of forward rolls and somersaults.

This was followed by a long line of zig-zags, running the length of the park and then by broomie-hops all the way back, as she made her broom jump up and down like a bunny rabbit.

She then went into an amazing sequence of manoeuvres performed to the tune of 'Come Fly With Me', by her old favourite, Frank Sinatra, and then finished the whole performance by disappearing down the Chimney Chaser, sitting at the bottom and then shooting out of the top accompanied by fireworks, which weren't set up right now, but which would undoubtedly merely add to the drama of the whole routine.

Having finished her act, Bef felt full of energy and good spirits. She gracefully brought her broom down to land in the middle of the park and awaited a round of applause from Jeremiah. Nothing came and she felt ever so slightly peeved. A shout of 'bravo' came from a workman fixing one of the rides, but absolutely nothing from her best friend Jeremiah.

She looked around and saw a stream of people arriving for the costume fitting. She also spotted Mel and Gaspar returning. They waved to her and clapped their hands in the air.

'Saw some of the show from on the hill,' shouted Gaspar. 'It looked wicked, but then Jeremiah sent us to get the volunteers, while he fitted the costume of one who'd turned up early.'

Bef puffed her chest out with pride. She was

sure her performance had been brilliant, but it was nice to hear it from someone else. Her skirt, however, definitely needed a bit of adjustment, as it felt around two inches too long and Jeremiah would need to alter the one he was making in gold for the opening ceremony, as it was exactly the same length. She barged in to the entrance to Candymonium to tell him that right away.

'Jeremiah,' she yelled. 'Did you see my act? What did you think? I saw you scurrying around beneath me and almost dive-bombed you, but thought you'd be scared witless! Are you in the changing room?' she asked bossily.

She pulled back the red velvet curtains, expecting to find Jeremiah fiddling around with pins and tape measure, but the room was empty. Mel and Gaspar entered, calling out to Jeremiah to say that the army of volunteers had arrived. They too couldn't seem to find him.

'Where on earth is he?' fretted Bef. 'He was acting most peculiarly after you'd left, but assured me he wasn't the sugar lump. I saw him running around as actively as an ant, but now he's disappeared.'

'Maybe he's dealing with the volunteer who arrived early,' suggested Mel. 'She said her costume looked a little bit too brief.'

'No, she didn't mate,' laughed Gaspar. 'She said bweef,' because I couldn't work out what she was talking about at first.

Bef's ears pricked up. 'What!' she yelled. 'She couldn't say 'brief' … is that what you're telling me?'

'Well, I guess so,' replied Mel. 'I didn't really pick up on it.'

'Neither did I, until I just said that,' stated Gaspar. 'I hadn't even really been listening. I just realised she wasn't Capriccia and then … well, I can't actually remember what happened next. In fact, I can't remember anything about the minutes between that conversation and ending up on the hill with the other volunteers. It's as if my mind's gone blank.'

'O Dio!' yelled Bef. 'Mind games. Personality changing. I'd forgotten that's another of Fiery Tina's talents. Describe this woman that you saw to me.'

'Can't remember,' said Mel, blankly.

'Completely gone out of my head,' answered Gaspar.

Bef uttered a shriek that set all the dogs in the village barking. She kicked her feet into the ground in frustration and banged her fist into her head.

'I should have seen the signs in Jeremiah,' she exclaimed. 'It was a classic case of nastyurtium – a condition provoked by a vile fairy and one which takes over the personality of the victim. Capriccia may have been behind some of these kidnaps, but I can tell you now that Fiery Tina's prints are all over this one. 'Did this woman you saw have auburn coloured hair?' she demanded.

'No idea,' replied Gaspar. 'Sorry.'

'Who cares!' answered Mel. 'He was just a tailor after all. Hardly worth wasting any time on. As for that silly little chicken wire hat he wore, it was an absolute embarrassment. I couldn't bear to be seen with him.'

Both Bef and Gaspar looked at him with fright, wondering why he too had become so insensitive and cruel.

'Gaspar,' hissed Bef under her breath. 'Who spent most time with this woman who turned up for a costume fitting? Was it Mel?'

'Well, yes, I suppose,' answered Gaspar. He was whispering in the same tone as Bef, seemingly aware that Mel should not hear this.

'I fear he's been got at too,' said Bef. 'We must watch him like a hawk and see if any other unusual characteristics emerge.'

Gaspar nodded, with a dejected look on his face. Surely his other band mate hadn't been taken over by the enemies. Mel was bustling around on the stage on which 'The Three Kings' were supposed to perform for the opening ceremony of Befland. He seemed to be behaving perfectly normally now, so maybe they were fretting about nothing. Maybe he was just suffering the stress of it all.

'Where do you think Jeremiah can be?' asked Gaspar quietly.

'I have no idea,' replied Bef. 'I expect they will let us know before much longer.'

Gaspar looked around to suddenly see Mel heading to the Bonbon Bumper Cars at great pace. He grabbed Bef's hand tightly and pulled her along, following in Mel's footsteps.

'What's he doing?' he said to her. Bef looked puzzled and offered no reply.

Mel jumped into an Amazing Almond-flavoured car.

'I love thrills and adventure,' he shouted, as he began to drive it at a furious pace around its circular arena. 'Nothing like an adrenaline rush,' he yelled, as he began to bump it into other cars. 'It drives me nuts, just like the flavour of this car.' With that, he put his foot on the accelerator and started to head straight down the centre of the track.

'He's going to crash into all the parked cars,' shouted Gaspar. 'He's not going to brake.' Sure enough, he didn't. Gaspar awaited a major crash and was ready to run to Mel's aid, but as his band mate came to just within six inches of the parked cars, he vanished into thin air, leaving Gaspar open-mouthed and in a state of shock.

'He's just disappeared,' he said to Bef, stating the blatantly obvious.

'Indeed,' replied Bef. 'It would appear that he'd been semi-snatched when talking all that drivel earlier. It follows the exact same pattern as that of Jeremiah.'

'What do we do now?' asked Gaspar in an absolute panic.

'We have to wait,' replied a grim-faced Bef. 'They and not we are in control of this game and they are making all of the rules. We are the pawns and they are moving the pieces.'

Chapter Thirteen

Bef launched an immediate search for Jeremiah and Mel, asking the townspeople, who had arrived for the 'Bef Rehearsal' to scour the park and then the village, to try to find their statues. It came up with absolutely nothing. Drained and weary, she and Gaspar eventually gave up and returned home with her broom.

A few miserable hours followed, as they sat twiddling their thumbs and feeling helpless. There was nothing they could do at this precise moment in time.

'Shall I make some tea?' asked Gaspar, trying to break the silence. Bef just nodded, seemingly too dumbstruck to speak. He started rattling around. 'Where is the acorn tea?' he asked.

'Third brown pot on the fourth shelf,' replied Bef.

Gaspar opened the pot and stared in amazement at the contents.

'There's a bit of paper in here,' he said. 'I think it's another riddle and a letter.'

Bef bustled up to him. 'You're right,' she said. 'Fetch it out.'

Gaspar did as instructed and began to read,

'Jeremiah was a little inferior,

So he's now sitting back in Siberia.

So near to your coal,

But no use at all:

Now he simply can't feel any wearier.'

There was a tiny, weeny letter printed on the page, which neither Bef nor Gaspar could make out. Bef waved her hand across the page.

'Ingrandimento!' she declared. Instantly the letter was enlarged and the pair of them saw that it was a letter L.

'There's no L in Bürstenfrisür,' declared Gaspar. 'That can't be the word we need to spell out.'

As they continued to stare at the piece of paper, a blurred image started to appear, which became clearer and clearer the more they looked. Gradually, they made out a snowy landscape and a place they both knew really well – Jeremiah's prison cell in Siberia. The focus then moved inside the building and they saw the fabulous furnishings and decorations that Jeremiah had sewn and knitted. Slowly, they began to see Jeremiah himself, cast in stone and sitting in a rocking chair with knitting needles and wool in his hand.

'Poor Jeremiah,' said Bef. 'I was a little tetchy with him today and it wasn't his fault at all.'

Gaspar put the paper down.

'If this clue is in the acorn tea jar, we may find a clue about Mel's whereabouts somewhere else, if we logically think where that may be,' he suggested.

The pair of them looked blank for a while.

'How about in the toilet?' asked Bef. 'He seems to have spent a lot of time in there lately!' They both headed up the stairs, but found nothing at all.

'What about in the car?' asked Gaspar. 'He was snatched from a car, after all.' Bef looked dubious.

'It's really Thaz's car, though,' she said. I'm not sure they'd put a clue there, especially as it's parked up beyond the town walls.'

'Well, he's never had his head out of that travel brochure for New Zealand,' said Gaspar. 'Perhaps we should look in there.'

Gaspar rooted around and found the magazine on a stool in the living room. He flicked through it and saw nothing. Then he lifted it up by the spine and shook it. Something tumbled to the floor, landing by Bef's feet. She stooped to pick it up.

'Ecco,' she said. 'Here we have a riddle.'

'Mel believed he was truly a hero,

But now he's reduced to a zero.

He's hanging around,

But where to be found?

He's as past-tense as Emperor Nero!'

Once again, the pair of them looked solemn.

'Do the Ingrandimento thing again,' Gaspar instructed in an urgent tone.

Bef waved her hand and a letter A appeared. They continued to stare at the paper just as before and another image gradually came into focus. Mel had been turned to stone while suspended from a bungee rope.

'He's at that place he wanted to visit in New Zealand, where they do that incredible bungeeing into a canyon,' explained Gaspar.

'So they are now moving our friends around the world,' said Bef solemnly. 'That suggests that the magic is getting more powerful and the sorceress increasingly evil. These are worrying signs indeed, Gaspar. Worrying signs.'

Up at Fiery Tina's base camp, trouble was brewing. Tempers were fraying, to say the least, and Capriccia was NOT amused. Her Northern Highlights had changed to become a deep orange colour – not quite at her most annoyed setting of red, but close enough to spell danger. Sly had already taken cover under a table, pretending he needed shade from the sun. In reality, he knew Capriccia was about to spin and that meant getting out of the way fast, as she had little or no control over her movements when she did. He chortled to himself, knowing that Fiery Tina knew nothing about this – that would teach her to leave him out of her charmed circle and whisper things to the others so that he couldn't hear what they were talking about. Little did they know how razor sharp his hearing was, thanks to his pointed elf ears. He could hear every word, whether they whispered it or not, if he tuned in correctly.

Sly had become increasingly angry at their combined behaviour and their total ingratitude. They played their silly snatch and conundrum game and slapped themselves on the back each time they snatched a victim. They were all self-obsessed, vile creatures and he'd had enough of them. But he could bide his time and turn the tables on them, when the right opportunity arose.

He glanced at Capriccia. She was building up to a rant. He could see it in her eyes. She glared at him and he shrank back a little under the table. He was happy to keep out of her way. Sure enough, her feet began to turn in the red, sandy gravel. Her ankles started to draw together and the turning started, at first slowly and then accelerating into a very fast spin. She was moving so fast that she couldn't stand still on the spot, so began to move towards the hopscotch court as fast as a tornado.

Sly put his hands across his eyes, peeping through his fingers and fully expecting her to wipe out Fiery Tina in one furious spin. Amazingly, however, she stopped abruptly, right in front of the person she sought to confront and about two inches from her toes.

'Why did you do that?' yelled Capriccia. 'I was perfectly capable of snatching that ridiculous tailor in the silly hat, not to mention that boy who likes adventure. You had no right to come steaming in and taking over from me.'

'I think you'll find I did,' replied the fairy, tilting her head to look Capriccia in the eye. 'I'm your teacher and I was getting bored with doing nothing. Anyway, you hadn't developed a stwategy and I fancied performing some of my mind twicks. Twicks that you haven't yet perfected, as you are such a lazy pupil.'

Capriccia was getting angrier and angrier and her Northern Highlights were now scarlet. Sly shuffled back under the table a little. Capriccia was one thing, but what would the totally unpredictable fairy do?

'My magic was strong enough to send one to Siberia and another to New Zealand,' yelled Capriccia.

'A widiculous thing to do,' said Fiery Tina. 'If they'd been closer at hand, the Bef woman would feel more pain. Now, she can shut them out of her mind. She can only see them if she uses magnification. I have no idea why you chose to do such a stupid thing.'

'To show how clever I am,' yelled Capriccia, her feet beginning to turn again. 'I'm much better at magic than you give me credit for now and I've been learning things without your help, thank you very much. I can do more than you even realise.'

'It would be quite some thing for you to become clever, Capwiccia,' answered Fiery Tina, giggling in a way that infuriated Capriccia even more. 'You are one of the dumbest people I've ever met. You're also very awwogant and without any basis. You are not good at magic ... just incwedibly averwage.' Fiery Tina turned her back on Capriccia and started to hop once more.

'At least I'm not addicted to a children's game,' shouted Capriccia. 'That's just pathetic.' Her ankles came together and she began to spin again, this time in reverse, heading back to the spot at which she'd started her journey. Sly curled up into a ball, trying to avoid the storm of dust that she was creating. She came to a stop by a plastic chair, began to unwind, shook herself out and plonked herself into it. 'Bilberry juice. NOW!' she yelled, clicking her fingers three times. Amazingly, a glass of bilberry juice appeared, which she grabbed and downed in one gulp. 'ANOTHER, NOW!' she yelled.

Sly misjudged the situation, believing she was now calming down and in need of a true friend. He sidled over to her in his usual creepy way.

'Mistress,' he said humbly. 'Could I possibly

suggest something that could be advantageous to both of us?'

Capriccia looked him in the eye with a withering look that made him shrink a bit.

'No,' she answered rudely.

'Please, mistress,' Sly continued. 'We have come a long way together and I have ideas of how we could exploit the situation to our advantage.'

Capriccia looked vaguely interested. For a start, she never had any ideas of her own. Secondly, she liked the word 'exploit' – it was something she was very good at.

'What is it then?' she said, yawning in his face as normal. Sly beamed a little. He didn't usually get her attention so easily.

'It's about the Casa,' he said, knowing this would instantly increase her interest in his words. 'And your wonderful shoe collection, of course,' he continued. 'You know that I've always had your best interests at heart, which is why I came to find you when I discovered the horrific situation with the moths.' He paused and then realised that was the wrong thing to do. He needed to talk without allowing her to interrupt.

'Well,' he continued quickly. 'I think it would be wise for us to forget this conundrum business and head back to your Casa as soon as possible. Who knows how many pairs of shoes will have been eaten away by the moths if we don't! We can take back control of the Casa and set up camp there. I can be in charge of running the Casa for you, setting up all the security, so that nobody can oust you and dealing with all day-to-day matters, while you just enjoy your clothes, your accessories, your perfumes and, of course, your shoes. What do you say?'

Capriccia looked him up and down and down and up before bursting into cruel laughter.

'I would say,' she said, 'that you couldn't even organise affairs in Santa's Post Office, let alone my fabulous Casa. You were so thick that you couldn't even reveal the identity of the Bef woman. You were so incredibly bad at detective work that Santa demoted you and you were then so useless that you were left bouncing up and down on a bed on the Casa's roof. I would say that you are a silly, insignificant little elf who isn't fit to breathe the same air as Capriccia Claus.'

With that, Capriccia picked up the second glass of bilberry juice that she had just ordered and poured it over Sly's head. Dripping in bilberry juice and wounded by her words, he stood dejected and heartbroken in the middle of Fiery Tina's garden, with tears welling up in his eyes. Capriccia had always been rude, but never quite so hurtful. He shuffled off, without another word, to hide in shame back under the table.

'Ha, ha, ha,' said a voice from the bushes. 'Zat was just what he deserved and if you hadn't done it zen Bernhardt Bürstenfrisür would have stepped in.

As if zat fool could run your Casa of Contentments. What you need there is a real man, like myself.'

Capriccia looked dubious, but said nothing. That slightly annoyed Bernhardt, as he had expected a few compliments. He drew breath and started to speak once more.

'I have excellent news,' he reported. 'News of ze biggest proportions. News zat will make your toes curl, in or out of your rather over-ze-top shoes!'

Capriccia scowled. 'What news?' she asked, hoping she could hear it before Fiery Tina stopped playing hopscotch.

'I have developed an exact replica of ze Bef woman's broom,' explained Bernhardt as, to Capriccia's disappointment, Fiery Tina hovered above them and landed next to the Most Fearsome Feller in Folklore.

'Do tell us more,' she said, simpering in his ear.

'It is exactly ze same size and shape as her current broom,' he explained, 'despite ze fact zat I made ze original over von thousand years ago and did not note down every detail in those days. Not only have I used ze same wood, planed ze wood in ze same way, treated it in ze same colours and even replicated where it was damaged by water when it crashed into ze Adriatic in ze 1700s, I have even replicated ze enhancements I made to it for her and zat strange boy, Gaspar. Am I, or am I not, ze best broom artisan ze world has ever known?' He flung his arms up and out wide, looking up to the sky, awaiting a round of applause that didn't come.

'What use is this?' asked Capriccia bluntly.

'What use? What use?' shouted Bernhardt angrily. 'It is our main weapon! It is our way of humiliating her once and for all, of getting her driven out of her village by ze people who live in it, of making ze whole world see what a ridiculous woman she is!' He was so angry, his legs were shaking like jelly and his top lip was quivering.

'When?' asked Fiery Tina. 'When will all this happen?' She tilted her head to look down at Bernhardt like a giraffe with a crook in its neck.

'Ze opening ceremony of Befland!' declared Bernhardt. 'Zay are going ahead with it and by swapping von broom for another, without her realising it, we can completely ruin her plans. She thinks she is going to perform a fabulous routine in ze skies above Befland. Believe me, it vill be anything but triumphant, or my name is not Bernhardt Bürstenfrisür. Once she has been humiliated, ze folk vill see zat she is bad for business and zay need a much better figurehead for ze village.' He looked at Capriccia and smirked, 'Maybe a figurehead with better fashion sense and more beauty,' he suggested.

'I think I'll be too busy for that,' answered Fiery Tina, suddenly appearing behind him and completely missing the fact that he was referring to Capriccia and not her. 'I just want my VIPB patch in Flo-wence and then I shall be happy,' she added.

Capriccia's mind was whirring. Why shouldn't she become queen of Bef's village? What better revenge could there be than that? Bernhardt's plan was beginning to appeal to her more and more. She sensed that she needed to side with him as fast as possible. If he could make this happen, he could also surely get control of her Casa back and deal with Santa and his troublesome elves. She smiled sweetly at Bernhardt, a smile that Sly, sitting under the table, knew was the insincere smile that she painted on her face when she wanted to use someone. He had seen it many times before and that wounded him.

'Bernhardt,' whispered Capriccia. 'When are you swapping the brooms?'

'I am not!' he replied. 'You are! It's part of ze conundrum!'

'Yes, indeed, Capwiccia,' said Fiery Tina, in her most annoying voice. 'You need to get your thinking cap on, as you are now supposedly so good at magic. You can decide how you are going to not only get hold of something the Bef woman never lets out of her sight, but also work out how you can possibly swap it for another one. I can't wait to see your feeble little bwain work that one out!'

The Northern Highlights turned to amber, as Sly watched the whole scene. He almost wanted to warn the Bef woman what was going to happen. He'd lost any affection for the people surrounding him and wished he could run away. But to where could he run? He had no home, no job and no friends. His only focus had been Capriccia.

As he pondered all of this, Capriccia strode towards the table. She lifted her foot and kicked its leg as hard as possible, setting cups and saucers crashing and tea slopping out of a teapot's spout.

'Get out from under there, elf,' she ordered rudely, 'I need ideas.'

Sly poked his head out from under the table very tentatively indeed. At that moment, a sugar lump bopped on top of it and tumbled to the ground.

Chapter Fourteen

Lars was bitterly cold. The weather in the mountains of Lapland could be truly unforgiving and a blizzard had sprung up, which was blinding his eyes, as the biting cold sank its fangs into his skin.

He had been trekking for three days now – or was it four? He had lost track of time and also sense of direction. Everything was white. Everything looked the same. How on earth was he going to find the Rock of Erik the Enraged in this climate?

He was being defeatist and he knew it. He had to snap out of it and battle on to find the Rock. It was part of the landscape: part of the soul of the world. It would not fail him, he was sure. He just needed to get his bearings.

There was nothing else moving out here, apart from him, so the sight of a flash of reddish brown within the falling snow caught him totally by surprise and off guard. He lost his balance for a moment or two and then regained his composure. But there it went again! Was he imagining this, or was there something out here with him?

He received the answer. A small bird landed on

his arm and he shepherded it towards his chest, to protect it from the blizzard.

'Who are you, friend?' he asked, in the language in which he spoke to the Arctic Warbler.

'I am the Siberian Jay,' twittered the bird. 'Your friend the Arctic Warbler has sent me to guide you. I believe the Arctic Fox called me a 'meddlesome bird'. I am here to prove that my intentions are true. I have been turning the sky red to warn everyone of impending danger. I predict trouble of enormous proportions and everyone must be on their guard.'

'Is this something to do with Capriccia Claus?' asked Lars, 'and maybe also Bef, who finally sent her packing, quite literally?'

'I feel in my feathers that it is,' replied the Siberian Jay, 'but you need to consult the Rock of Erik the Enraged and I sensed that you could not find it.'

'Indeed,' said Lars, 'you are a very perceptive bird.'

'Come,' said the Siberian Jay, 'I will try to battle against the falling snow and guide you on your way. Only the rock's tip is exposed, but I perch on it often, when I am seeking wisdom and guidance as to whether to turn the sky red or not. I know the surroundings well, so should be able to take you there with a bit of luck and a following wind.'

Lars unloosened his coat to let the bird flutter out. It struggled to fly at first, but eventually forced its wings to beat fast enough to surge forward against the driving snow, before hovering and waiting for Lars to catch up. In this manner, they made their way up the mountain in a completely different direction to that which Lars had imagined.

Onward and upward they climbed for a good half hour before the bird came to land in the snow.

'The rock is ahead,' it said to Lars. 'Do you see the small point of it sticking out of the snow?'

Lars cleared his eyelashes of snowflakes and focused.

'Yes, I think so,' he replied. 'I will need to clear more of its surface of snow before I can consult it.'

'Maybe and maybe not,' replied the wise bird. 'Once you call upon its help, it will rise up anyway, so you may not need to do anything. Simply place your hands on the top and ask the rock for the knowledge you seek.'

Lars trudged forward and reached the famous Rock of Erik the Enraged. He brushed snow off the surface as gently as he would have knocked it off the back of one of his beloved reindeer and got on to his haunches. He cleared his throat, preparing to speak and consult the mountainous oracle.

'I come here, oh wise Rock of Erik the Enraged, to seek guidance,' said Lars in a clear, loud voice. 'There is talk of great danger for our land, if it suffers the return of the dreadful Capriccia Claus. It is said she is becoming more powerful and to be found in a location in Italy, where a woman has been turned to stone and is hanging like a bat in the bell tower. I fear this may be my friend Bef, who drove Capriccia out of Lapland, to help save the reindeer. I come here to ask you to guide my thinking and help me understand what may be happening.'

For a few seconds, there was no response to his plea, but then a rumbling noise could be heard, at first sounding like the babbling of a brook, but then stormier, like a raging sea. The rock lifted, as Lars stood back and watched in amazement. Snow tumbled from its crevices as it soared up around two feet and then opened up, revealing a cavern into which Lars could peer. Inside the rock, he saw a sea of rich purple. The Siberian Jay fluttered by his shoulder.

'It's amethyst,' it said. 'The rock wants you to take some.'

Lars plunged his hand inside and grabbed a handful of amethyst, which he pulled out and immediately put inside a bag slung casually around his waist. He went back for a second handful, having no idea how much he needed. The Rock of Erik the Enraged then began to close again, until the opening was just a few inches in diameter. The purple colour faded and Lars thought its guidance was over, but suddenly up shot a stream of colour, which lit up the sky above it as almost a miniature version of the Northern Lights. The colours moved and swayed and altered in shape until they began to form images.

The first was that of a tiny little man who Lars instantly recognised.

'That is Tomte,' he said boldly. 'Another VIPB! I must find Tomte and take him with me.' The second showed Bef in front of a hillside on which letters were strewn. 'That means nothing to me,' said Lars, 'other than the fact that she is not turned to stone or hanging like a bat.'

He breathed in deeply, trying to concentrate hard as the third image appeared in the sky. This showed a clock and then a host of tiny men marching into a mine.

'The Gnomes of Zurich,' declared Lars. 'I met them once. But why do I need them now?' He shook his head, confused by these varying images that seemed to have no logical connection.

'Concentrate,' said the Siberian Jay. 'Another image is appearing.

The final image to appear in the sky was that of a man – a man Lars had never seen before in his life: a man dressed in long robes and with long, curly grey hair. He was turning the pages of a book and the title of the book appeared – The Grandissimo Libro di Scongiuri.

'That's Bef's book,' declared Lars. 'Why would it be in the hands of another? Who is this man?' He stared at him in wonderment.

'Quick,' said the bird on his shoulder. 'Do you have a bottle or something similar?'

'Yes, I have some water,' replied Lars. 'Why?'

'Capture the image in the bottle and secure the top quickly. The image will stay trapped in the bottle and you can refer to it when you need to.'

Lars did as instructed, emptied his water into the snow and scooped the image inside.

'I just have no idea who this man can be,' he said in a confused manner. 'I have never seen him before and yet there is something familiar about him.' He stared at the bottle. 'This way madness lies,' he said, putting the image away into his bag. 'I must seek out Tomte and then prepare the reindeer, though to where we are flying, I have no idea.'

'The bottle will help guide your course,' said the bird. 'It will steer you to where you need to be. Keep it with you and it will guide your thinking. That is why the Rock of Erik the Enraged allows one image to be captured. Fear not, its guiding powers will stay with you as you journey.'

'I cannot thank you enough,' said Lars. 'You are far from being a meddlesome bird and I understand why you are such good friends with the Arctic Warbler. You are both birds with good hearts and sensible heads.'

'Enough of the praise,' said the bird. 'I am glad my decision to turn the sky red has proved to be the right one. We must all be on our guard, but at least we now have Lars the Reindeer Whisperer to help fight the evil that is out there. Follow me back down the mountain and then do what you have to. I sense we do not have time to waste.'

The two wanderers watched the Rock of Erik the Enraged sink below the snow again, as they made their way back down the mountain, Lars slipping here and there, but always watched over by the Siberian Jay. Both knew there would be much work ahead and much danger too. The Jay would be turning the skies red for some time to come.

Chapter Fifteen

Bef was taking her mind off things by doing what she did best – cleaning. She had swept the floor at least eight times, even by Gaspar's estimation and he had only been up a few hours. If not brushing, she was dusting everything that didn't move, which saw Gaspar leaping from chair to chair to prevent his nose being tickled.

Bef was also singing at the top of her voice – almost anything that came into her head from her repertoire of broom songs. This ranged from 'Fly Me To The Moon', to 'I Believe I can Fly'. Gaspar thought it very impressive that Bef even knew the latter, but was really scratching his head as to why she kept breaking into 'Boris the Spider'.

'Why do you keep singing that song about the spider?' asked Gaspar.

'What song about a spider?' asked Bef.

'The one about Boris,' explained Gaspar.

'Don't have a clue what you're talking about,' replied Bef. 'Don't know any songs about Boris or spiders.'

'That's very curious,' thought Gaspar, but he

decided to let it drop. 'Why are you singing so loudly,' he asked, changing the subject and almost having to put his hands over his ears thanks to the volume.

'So I don't hear the toilet flush,' she explained. 'Our enemies have infiltrated the Flush Telegraph communications system used by VIPBs and pictures of Marianna, Mr Passarella, Thaz, Jeremiah and Mel keep flushing out. They all look so stony-faced.'

Gaspar rushed into the toilet. Sure enough, within seconds, another message came out with a mighty flush, this one picturing Jeremiah in his Siberian cell. Although Gaspar was upset to see it, he had something else on his mind. He rushed back into the living room.

'I'd completely forgotten about the Flush Telegraph,' he said. 'Why don't we use it to our advantage and send a message to other VIPBs to ask them to help?'

'I don't want to publicise my misfortune to all and sundry,' said Bef rather haughtily. 'If some got a sniff of what's going on, they'd be charging in trying to take over my VIPB patch and it's enough that Bernhardt and Fiery Tina are doing that.' She almost added 'and Capriccia,' but could not, for the life of her, imagine that Capriccia could seriously ever think that she could be a VIPB.

'Very well,' said Gaspar. 'But what if we just ask one VIPB for help?'

Bef looked bemused. 'Who did you have in mind?' she asked.

'Natalia Lebedev,' replied Gaspar, which wasn't difficult for Bef to guess, as it was the only VIPB he knew other than Santa.

Bef pondered his suggestion. Whilst at face value the suggestion seemed preposterous, there was some sense in it. Natalia had been very angry with Bernhardt when she'd last met him and it had been she who had voted against him, to stop him from becoming a VIPB. Bef had tried to prevent Bernhardt from discovering this fact and it had not been her fault that he'd managed to work out the anagram she gave to him, when she needed to escape from his clutches.

Natalia was already a recognised VIPB, so should actually come to the assistance of another VIPB if asked to do so. Added to that, Bef could not imagine that she would have any respect for either Fiery Tina or Capriccia. In fact, the more she thought about it, the more Gaspar's suggestion made sense.

'I actually think you could be on to something,' she said to Gaspar, beaming at him for the first time in days. 'But we need to send a message via her friend Penelope Popov. She's a very minor VIPB, but one who never fails to check her Flush Telegraph inbox. She'll be contacting Natalia within seconds to alert her to what's happening.'

She began to scurry around. Opening drawers

here and there and slamming them again, she was desperately seeking something.

'What are you looking for?' asked Gaspar.

'A Flush Telegraph capsule,' she replied. 'It's so long since I've used the system that I don't know where they are.'

Gaspar looked around the room. 'Is that rose on the window sill growing in one?' he asked.

Bef spun round.

'You clever, clever boy,' she said as she tipped the rose out and began to dry the capsule. 'Just need a stopper now,' she said, rummaging in her drawers once again. 'Ecco,' she said within seconds. 'Now, let's compose the message.'

She sat down at the kitchen table and started to write. After a few minutes, she pushed the piece of paper across the table to Gaspar.

'What do you think?' she asked. He read the note.

'Dearest Natalia. I hope your face has recovered from having all that coal fly into it during my last visit to Russia. It really wasn't my fault and I wasn't to know you would climb through the coal trucks in the belief that I had snitched on you – which I never did – as I am sure you now realise. Now, we may not always have seen eye to eye, but as a fellow VIPB, I am in dire need of your assistance. My friends and I are

victims of a very nasty conundrum, which is backed by statuefication and, added to this, that miserable little nincompoop, Bernhardt Bürstenfrisür is partly behind it. You may also be aware of a spiteful, deranged Fairy called Fiery Tina, who is the architect of the conundrum, while you will undoubtedly be glad you are not aware of a vain goose of a woman called Capriccia Claus, who is also part of the skulduggery. As one VIPB to another, I beseech you to ride to my assistance here in Italy and help me fend off this terrible attack on all that I love.'

The note was signed at the bottom, 'Your dear friend, Bef.'

'Sounds OK,' said Gaspar, 'but not sure you should remind her of the coal mine episode in such detail. I seem to recall that she wasn't too happy with us.'

'Nonsense,' said Bef. 'She will appreciate my honesty and realise that I wouldn't crawl to her in this way, in fact not in a million years, were I not truly desperate.'

'OK, if you say so,' said Gaspar, a little offended to be slapped down so hard. 'So how do we get it to her?'

'I need to consult the Flush Telegraph Directory,' explained Bef. It will tell me how many flushes to give to get it to its intended recipient. She reached for a book on her dresser and flicked through until she reached P for Popov. 'Now,' she said, 'we need to put the note inside and ask Penelope Popov to forward it to Natalia. That will give Penelope something to do for once. Let's just hope Natalia's in a good mood.'

She rushed to the toilet, being almost hit in the face by another message from her enemies, which this time featured Mel on his bungee rope. Gaspar picked it up and looked glum.

'Yes, let's hope she comes to help,' he agreed.

Bef popped the capsule into the toilet and gave three sharp flushes of the chain, followed by one long flush.

'One more flush after precisely two minutes,' she said, urging Gaspar to study his watch.

He counted down the seconds and raised his thumb when the two minutes was up. Bef gave another big flush and then sat on the toilet seat.

'Ouch' she yelled, as another message hit her on the bottom! 'We'll come back and check in thirty minutes. That should be plenty of time for Penelope to have forwarded the message to Natalia and for Natalia to have replied.'

The pair of them sat at the kitchen table watching the minute hand of the clock on the wall move. Silence reigned and even the messages from their enemies had stopped appearing, making Bef fearful of what else they might be up to instead. They sat quietly, secretly praying for a positive response from Natalia. As the minute hand clicked to the 30-minute mark, they both rushed into the toilet. Gaspar entered first and just as he got inside, out popped a capsule that hit him on the forehead. Instead of moaning about it, he grabbed it quickly and realised it didn't contain a picture of one of their stony friends.

'I think she's replied,' he shouted. 'Let's just hope she's on our side.'

Bef uncorked the capsule and took a note out. It read,

> *'Dear Bef, this is Penelope Popov replying on behalf of Natalia Lebedev. Natalia has considered your note and graciously decided to let bygones be bygones. She has taken to her broom and is riding to your assistance now, being absolutely determined to prevent that, and I quote, 'little pipsqueak' Bernhardt from becoming a VIPB. To speed up her arrival, she has asked me to send you this note. She is unsure of the direction of the wind, but you can expect her within a few hours, if it is favourable. She will rap on your door seventeen times as a sign that it is her seeking entrance. Await this signal and accept no other.'*

'Goodness, she's thorough,' said Gaspar reading the note.

'She's an official minute-taker at VIPB conferences,' explained Bef. 'She's a bit of a mardy bottom, but never takes notes down wrongly.'

Gaspar grinned to himself. It was good to have some light relief for once.

'I guess we sit and wait then,' he said.

Bef seated herself at the table and started drumming her fingers to pass the time. After a few seconds she sat up.

'We'll go absolutely mad if we sit here and do nothing,' she declared. 'Let's get Jeremiah's knitted dominoes out and play a game or two.'

'Agreed,' said Gaspar, having quite developed a liking for the game.

After four games, Bef was 3-1 up and Gaspar was determined to catch up, but a knocking at the door interrupted things. They looked at each other anxiously.

'That was only eleven knocks, followed by one further knock,' said Gaspar cautiously. 'That cannot be Natalia.'

Bef stood up. 'Go upstairs for a minute Gaspar. I need to speak to this person alone.'

'Are you sure it's safe?' asked Gaspar. 'You don't know who it is.'

'I do,' confirmed Bef.

Once Gaspar was upstairs, she opened the door a little.

'You took your time,' said a gruff voice.

'Things are serious, Lorenzo,' she explained. 'We have to be cautious. Have you found anything in the Grandissimo Libro di Scongiuri?'

'Yes and no,' said Lorenzo. 'I found some hand-written notes scribbled on one page, which seem to have been in mother's writing. They don't tell me how to undo a statuefication spell, but they do hint how to protect against statuefication.'

'Come in and tell me more,' whispered Bef.

'No, we can't risk it,' said Lorenzo. 'When I leave here, I want you to give me a bulb of garlic, to make it seem as if I came to borrow some.'

'Va bene,' said Bef, agreeing with her older brother. 'What is the protection?'

'Amethyst,' said Lorenzo. 'A small amount needs to be used to create an elixir in water. Do not swallow the crystals: their power will transfer to the water if you leave them a while and will offer you protection. This must only be done in the most pressing of circumstances, if one fears statuefication, but I think these are those times. The issue is, of course, where to find any amethyst. With that, I cannot help.'

'At least it's something,' said Bef. 'Keep going through the book and you may discover more. For now, I will rack my brains as to where to find some.'

'Take care, sister,' said Lorenzo. 'I have heard news of further statuefications. Make sure it's not you next, or me for that matter. Now give me some garlic.'

Bef rushed inside and fetched a bulb, pressing it into her brother's hand.

'Thank you, Lorenzo,' she said. 'You have been most helpful.'

'Thank you gracious lady for the garlic,' announced Lorenzo in a loud voice that even Gaspar heard upstairs. 'My recipe would not have been the same without it, so I thank you for your neighbourly act and for helping an old man in his hour of need.'

'Prego,' said Bef, which Gaspar knew meant, 'don't mention it.'

Bef shut the door and Gaspar came down the stairs.

'Who was that?' he asked.

'Just a neighbour needing a bulb of garlic,' she replied, looking very thoughtful.

She bolted the door behind her and they sat and waited once more, completing another two games of knitted dominoes, which allowed Gaspar to equal the score, though he had the feeling that Bef's mind was somewhere else entirely.

Hours ticked by and the waiting became unbearable.

'Do you think she's lost?' asked Gaspar, echoing Bef's thoughts entirely. Her answer was delayed, however, as a harsh scraping noise was detected on the roof.

'What was that?' asked Gaspar nervously.

'We must wait and see,' said Bef, not sure herself whether it was a stray cat, Natalia or one of their enemies. Within seconds, there came a knock on the door. Bef and Gaspar began to count: 15, 16, 17 … the knocking stopped.

Bef tentatively went to the door and moved the spyhole. She noted a very tall woman with long black hair and instantly recognised her.

'Natalia, come in quickly,' she said, ushering her through the door. 'You may remember Gaspar.'

'Indeed,' said Natalia, 'but we had better not dwell on that meeting!' She looked around. 'So zis is where you live, is it? I had expected something a little grander, I have to say. But never mind, I zink we have some catching up to do. You had better start at the beginning and finish at the end, sparing no details and giving me the facts and no fiction. I need to know what we are dealing with.'

Gaspar went to put some water on to boil, while Bef tried to explain all that had happened, the statuefications that had occurred and the riddles and letters that had been received, but even she didn't know what to tell Natalia, being at a loss as to what was really happening herself.

Natalia looked thoughtful throughout the tale, uttering the words, 'I see, I see,' at frequent intervals. The tale concluded.

'Well that little nincompoop could not be masterminding zis alone, zis is true,' declared Natalia in a very heavy Russian accent. 'However, I know nothing of zis woman Fiery Tina, other than what I've heard on the grapevine. That is not good, I have to say. I hear she's one sequin short of a shimmer. As for Capriccia Claus, I believe that she's not the brightest button in the box, so I have to question who is pulling the strings.'

'My broom believes it to be Capriccia, as I told you,' said Bef. 'I have to believe it.' She glanced at her broom, expecting it to leap up in agreement, but it lay lifeless on the rug. 'Odd,' she thought, then dismissed it as her broom feeling as depressed as the rest of them.

'Is there anything else?' asked Natalia.

Bef's mind strayed to Lorenzo, but she kept schtum. Some things were best kept secret, even from Gaspar.

Natalia's brow was furrowed with concentration.

'So we have to get Befland opened,' she said. 'Making plans to do that despite all of zis will perhaps flush them out and, once they are out in the open, we can perhaps defend ourselves better.'

'Do you know anything about statuefication?' asked Bef.

'Nothzing at all,' replied Natalia, making Gaspar's heart sink. At least they had another VIPB on board, however, which had to be good thing.

A faint noise was heard at the window – a sort of scratching and tapping.

'What's that?' asked Gaspar, full of fear at every single noise and knock he picked up these days.

'I have no idea,' said Bef and Natalia at exactly the same time. All three turned round to face the window as the tapping continued. Bef boldly peered through the glass into the darkness outside. Natalia shuffled her out of the way and did the same.

'It appears to be a bird,' they both said at once.

'Shall we let it in?' asked Gaspar. The two women shrugged their shoulders, slightly non-plussed. 'Here,' said Gaspar, trying to take the lead. 'These are phials of the potions that Mel and I worked on just before he disappeared. Take one in your hand and be prepared to use it immediately if anything terrible happens when I open the window.'

He bravely went to the latch and tentatively unlocked it. Immediately, a little bird flew in. It flew around the room several times, getting its bearings before fluttering down to rest on the kitchen table.

'It's got something attached to its leg,' said Gaspar. 'And it's also carrying something in its beak.'

'I've seen this bird before,' exclaimed Bef. 'It's the Arctic Warbler. The very same one that talks to Lars, if I'm not mistaken.' She slowly reached out and let it hop near, before undoing a little pouch attached to its leg. As she gently unwound some cord, it dropped a few pieces of purple rock on to the table from its beak. She delicately picked up a nugget and held it up, letting light fall through it so it shone bright purple and appeared absolutely splendid, as if it were the greatest jewel in the world.

Bef's eyes lit up and she beamed from ear to ear.

'It's amethyst,' she enthused. 'The Arctic Warbler has brought us amethyst!'

CHAPTER SIXTEEN

The nervous gang of three spent many hours debating their next move, but one thing they were all determined to do as fast as possible was to use the amethyst. Natalia and Gaspar had both been clueless as to what to do with it, but Bef stepped in and explained that they needed to make what she called an 'elixir'. What she didn't mention was Lorenzo and his advice.

First, they sprinkled the crystals into a jug of water and left them soaking for several hours. Once the crystals had worked their magic, each of them took the jug to their lips, being careful to sip only water and not the crystals themselves. Once each had drunk their share, they sat back, wondering in their hearts if it had offered any protection or not. Time would surely tell.

The next thing on the agenda was the opening of Befland. The grand plans were now, of course, scaled down and were almost miniscule in proportion. Only Gaspar could perform on stage, so had to change the routine that 'The Three Kings' had intended to perform together. Bef could still enthral with her marvellous broom routine in the skies above Befland, but would have to wear a half-finished costume, with a hem turned up by Bef and Natalia using Jeremiah's needles and thread. The rides could operate as intended … with the notable exception of the Coaler Coaster.

Bef was particularly subdued as the plans for the rides were discussed. There were enough park attendants and villagers to operate them, but despite that she was depressed and downbeat.

'Come on, shake yourself out of it!' demanded Natalia, as Bef shuffled around in her big floppy shoes not displaying the steel needed to show their enemies that they could not be defeated.

'What is wrong with her, apart from the obvious?' asked Natalia.

'The Coaler Coaster,' Gaspar explained. 'It's always been her baby. She's cut up that we can't get the coal. Jeremiah even offered to knit some.'

Natalia looked pensive.

'Does it really make that big a difference to her?' she asked.

'She wanted it to re-enact our previous meeting,' explained Gaspar. 'It was to be the star attraction and something absolutely unbelievable for families.'

'I see,' said Natalia. 'I see.'

Throughout the day, there were various knocks at the door to deal with. All three of them answered the door together, with Gaspar's potions in hand. In every case, the caller was just a villager, checking if the opening really was still going ahead given what had happened to Marianna and Mr Passarella.

The mood in the town was more subdued than should have been the case, with all residents fearful of the strange things that had been happening and, of course, the fact that two of their friends and one of 'The Three Kings' were now sitting around the town, and at Befland, as statues. As Fiery Tina had said, if Capriccia had used her brain and kept Jeremiah and Mel in the town, the fear factor would have been massive.

As it was, the thought of having a go on rides that had been talked about for months and the expectation of Bef's marvellous broom antics above the park were enough to convince everyone that they should turn up for the grand opening ... everyone that was with the exception of Lorenzo, who never left the house unless he absolutely had to. He was still curled up with the Grandissimo Libro di Scongiuri and Bef knew full well that she would not see her brother's face in the crowd. Not that she wanted him there. Lorenzo's safety was of huge importance.

After the procession of people arriving at the door, the two remaining members of the Befland team and their new VIPB recruit really weren't expecting any other visitors. When the knock came, just three hours before the opening was scheduled, they were all immediately put on edge. Each clung on to their potions tighter than they had all day. Bef moved the spyhole and saw a man – a man with a dirty face.

'Who is it?' whispered Gaspar.

'I have no idea,' said Bef.

The man started to shout for attention.

'What on earth is he saying?' asked Bef. 'I can't understand a word.'

Natalia pushed her out of the way. 'Luckily, I do,' she stated in a matter-of-fact way. 'I think we can open the door.'

Gaspar did as instructed and moved the latches back. He tentatively inched the door open. A muscular man in blue overalls – blue overalls stained in soot – stood on the step. Natalia pushed past Gaspar and spoke to the man in Russian. He nodded and clearly thanked her. He turned away, leaving Bef and Gaspar none the wiser.

'Bef, my dear,' said Natalia. 'I am not sure how this has happened, but you have your heart's desire. That man has just transported truck loads of coal from Russia. Your Coaler Coaster will be full of it for the opening.'

Bef beamed with delight.

'Mr Passarella must have found a supply before he was turned to stone. Either that or Jeremiah managed it, though I am sure he would have preferred to have knitted lumps. At last, something is going right! What do you think broom?'

Her broom didn't respond. She stared at it,

slightly peeved. It hadn't reacted to very much lately, which was a worrying sign. She could only think it was extremely depressed by all that had happened. It was probably also still very fearful of having to return to Bernhardt. Bef could only hope it would be up to the performance they had to give in just a few hours time, but then the broom had been fabulous at the 'Bef Rehearsal' and the statuefications had already started then. She was probably worrying unnecessarily.

Natalia seemed puzzled.

'I shall try to keep watch while you both perform,' she said, after several minutes had passed. 'I need to find somewhere to hide, where I can observe the park, but without attracting attention. We don't want our enemies to know that I am here. Have you any idea where I could be situated?'

Bef looked at Gaspar and Gaspar looked at Bef. Together, they blurted out, 'In the Coaler Coaster.'

Natalia looked bemused. 'Explain more,' she said.

'Well,' said Gaspar, taking the lead. 'Originally, Bef had the idea that a replica of you could appear during the Coaler Coaster ride, to add to the drama. It may be that our enemies know that. So, if you now appear at the ride, they will just assume that you are the replica that we planned. It's a perfect place for you to stand.'

Natalia didn't know whether to be flattered or

slightly peeved about the original plans, but had to agree that it was a great suggestion.

'It's actually genius,' she said. 'We just need to make sure I can get to the park undetected.'

Gaspar looked at Bef.

'Do you think you could perform a spell for long enough so that we could load Natalia into a vehicle, as if a dummy, and then get her in place at the Coaler Coaster?'

Bef thought about it.

'I could try a variation of the Pietrifisico spell, which would freeze her in motion for a while. It's called the Pietricongelato Spell.'

Natalia looked rather dubious about this suggestion. Gaspar felt the need to explain.

'It's perfectly fine,' he said. 'She's pretty useless at the Pietrifisico spell, so can't be much better at this one. I reckon you'd only be frozen for a maximum of ten minutes. It's just a way of fooling our enemies.'

'OK,' said Natalia, a little reluctantly. 'When do I become frozen?'

'We need to get you to the car,' said Gaspar. 'But I've been thinking about that. Bef's gold dress is absolutely huge at the bottom, with a flowing train too. I believe you could hide under the dress, if I carried the train, and we could walk down to the town walls and then get you into the car in a place where you won't be seen. We can drive to Befland and Bef can perform the spell. We can then get some of the workmen down there to carry you to the Coaler Coaster and put you in position at the platform where the dummy of you was supposed to appear. The spell with then wear off and you will just have to pretend to be the dummy, unless, of course, you need to act and protect us.'

Natalia looked at him quizzically. 'Do you know, young man,' she said, in a slightly patronising tone, 'I thought you were rather stupid, but you're actually brighter than you look.'

Gaspar beamed and Bef applauded.

'That's a brilliant idea, Gaspar,' she said. 'Let me get into my dress and we can get on.'

A heavenly vision appeared at the top of the stairs just fifteen minutes later, with Bef looking every inch the golden angel that Jeremiah had predicted.

'If only Jeremiah were here to see you now,' said Gaspar. 'He would be so proud.'

'We must do everything we can to get the poor man home and in one piece, rather than in stony segments,' stressed Bef. 'Perhaps our enemies will lose interest, once they've seen that we've opened the park, and give our friends back to us.'

'Indeed,' said Natalia. 'We just need to keep them at bay tonight.'

As they left the house, with Natalia hiding under the many folds of Bef's voluminous dress and Gaspar carefully holding the beautiful, golden train to prevent her being spotted, they joined throngs of villagers heading towards Befland. Many doffed their caps as they passed the statue of Mr Passarella – a statue neither Bef nor Gaspar could look in the eye.

As they themselves walked past, Bef muttered under her breath, 'I swear to you, Luigi, I will get you home soon.' It may just have been Gaspar's imagination, but he could have sworn Mr Passarella's clipboard moved.

Bef tried desperately to prevent people standing on her dress as they came forward to wish her well, fending them off with her broom. Several managed to tread on Natalia's toes, leading to a few strange squeaks coming out from under Bef's dress.

'That Jeremiah Needlebaum is so clever he's managed to sew squeaking mice into Bef's dress,' said one man.

'Do my eyes deceive me, or are those stitched snowflakes?' said another.

They reached the car park and Gaspar took charge.

'Stay here! I'll bring the car into the shadows,' he said. He dashed off and reappeared within seconds. 'Try and shuffle inside, quickly' he said. 'I'll shield you.'

Bef and Natalia got into the car, which in true rock star style had blacked-out windows. Gaspar jumped into the driving seat.

'I'll drive to Befland and as we approach you can do the Pietricongelato spell. I'll then yell for help and we'll get Natalia to the Coaler Coaster and in position. Is everyone set?' he asked, with urgency in his voice.

'Yes,' replied Bef.

'Affirmative,' said Natalia.

All went to plan. The moment they arrived at the gates, Bef looked Natalia in the eye and uttered the word, 'Pietricongelato', in as bold a voice as she could muster. Natalia instantly froze.

'Quick, please,' shouted Gaspar to some of the park employees. 'We need to carry this dummy to the Coaler Coaster.'

As men came scurrying, Bef giggled to herself. Natalia would hate being called a dummy! The men quickly carried her and got her into place, on a platform halfway through the ride. Her head and shoulders stuck out at the top of a sentry box, which would give her a perfect view over Befland and of the skies above it when she unfroze.

Bef turned to Gaspar.

'I shall make my way to the hillside and watch your performance from there. As soon as you have finished singing, I will start my routine.'

'Good luck,' said Gaspar, wondering if anything might happen to either of them.

'We have the assistance of the amethyst, remember,' said Bef. 'Don't be too nervous.'

Once the crowds had entered Befland, loud music struck up and an announcer started to inform the audience what was happening during the evening. There would first be a performance by Gaspar, one of the famous 'Three Kings', followed by a demonstration of the wonderful Coaler Coaster and then a dramatic aerial performance by the village's most famous resident, Bef herself.

Natalia began to unfreeze just as the announcements were being made. Nobody had informed her, Bef or Gaspar that the Coaler Coaster was going to be demonstrated. Mr Passarella must have decided this after he'd discovered that he'd found some coal, but had probably been turned to stone before having a chance to tell Bef. Natalia was now a key part of a ride that would have everybody's eyes upon it. Even from where she was standing, she was sure she could hear Bef on the hillside uttering the words 'O Dio!' Had Bef known what was happening behind rocks on another hillside, her cries would have been even louder.

Capriccia, Bernhardt and Fiery Tina had all taken up spying positions, with Sly dragging along behind them not in the mood for their games. Bernhardt had promised Fiery Tina a feast for the eyes, but had also kept winking at Capriccia in a very strange and all-knowing way.

As the announcer read out the plans, Fiery Tina stomped her feet.

'I am NOT pwepared to watch that women showing off on her bwoomstick,' she declared in a hissy fit.

Capriccia sniggered, causing Fiery Tina to glare at her in a particularly frightening manner.

Capriccia stopped laughing and glared back.

'If I were you, Capwiccia,' said Fiery Tina in a very strict tone, 'I would pull my socks up and get on with snatching the next thing that the Bef woman loves.' She put her hands on her hips and looked very smug at putting her pupil in her place.

'Already done it,' said Capriccia triumphantly. 'You see, I'm so clever that you didn't even realise.'

'What are you talking about?' snapped Fiery Tina. 'Nobody else is missing. That lovely boy is singing, she still has her shoes on her feet and she's about to ride her bwoom! You are talking nonsense, as usual!'

Bernhardt and Capriccia both broke out laughing at once, annoying Fiery Tina even more. Sly just rolled his eyes, thinking how childish all three of them were. As Fiery Tina's eyes smouldered with anger, Bernhardt chipped in.

'Just wait and see. Just wait and see.'

Gaspar was already part way through his routine, strumming his guitar and singly beautifully, even though he felt very self-conscious. He wasn't used to appearing on his own on stage without Mel and Thaz. Nevertheless, the audience broke out into rapturous applause and Gaspar took a bow. He stared into the sky and could see no sign of anyone waiting to whisk him away. With great relief, he handed the microphone to the announcer.

'And now for the demonstration of the Coaler Coaster,' said the man, his voice booming out over Befland.

Capriccia, Bernhardt and Fiery Tina all peeked over the rocks. Each wanted to see the ride in action, but felt very differently about it. Capriccia felt jealous. Bernhardt couldn't help but remember the scene in the Russian coalmine where he'd chased Natalia out into the snow. Fiery Tina steamed even more, as she realised that they'd found coal somewhere, despite her best efforts. Her mind went back to her lovely white tutu and the days when she was quite a good fairy, for at least three days a week anyway!

Bernhardt whipped out the binoculars. Super-excited volunteers were seated in the trucks rattling up and down the Coaler Coaster and coal was flying around at all angles, just as Bef had wished. The trucks were heading towards a sort of tower and something caught Bernhardt's eye.

'Nein,' he shouted loudly. 'Zay have created a dummy of ze woman who stopped me becoming a VIPB. How dare zay!'

At this point, Natalia was attempting to stay stony-faced, but the trucks were hurtling towards her at some speed. Up on the hill, Bef was watching anxiously.

'Keep still, Natalia. Please keep still!' she muttered.

She could detect Natalia twitching and was

worried to death. Natalia would give her presence away before long.

'There's nothing for it. If I don't do something, she'll move,' she thought. In an instant, Bef yelled out at the top of her voice, 'Pietricongelato!' This was total desperation, as her spell was wonky at the best of times, but amazingly she saw Natalia stop twitching. She was temporarily frozen once more – and just in the nick of time, as the coal trucks started to rumble through underneath her.

'It's an amazing likeness,' marvelled Bernhardt. Capriccia kicked him hard. 'Ouch,' he yelped. 'What was zat for?

Capriccia nodded towards the hill. 'It's the Bef woman we're here to watch,' she said. 'Not some dummy.'

Bernhardt nodded and took his eyes off Natalia just as she began to unfreeze. That was a blessing as she shook uncontrollably as she regained the ability to move and then flung her arms around madly, before coming to her senses, realising what had happened.

The Coaler Coaster stopped running and the crowd applauded once more. Kids were already begging their parents to let them queue for it, but everyone's attention soon switched elsewhere as the announcer came back on the microphone and said, 'And now for the star of the show – our very own, fabulous Bef, the Queen of Befland!' His voice rose at the end of the sentence, making everyone extremely excited about what they were about to see.

Bef started the music playing and leapt on to her broom.

'Come on broom,' time for us to show off our talents,' she declared. 'Andiamo!'

She took off, but not with the normal sort of pace she would have expected after a 'Let's go' instruction. This led her to go into her first manoeuvre – luckily just a simple loop – with far less speed than anticipated, which caused her to wobble. She tucked her legs in to give her broom the hint that it needed to speed up. That was essential, as the 'broomies' were next and they needed a good degree of force behind them.

She tilted the broom up, ready to launch into her famous trick, but her broom had other ideas and instead tilted violently downwards, forcing her to perform her broomies upside down and clinging on for dear life. Her voluminous dress blew out, revealing her bright red knickers, much to the amusement of the crowd. She bounced up and down in this fashion, becoming decidedly sick and desperately trying to make her broom turn back up the way it was supposed to be pointing.

'Mamma mia!' Bef cried. 'What are you doing to me, broom?'

Instead of getting a response, as would normally be the case, she got no reaction at all. She struggled hard and managed to force the broom back upright, but things went from bad to worse. As she made her mouth shapes, the broom spurted out hot air of its own. Instead of creating the Colosseum, she got something that looked like an oddly squashed plate. Big Ben became a wonky cheese grater. The White House just looked like a wobbling blancmange and, as for the Taj Mahal, it just appeared like a melting ice cream.

'What was that supposed to be?' asked hundreds of people in the crowd simultaneously.

'Absolutely no idea,' replied hundreds of others. Some even began to jeer.

'Broom, we must perform the bunny hops properly,' shouted Bef. However, instead of hopping down the centre of the arena as at the 'Bef Rehearsal', the broom zigzagged in a manic fashion, crashing Bef first into a hard flagpole and then into the Chimney Chaser.

'Ouch,' she cried. 'Stop bumping me around!'

Murmurs of displeasure came from the audience below, as the broom suddenly took complete control and, rather than performing serenely to the music, began to zoom down towards the poor frightened people below, only missing their heads by a few feet before zooting back up again.

Next, it rushed straight through the Bonbon Bumper Car area, flying just inches off the ground and bumping Bef's floppy shoes along the arena flooring, before lifting itself upright and almost tipping her off in the middle of Aniseed Alley. Bef saw some men touch their head, just to check that their toupee was still on!

Bef began to cry.

'This is an absolute disaster, broom,' she sobbed. 'Why are you behaving like this?' Rather than heed her words, the broom shot in and out of the Chimney Chaser, setting off fireworks that shot into the crowd and badly singed Bef's dress.

Boos from below were now accompanied by screams of women and children and the angry shouting of men who had only escaped being hit on the head by a fraction. People began to flee the park, as increasingly violent swerves and swoops were performed by the mad woman on the broom.

But finally, after much humiliation and an appalling display of broom flying, something even worse occurred. The broom started heading straight towards the metal top of the Coaler Coaster. Gaspar, who had heard all the commotion and come out from behind the stage to watch Bef's antics in sheer horror, suddenly gasped hard.

'It's going to crash Bef into the Coaler Coaster. She's going to be crushed.'

Sure enough, the broom was speeding up and steering a direct course towards the roller coaster's metal framework.

'She hasn't got a prayer,' yelled Gaspar. 'Someone needs to do something!'

Bef herself feared the worst. She had absolutely no control over her broom and was powerless to prevent it crashing her into the hard, steel loops of her star ride. She shut her eyes, expecting to feel enormous pain and then a swift tumble to the ground, but it didn't come. Instead, she heard an almighty swooshing noise and felt herself lifted off the broom. Somebody then grabbed her arm and pulled her sharply. Seconds later, there was an almighty smash. The broom had hit the Coaler Coaster, but without Bef on board. She was in the arms of Natalia Lebedev and now standing in the turret in which Natalia had been positioned for the whole evening.

Bef stared downwards as the broom tumbled down to the ground, causing families to scatter, with sheer pandemonium raging below. Hundreds of people could be seen stampeding out of the gates of Befland, shouting, screaming and shaking their fists at Bef. It was almost like looking down into an angry nest of hornets.

'My poor broom,' cried Bef. 'I knew it hadn't been feeling well.'

'I would wager anything that the broom down there is NOT your broom,' answered Natalia. 'I zink your broom has probably been missing for a few days now. Have you noticed anyzing different about its behaviour?'

Bef scratched her head.

'Yes,' she replied. 'It's not been answering me, or responding to what I say. Normally, it gives a little shake or a shuffle, or rises up a few inches. It's done none of that, but in appearance, it's exactly the same.'

'I am sorry to have to tell you zis,' said Natalia, 'but I have a strong suspicion that your broom is back in the hands of Bernhardt. Only he could have made a broom almost identical, but he wouldn't have known the personality traits that it has picked up in all the years that it has lived with you. Only he could have given you a rogue broom that has behaved like that one now lying down there. What you think is your broom, is actually another one altogether.'

Bef was heartbroken. She and her broom were so close – closer than anyone could ever imagine. She was already sobbing by the time Gaspar rushed over. He put his arms around her, as she wept buckets of tears into his pristine white shirt. As she clung on to him, a piece of card fell into the sentry tower. Gaspar picked it up and turned it over. 'It's an A,' he said. 'They've got Bef's broom.'

On the hillside there were three jubilant enemies. Fiery Tina had uttered the word 'Oops' about 97 times as Bef had performed her terrible routine, much to her own great amusement. Bernhardt had laughed so much that he had fallen to the ground rolling around and holding his ribs. Capriccia was cruelly cackling. None had realised that Natalia had reached out and grabbed Bef: their mirth had got the better of them and their powers of observation had been lacking.

'Bwilliant, Bernhardt,' shouted Fiery Tina. 'How did you manage that?'

Capriccia arched her back. 'Actually,' she said, 'I was the one who made it possible. I took away the thing the Bef woman loves most in the world.' Bernhardt looked at her a little in amazement.

'Well, Capriccia, actually it was I who told you that ze broom had to return to me, if I called it back, under ze terms of ze 1020 rule. And it was I who sent ze other broom back to take its place.'

Capriccia digged him in the ribs, to tell him to shut up. It was true that she'd done very little, but she had helped call Bef's broom back to its master – well, at least once.

Fiery Tina seemed stuck on a loop of 'Oops' and didn't really take any of this in, much to Capriccia's relief. She was off the hook.

'Six down, two to go,' declared Capriccia callously. 'Just two more things for the Bef woman to lose and then she will be ruined once and for all.'

In Bef's eyes, as she looked at all the thousands of visitors streaming like little ants back to the town, all grumpy, angry and disillusioned with Befland, she was already finished.

CHAPTER SEVENTEEN

No amount of frenetic cleaning could take Bef's mind off the absolute disaster of the previous evening. She was so embarrassed, she didn't dare show her face outside and a few angry notes had been pushed under her door by parents who were not impressed at the way she'd terrified their children. Gaspar felt helpless, not knowing how to console her. Natalia was occupied with other thoughts.

Suddenly, Natalia broke the silence.

'What do you know about the 1020 year rule?' she asked.

Bef looked thoughtful, trying to remember what it had said on the document housed in the Casket of Confirmations in her brother's house. She pulled up the text of the document in her mind, having cast a special memory spell while reading it, so it was lodged in her brain. She stared straight ahead without blinking while her mind scanned the document. She then spoke.

'It says a master can call a broom that they originally crafted back to their home after 1020 years.'

'As I thought!' declared Natalia triumphantly. 'There's a crucial bit of information in that sentence.'

'Yes, we know ... 1020 years,' said Gaspar, in a dejected fashion.

'Wrong!' shouted Natalia. 'The important bit is 'back to their home.' Your broom must be in the Black Forest at Bernhardt's home, rather than anywhere around here. It won't be statuefied, as it's just been called back. If we travel to Germany, we may be able to retrieve it!'

Bef's eyes shone for the first time that day.

'You are right, Natalia,' she said. 'It will be in his treehouse.' She then looked upset once more. 'But we have no means of getting there,' she said.

'Wrong!' said Natalia for the second time in two minutes. 'We can travel on my broom. I doubt whether Bernhardt will even be there when we arrive, so we can break into his home and get your broom back. It should be a relatively easy snatch.'

'Can you carry three people?' asked Gaspar. 'I can't let Bef travel alone.'

Natalia looked thoughtful and began to scribble calculations on a piece of paper.

'I think we shall be fine,' she said after a while. 'I've worked out the distance and the drag that three people will put on my broom, but it all seems to suggest that there won't be a problem. We need to pack bags full of things we need – tools to break in with, Gaspar's potions, maybe extra amethyst, water, a compass and anything else you can think of. Let's get on with it!'

Whilst Bef, Natalia and Gaspar were scurrying around packing their bags, other things were happening at the ruined castle at which their enemies had taken up residence.

Bernhardt was absorbed in the study of a document – one written on a parchment roll and one that he hadn't read for many hundreds of years.

'What genius it was for me to remember this document,' he shouted with glee. 'We have taken away ze thing ze Bef woman loves most and I can almost feel her pain from here. Added to zat, we have made her look absolutely ridiculous. What a success yesterday was!'

The other three looked at him with bored expressions on their faces. Bernhardt had said the same thing repeatedly and self-praise was rather wearying after a while.

Bernhardt looked peeved.

'Very well, if you don't wish to congratulate me, I shall leave you here,' he said. 'I must travel home and secure the Bef woman's broom, so that it cannot escape.'

'What about our next move?' asked Capriccia, panicking rather a lot. Bernhardt had been the one who'd whispered ideas in her ear, to help her plan her snatches. She'd be useless without him.

Fiery Tina wasn't that happy either.

'We need to stick together,' she said, in a

matter-of-fact way. 'We have to plan the final stages of the conundwum. Now is the crucial time. Being one man down won't help at all.'

'Very vell,' said Bernhardt. 'Come with me and I vill throw a party to celebrate ze success we enjoyed last night. Befland is ruined and we should raise a glass of Fir Fizz to mark zat fact.'

'Ooh, I love a party,' enthused Fiery Tina. 'Sounds super-duper to me! I'll fly with Capwiccia and you can take the strange elf with you.'

Sly wasn't remotely interested in any party. He was quite surprised they'd even remembered him, but he wished they hadn't. He could have perhaps got away, if they'd left him behind. He wanted to escape their vile behaviour, but actually had no idea where he could go. However, there was no chance of that. Bernhardt was already mounting his broom and calling Sly over. Fiery Tina was sorting out her fairy wings and trying to attach Capriccia to her. Reluctantly, Sly jumped on board, feeling ever so sick as the broom soared into the air and he witnessed a flash of fairy lights as Fiery Tina came alongside.

The other group of people heading to the Black Forest were not as swift. Bef tried to pack as many of her gadgets as possible, so flitted around the house finding all manner of things. What she was really after, however, was her willow wand. Where the devil had she put it? The trouble was that she'd hidden it in so many places over the centuries, she now couldn't remember which was the most recent.

This process continued for a couple of hours, until Natalia, feeling very exasperated, decided to put a stop to it.

'We need to put this to bed right now!' she exclaimed.

Bef danced on the spot.

'That's it Natalia. That's it!' she declared, rushing up the stairs to her bedroom. She pulled a mattress off her bed and started to count the wooden bars of the bed's frame. She got to nineteen and started to unscrew the slat. It was stiff and hard to turn, but she used more force and eventually managed it. She peered down the hole in the slat and could see nothing. 'Fiddlesticks,' she said, thinking she'd got it wrong and the wand wasn't here. As a last resort, she tipped the bar up and shook it. Out shot a willow wand, about eleven inches in length. She picked it up triumphantly. 'Now we can fly!' she shouted.

The three of them gingerly headed out of the back door to where Natalia's broom was hidden.

'Sit still while I control our direction,' said Natalia, studying a compass. 'We shall have to try to fly into the forest undetected, so I shall drop our speed when I think we are near enough to glide. Do you have any idea where in the Black Forest Bernhardt lives?'

'In a big tree,' replied Gaspar, truthfully.

'And what use is that to me!' snapped Natalia. 'We need a better plan than trying to find one big tree in a the middle of a vast forest of trees!'

'I can only think of one thing,' said Bef.

'What's that then?' asked Gaspar.

'I could try and connect with my broom and send a message to it. If we can make it hum or send out a signal, it may be able to guide us to where we need to be.'

'It's our only hope,' said Gaspar.

They shot up into the sky at speed, with Natalia setting a general course for Germany, heading north and over the snow-capped Alps, where the chill made Gaspar shiver terribly, even though he was wearing the warm, furry suit that Jeremiah Needlebaum had once made for him. A resident of Dubai wasn't cut out for freezing conditions and he felt the cold terribly.

Next they flew over Lake Lucerne and then Zurich, causing Bef to wonder how the Gnomes of Zurich were getting on these days. She'd always had a great affection for them, but hadn't dropped in on any for centuries.

Having passed over Zurich, they began to spot a dense mass of trees that just had to be the Black Forest. Bef shut her eyes tight and began to hum, entering a deep trance and closing herself off from the rest of the world around. She hummed louder and louder and suddenly something strange happened. Natalia's broom started to respond to Bef stroking and guiding its direction with her legs and began to drop down foot by foot, altering its course from that which they had been following.

'She's getting messages from her broom,' cried Gaspar. 'It's helping guide us to Bernhardt's home. It's amazing!'

Sure enough, Natalia's broom started to glide and almost seemed to be floating to the ground. They drew nearer and nearer to the top of the trees below and the broom began to weave in and out of glades of dense thicket and dark trees, dropping all the time. Bef continued to hum and Natalia's broom carried on responding to whatever Bef's broom was saying in response. Within ten minutes, they were just a few feet away from the forest floor, hovering in the air as Natalia's broom decided which direction to take, according to Bef's strokes and leg movements.

Out of the blue, Gaspar muttered. 'I think I've just seen Bernhardt's home. I believe we've just passed it.'

Sure enough, the broom circled and headed back on itself, still continuing to bring them down and down. The massive tree that Gaspar had spotted was standing at the other side of a glade. Suddenly, the broom hovered and glided to a halt, landing behind a fallen tree, which hid them from the view of anyone looking out of Bernhardt's treehouse.

Bef snapped out of her trance and looked around her.

'Perfect,' she said. 'Get behind the tree and see if you can spot any movement in Bernhardt's abode.'

The three of them laid on the prickly forest floor with their chins resting on the rough tree trunk. They studied Bernhardt's home, but could see very little in the gloomy surroundings of the forest. Bef pricked up her ears and began to move her head slowly from side to side.

'Shhh!' she said. 'Stop rustling your feet Gaspar. I think I can hear something.'

Sure enough, they could all detect a noise – the sound of raucous laughter coming out of Bernhardt's tree.

'I think I can also see a dim light that's flickering now and again,' said Bef.

'Me too,' agreed Natalia. 'There are at least two people in the tree, judging by the laughter, but there may be more. I can hear different tones of laughter. I'm sure I can hear at least one woman. We need to edge closer, taking care as we go, to see if we can get a clearer idea what's going on.'

Very slowly, the three of them began to crawl on their hands and knees, trying desperately not to make leaves rustle, or hurt their hands on fallen branches and sharp twigs. Every minute or so, they stopped moving and signalled to each other to wait a while, to see if anything stirred ahead. Having checked that the coast was clear each time, they continued to crawl.

Bef clutched her willow wand in her hand,

clinging on to it for dear life. Gaspar was being equally careful with the potions, while Natalia fingered a lasso rope, which she had brought along with her. They edged up towards the tree.

'There's a window there. That's where the light's coming from. One of us needs to try to look in and see what's happening,' whispered Gaspar.

By now, they could hear the voices more clearly, each one echoing around the forest in a most eerie way.

'That's Bernhardt,' said Bef, hearing a male voice and thick German accent. She paused. 'I think there are two different female voices,' she said.

'Agreed,' said Natalia. 'I'd say that it's Fiery Tina and Capriccia.'

They listened hard again.

'I think there are only three of them,' said Gaspar, which was little consolation, as they had hoped to find an empty treehouse. Now things were very different. To retrieve Bef's broom, they would have to fight off their enemies.

Gaspar signalled to Natalia and Bef. He seemed to be indicating that he would go and look through the window. Bef raised her eyebrows in such a way as to tell him to be careful. Gaspar was not deterred. He moved forward in a stealthy manner and reached the base of the tree, below the window. Nervously, he began to uncurl and straighten his legs, assuming a crouching position beneath it. Finally, he stood up a little more and put his nose on a window ledge made of sharp tree bark that dug into his skin. His eyes were focused on the scene in the room into which he was spying. There, he saw Bernhardt pouring glasses of some sort of fizzy drink, while a woman with auburn hair and wearing a black tutu was hopping around on one leg and another, with long blonde hair, which appeared to be streaked with blue highlights, kept holding up her glass and demanding more fizz.

Gaspar sunk back on to his haunches and gestured to the other two to join him. He drew letters in the air with his finger. First a B, then an F and a T and then a C. Both Bef and Natalia knew exactly who was in the room, though he hadn't spoken a word.

'At least there are three of them and three of us,' whispered Gaspar. 'The numbers are evenly matched.'

'That's where you are mistaken,' said a creepy voice, which seemed to come out of nowhere. The three of them leapt out of their skin, almost forgetting they were hiding below the window.

'Who on earth said that?' asked Gaspar, scared witless.

'I did,' said a slimy-looking individual, who emerged from the left and moved around the base of the tree, heading towards them.

Bef rolled her eyes.

'O Dio!' she exclaimed. 'It's the 81st elf.' She pointed her willow wand at him.

'Was the 81st elf,' replied Sly. 'My name's Sly now ... and you can put that wand away: you won't be needing that. Are you here to try to rescue your broom?'

'Possibly,' replied Bef. 'I should have known that you'd be involved, helping your precious Capriccia to get revenge.'

'That was true,' said Sly. 'Not any more, however. I've seen her for what she is and it isn't nice. In fact, I hate all three of them. Each has a personality disorder of some kind or the other. I just have nowhere to go. Nowhere to head.'

Bef looked at her wand. It was retracting and lifting itself away from Sly. For some reason, the wand believed he wasn't an enemy.

Gaspar digged her in the ribs. 'Could this be the sugar lump?' he asked.

'I think it could well be,' replied Bef, still watching her wand. It still didn't wish to harm Sly in any way.

'Come with me,' said Sly. 'It's too dangerous to talk here. They could come to the window at any time. Round the back, we can enter the building through another door and they won't even know we're there.'

'This had better not be a trick, elf,' warned Natalia. 'I am equipped and can easily take out an imp like you.'

Sly scowled at her.

'I am not the enemy,' he muttered. 'Stay here

and be caught, if you wish, but I would suggest you would be safer coming with me.'

'They'll come looking for you after a while,' said Gaspar, as nervous as Natalia about the whole situation.

'They won't even notice I'm gone,' stated Sly in a dejected tone. 'They ignore me all the time. They are so wrapped up in themselves, they don't have time for others.'

Bef studied his demeanour.

'He's being honest,' she said, quickly adding, 'for once.' She grabbed Gaspar's arm. 'Come on. Let's go with him.'

Sly led them around the side of the tree. He bent down and opened a small door, which could hardly be seen, its hinges blending perfectly into the wood.

'You'll have to crouch,' he urged. 'It's a small door, but a safe area once you are inside.'

Bef, Gaspar and Natalia did as instructed and stooped to get through the opening. There was no furniture in the tiny room to mention, just a wooden bench seat running around it. All four of them perched their bottoms on this.

'Where is my broom?' asked Bef in a very direct manner.

Sly hesitated. 'Down below,' he said. 'But I know not where.'

'Do you mean in the cellar?' asked Gaspar. 'Bernhardt tried to put Bef and I down there.'

'No, that would be easy,' replied Sly shaking his

head. 'You'd merely have to overcome them and climb into the cellar. It's in a more tricky position than that. It's under the floorboards somewhere, in a cavity that Bernhardt won't mention. He's kept it a secret as to where he's put it. All he says is, 'under the floorboards'. Unless we know where, we can't lift the floorboards to find it.'

Bef's heart sank as she took in the information that Sly had delivered.

'Surely you can contact it and ask it to guide you?' said Gaspar.

'That's too dangerous,' replied Bef. 'If I am communicating within a certain distance of my broom, trained ears could pick up the signal, which becomes louder and fuzzy, like a crackling radio. My secret communication with my broom only stays undetected when we are over twenty-five feet away from each other.'

Gaspar scratched his head.

'Did you not see anything that might give you a clue?' he said to Sly.

'No,' replied the elf, in a dejected tone. 'They had locked me into Bernhardt's Broom Box where he ages his younger brooms. They thought it very funny to keep me in there for an hour, while they played their silly games. Bernhardt hid your broom at that point, so I saw nothing. I just heard him say it was now in a secret place under the floorboards and that nobody would ever find it there.' A tear rolled down Sly's cheek as he told this tale.

'He's genuine,' declared Bef. 'He's definitely the sugar lump.'

'Don't be so rude,' said Sly indignantly.

'I mean,' said Bef, 'that you are an outsider within this group of malicious people. You don't feel comfortable with their behaviour and you are ready to help those from another camp.'

'In that case, I am the sugar lump,' agreed Sly. 'I've had enough of them.'

'I suggest we sleep on it,' said Gaspar. 'Can we stay in here? Are you sure we'll be safe?'

'They've all drunk far too much,' replied Sly. 'They'll be asleep for hours themselves before much longer. They won't have a clue that you're here. If you knew where the broom was, it would be easy to creep in and take it back, once they fall into their Fir Fizz slumber. They'll be incapable of fighting back at present. It's such a shame that we don't know where to find it.'

'Indeed,' said Bef gloomily. 'Indeed. Getting some rest is the best we can do. A little sleep will give us some time to think.'

Sly smiled. Bef just couldn't work out whether it was a friendly smile, or a smug one.

Chapter Eighteen

The three travellers managed to get a little sleep, with one of them keeping watch while the other two dropped off, but none of them slept well. They were very aware of the fact that they were in the enemy camp. By the time it reached 3am, they were all wide awake. Natalia had prevented Sly from leaving them, so he too sat in their midst. The Russian VIPB was not as sure of his good intentions as Bef seemed to be. She was keeping her eye on him. One false move and she'd squash him flat.

'I've been thinking about it and tossing and turning while dreaming about it too,' said Bef. 'All we can do is enter the room in which they are sleeping before they wake up and then take them prisoner. They will simply have to tell us where the broom is hidden.'

'They will never do that,' advised Sly. 'And they are formidable. Fiery Tina has a lot of black magic up her sleeve and Capriccia has become a powerful witch. Bernhardt has various tricks too. No disrespect, but your spells don't work half the time,

I've never heard of Natalia and the boy can't do any magic. They would eat you alive.'

While Bef took a little umbrage at Sly's words, he was right. If it came to a battle, she and her faithful friends would lose every time. If she were reunited with her broom, however, it could be a different story.

'We can't attack them with all of our force while they are holding our friends in a statuefication spell,' advised Bef. 'We could creep in there and start to look around, to see if there is any sign of floorboard disturbance, but they could wake at any moment. What do you want to do?'

'I think we have to chance it,' said Natalia. 'It's our best option. We'll never find the broom when they are awake, so let's see what we can spot now.' She turned to Sly. 'How shall we get in?'

Sly moved away. 'Follow me,' he said. He had a smirk on his face, but Bef still could not decide if that was just his normal expression. Could he possibly be double-crossing them? Could he ever really have fallen out with Capriccia, when he had adored her so much? Was it a case of Sly by name and sly by nature? These questions pinged around her head as he opened the door of their hidey-hole and led them out into the darkness.

They crept slowly around the tree, desperately trying to not step on twigs that could snap and make a noise. They inched their way along like cats stalking mice, unable to hear anything from inside the massive tree. Shafts of light still shone through the open window. They would need to peer through and see how the land lay.

Bef made the move to peep. She sidled up to the window and slowly peered around the frame and into the room. Bernhardt and Fiery Tina were slumped over the table, with several empty Fir Fizz bottles dotted around them. Bef scanned the room again, wondering where Capriccia was. She spotted her blonde locks trailing over the arm of an armchair. She had to be slumped in it: she wasn't moving at all.

Sly had made it as far as the front door.

'I'll go in ahead and then signal to you when I've checked it's safe for you to follow,' he said in a hushed voice. Natalia looked dubious, but let him go forth. Bef's wand still wasn't regarding him as an enemy.

Sly entered, with Natalia just behind. He tiptoed into the room and aroused no attention from Bernhardt or Fiery Tina. Bernhardt was snoring. Fiery Tina's limbs seemed lifeless. He turned and signalled to Natalia to follow, who in turn beckoned to Bef, who gestured to Gaspar. All walked into the room in slow motion, hardly moving, so as to not create a disturbance in the air and with the intention of not making the floor creak.

They surveyed the boards as they trod on them. They couldn't see any sign of disturbance at all. They followed Sly's lead, as he stealthily moved towards the armchair in which Capriccia was slumped. Again, they placed their feet carefully and all was silent, apart from the rumbling noises coming from Bernhardt's nose.

Sly took another step, beginning to edge past Capriccia's chair. At that moment, an arm shot out and grabbed him by the leg.

'Not so fast, elf!' snarled Capriccia. 'I need a bilberry juice, NOW! My head is thumping, so I suggest you find me some quickly, or you will be my next stone victim.'

Sly quaked in his strange red pantaloon trousers.

'I am not sure where to find any, mistress,' he stressed, 'but I will do my best.' Capriccia slumped back into her chair, as he moved away.

Bef clicked her fingers and summoned up a glass of bilberry juice, which she handed to Sly.

'What was that noise?' snarled Capriccia, lifting her head once more.

'Just me fetching the juice,' stressed Sly. 'Here it is mistress.'

Capriccia grabbed the glass and downed it in one.

'Get me another,' she demanded, 'and make it quick! Why are you creeping around anyway?' she asked, as the other three froze, as if playing a game of musical statues. They passed another bilberry juice forward to Sly, which had this time been summoned by a wave of Bef's wand.

'So as not to disturb the others,' replied Sly

swiftly, reappearing by Capriccia's side and passing the juice to her. 'They are still sleeping.'

'Me too,' said Capriccia, much to Sly's relief.

She slumped back into the chair once more and shut her eyes tight, without even drinking the second bilberry juice. Sly gestured to the others to move quickly as he put the glass on the floor. They moved past Capriccia's chair in trepidation, never taking their eyes off her movements or their hands off their potions. All reached the end of the room safely and breathed a sigh of relief before moving into another. The treehouse was amazingly big and there were so many floorboards. It was anybody's guess where Bernhardt could have stashed Bef's broom.

They entered the second room, with the joy of knowing their enemies had not detected them. But again, they could see no signs of floorboards having been lifted. Gaspar got to his hands and knees and started to feel the floor. Suddenly, disaster struck: the floorboard he had touched started crying out in a horrendously shrill voice, 'Help me master! Help me! Help me now! Strangers in the house!'

'Oh goodness gracious, he's booby-trapped the place,' said Bef, having to think quickly. 'Silenzio!' she demanded, waving her wand at the crying floorboard. It stopped shrieking, but someone had definitely been alerted. Their hearts sank. There was a distinctive noise to be heard – someone was walking towards them, slowly and gently, just as they had, but approaching all the same.

'Get your potions at the ready,' warned Gaspar. 'Be ready to use them if needs be.' Natalia nodded and Bef also reached for her wand. The footsteps got nearer. A shadow fell across the door: the shadow of a reasonably tall person, definitely not Bernhardt.

'Could be Capriccia,' whispered Gaspar.

'No,' said Sly. 'She'd never remove her shoes and they would clonk on the floor.'

'Who is it then?' hissed Natalia. 'Who else would come here?' She glared at Sly, as if he'd tricked them by failing to inform them of a fifth person in the house.

'Search me!' said Sly.

The shadow changed shape as the man came and stood in the doorway and faced two VIPBs and a boy band member, all carrying potions and ready to use them.

'Not the welcome I'd quite expected,' he said, slightly bemused.

'Lars! What the devil are you doing here?' whispered Bef, delighted to see her friend the reindeer supremo.

'I'll tell you the whole tale once I've got you all out of here,' he said. 'Just quickly tell me what's going on.'

'It's a long story,' whispered Bef, 'but they've called my broom back as part of a malicious conundrum they've dreamt up. They've also turned five people into stone statues. I need to rescue my broom from the clutches of Bernhardt. Although he has the right to call it back, that's not supposed to be for malicious reasons or, at least, I think that's the rule. Trouble is, he's hidden it somewhere beneath the floorboards and we haven't a clue where to find it. We've no idea what to do.'

'Now something makes sense,' replied Lars. 'I consulted the Rock of Erik the Enraged and it showed me someone, who I then went and sought out, as I felt I was being advised to request his help.'

Bef looked puzzled. 'Who pray is this person?' she asked. 'And where is he?'

Lars opened up his big thick coat to reveal a tiny little man of only eighteen inches in height, with a long white beard, a tunic of bright jasmine yellow and a woollen tangerine hat. He jumped down on to the floor, almost as if he'd been housed in Lars's chest pocket, causing Sly to shout out, 'Be quiet, you fool,' as his feet hit the floorboards.

'Bef,' said Lars. 'Meet Tomte.'

Tomte bowed down in front of Bef, removing his woollen hat as he did so, before going over to Sly, jumping up into the air and boxing his ears.

'Ouch,' said Sly. 'That hurt.'

Lars looked at him.

'How surprising to see you again. I suppose there's no point trying to control your actions, as you don't speak Lynx, but be warned ... Tomte is a sweet little fellow ... unless crossed. If you offend him, he will have your guts for garters.' Sly looked at his knickerbockers and quivered.

'Is this the Tomte who brings presents to children living on farms in Sweden?' asked Bef. 'The one who lives under the floorboards?'

'The very same,' said Lars, 'and now that you have explained your quandary with your broom, the advice of the Rock of Erik the Enraged makes sense. If we can get Tomte under the floorboards, he can work his way through the network under the floor, until he finds your broom. If he then taps on the boards above your broom, we can get them lifted and get it out.'

'Delighted to meet you,' said Bef, stepping forward to shake Tomte's hand. 'I believe I may have met your father at a VIPB conference, at least, I assume it was your father?' Tomte nodded in agreement.

'We must be quiet,' said Bef. 'How shall we get Tomte under the floorboards?'

'No need to worry about that,' replied Lars.

As Bef and her friends watched, Tomte began to change shape, morphing into a very thin, vaporous looking cloud, which slipped between the gap in the floorboards and out of sight.

'Now we have to let him explore,' said Lars. 'That's the tricky bit. All be quiet now, as he lets us know in which direction he's moving.'

They all listened hard. An extremely light tap could be heard, followed by another.

'He's moving to the back of the treehouse,' said Lars. 'We will now get another signal.'

Sure enough, every so often, a small cloud of vapour rose up between the floorboards, causing Bef to whisper, 'He's over there!' or Lars to signal a change in his direction.

Natalia was watching over their sleeping enemies, with Gaspar close behind. Sly just sat in a corner, grouching about how much his ears hurt. Natalia still distrusted him, so scowled, putting her finger to her lips and uttering a loud, 'Shush!'

Bef and Lars tracked Tomte's winding movement, until he had covered the whole of the back of the house.

'He's found nothing,' stated Lars, as he saw the vapour clouds moving back towards them. 'That can only mean that it's in the main room. This means trouble, I'm afraid. We surely cannot retrieve the broom without waking them up.'

'Gaspar has potions,' said Bef, 'but who knows if they will be strong enough to knock out three opponents. We weren't tackling the magical powers of Fiery Tina before. That could be disastrous. Trust Bernhardt to house my broom close to his person. I might have known!' She tutted loudly, causing Lars to raise his eyebrows. 'Sorry,' she whispered, 'I'm just exasperated.'

The pair of them followed Tomte's signals and eventually re-joined Natalia and Gaspar.

'Any sign of life in there?' enquired Lars.

'So far, so good,' replied Gaspar. 'Any luck?' He answered his own question as he saw Tomte's trail moving through the floor and into the main room. 'Oh no,' he muttered under his breath. 'Tell me it's not in there!' He unscrewed the top of his potion bottle a few notches, urging the others to do the same. All watched the vapour trail moving its way under the floorboards and shooting up miniscule clouds now and again. It seemed that Tomte was still unable to locate the broom, much to Bef's despair.

But then something changed. Tomte started to circle the boards under Capriccia's chair, moving inwards and ever closer to her with every passing second.

'I think it's under Capriccia,' whispered Gaspar. 'But Tomte's not yet given us the sign.'

Just as he spoke, a slight tapping could be heard. It was only minor, but enough to cause Capriccia to turn in her chair.

'What was that?' mumbled Capriccia. 'What's that noise?' Before anyone could act, Tomte emitted a massive cloud of vapour right under her massive platform shoe with the liquorice laces. She sat up bolt upright with a jolt, yelling 'What on earth is going on?'

Simultaneously, Bef, Gaspar and Natalia piled into the room. Natalia reached for her lasso rope and swung it around her head wildly. The rope fell around Capriccia and Natalia pulled it tight, capturing the diva in her chair. At the same time, Gaspar put his hand over her mouth to stop her yelling out. Within milliseconds, Bef uttered the word, 'Pietricongelato'. Capriccia froze.

Lars rushed to the chair and gave Gaspar the signal to help him lift both it and Capriccia up and off the floorboards underneath. Having moved her out of the way, they sank to their knees and Lars reached for various tools housed in a pouch around his waist. He began to lift the boards, with Gaspar's assistance.

Despite trying to be quiet, there was no way they could avoid waking the other sleeping beauties in the room. The minute the boards started to lift, Fiery Tina raised her head, at its usual crooked angle, and glanced across the room.

'Bernhardt, wake up!' she shouted, as she began to shake him. Bernhardt jumped up and immediately rubbed his head.

'Too much Fir Fizz,' he said, feeling decidedly groggy. 'What ze devil is ze problem? He looked up to see Bef pointing a wand in his face, with Gaspar just behind her. Natalia was watching over Capriccia and Lars was lifting the floorboards. Out jumped Tomte from under the floor, just before Lars put his hands under the boards and retrieved Bef's broom. 'Bef, I've got it!' he shouted.

Bef nodded. 'Gaspar, are you ready?' she asked, keeping her silver wand firmly fixed on Bernhardt and Fiery Tina.

Gaspar knew she was intending him to use the potions. He nodded and flung them up into the air, aiming for the nostrils of both enemies. He waited for them to slump down, but nothing happened. Fiery Tina got to her feet, holding her own wand in a most menacing fashion. She uttered the statuefication spell, while pointing it at Bef, but failed to turn her to stone. She tried the same with Gaspar, but was again unable to statuefy him.

'What's going on?' she asked, leaving Bef and Gaspar in no doubt that the amethyst was offering protection.

But then something else happened. Tomte began to leap across the floorboards, tracing something out in vapour, which then settled and marked the floor in the pattern that he'd created. The movement caught Fiery Tina's eye and she lowered her wand, dancing towards Tomte in delight.

'Goodness me,' thought Bef. 'He's drawn her a hopscotch court.'

Bernhardt jumped to his feet. 'You can NOT take your broom back,' he said. 'It is against VIPB law. After 1020 years, ze broom MUST return, if its maker demands it.'

'Not if it is being used for evil purposes,' shouted Bef in his face. 'It is part of your sick game and so I am taking it back. You are manipulating it. Consequently, you have broken the terms of the agreement. It's coming back with me.'

All of a sudden, both Bernhardt and Fiery Tina

slumped to their knees, collapsing like crumbling buildings, as Gaspar's potion finally took effect.

'I think all the Fir Fizz they've drunk may have given them some protection,' he explained, trying to make an excuse for his potion's delayed success. 'Let's get out of here now.'

All of the attention had been focused on Fiery Tina and Bernhardt and then on Tomte, the broom and Lars. For split seconds, Natalia had stopped watching Capriccia and had not seen her get to her feet as the Pietricongelato spell wore off. She was staring at her feet as she picked up the glass of bilberry juice that Sly had left on the floor. Her face was as angry as Sly, who had slipped into the room to hide in a corner, had ever seen it. It was the colour of the bilberry juice itself. In a split second, she moved up behind Tomte, tipped the glass of juice up and poured it all over the little gnome's head.

'That's for ruining my shoes with your dirty vapour,' she said menacingly.

Sly was secretly pleased, still feeling his ears smarting from the blows Tomte had given him, but also remembering that he too had suffered the same fate. At least he wasn't alone in that regard now. However, he had no idea what would happen next. Only Lars had an inkling.

'Quick,' yelled Lars. 'Get out of the door fast and scarper. Leave Tomte to deal with things now. Believe me, he's more than capable.'

He virtually pushed Bef and Gaspar out of the door with Bef's broom, as Natalia followed hot in pursuit and Sly lagged behind.

'Please take me with you,' he begged. Bef looked at him and took pity on him, knowing Natalia would give him no room on her broom. She signalled to Sly to jump on to her broom with Gaspar, before turning round to see where Lars had gone.

Lars came tearing out of the treehouse just seconds later.

'You go,' he yelled. 'I've some reindeer waiting just across the glade. I'll wait for Tomte and take him back home. I'll then come and find you. This whole messy business is far from over.'

Bef jumped on her broom, as Sly began to repeat, 'He'll have your guts for garters,' again and again.

An almighty crashing came from the treehouse as Tomte's famous temper began to be demonstrated in the worst possible way. He whizzed around the room like a hurricane, wrecking the timber structure all around Bernhardt and Fiery Tina, as they lay motionless, still under the influence of the potions, unaware of what was happening as pots and pans crashed to the floor and mirrors and glass were shattered.

Capriccia was screaming loudly, begging the other two to wake up and claiming she was in the presence of a poltergeist. Getting no response, she lifted her feet and tried to crush Tomte, just as she had done the spider in Hamburg, but Tomte jumped out of the way, leaving Capriccia with her foot wedged in the gap in the floorboards that Lars had created when reaching the broom. No matter how much she tugged, she couldn't release it. Tomte rushed to the door and out into the dark forest, just as Capriccia had grabbed her silver wand and tried, unsuccessfully, to turn him to stone.

She managed to pull her foot out of the trapped shoe, leaving it under the floor, in all of its gaudy glory, as she ran to the door in a lopsided manner with just one platform shoe on her feet. She looked into the sky and saw Bef on her broom, already airborne and flying away. Capriccia cursed under her breath and then uttered some much more hateful and vile words, directing her silver wand towards Bef in a most purposeful manner.

'Got you,' she said, as she saw what resulted. 'Got you good.'

CHAPTER NINETEEN

Bef did not know whether to laugh or cry. On the one hand, she had her precious broom and best buddy back in her possession and was as happy as if a lost pet had been returned to her. On the other, she had nothing on her feet and felt as if she had been robbed or mugged. Her precious, floppy shoes that flapped and slapped and slapped and flapped had been whipped off her feet by Capriccia and had disappeared into the ether. She'd felt them being tugged away and had circled furiously on her broom, to see if she could see them flying through the skies above the Black Forest, but they had disappeared without a trace.

Without them, she simply wasn't Bef. Even when she had been rejuvenated by Old Father Time and become a much more fashionable witch, she had refused to swap her old faithful shoes for trendy ones. They were part and parcel of her: a big piece of the puzzle that was her personality and a habit that couldn't be broken. She even slept with them on her feet!

She, Gaspar and Natalia returned to her house

subdued, but with the satisfaction, at least, of knowing they'd managed to fight back to some extent. It was a big advantage to know that Gaspar's potions worked and that the amethyst did indeed provide protection against statuefication. It was even some consolation for the latest snatch, however much that hurt.

As for Sly, Bef reluctantly let him stay in the house, realising he had nowhere else to go. Natalia tried to argue with her, stressing that he couldn't be fully trusted, but Bef was far too tired to debate it. Her wand wasn't seeing him as an enemy, so she gave him the benefit of the doubt.

'We haven't had a letter yet,' said Natalia. 'Maybe your shoes are not part of the conundrum plot. Maybe Capriccia just lost her temper and grabbed what she could.'

'Who knows?' said Gaspar. 'I'd thought they were only after humans, but if the broom was part of the plan, then maybe the shoes are too. Perhaps they planned to take the shoes at a different time, not knowing that we would arrive in Germany. Maybe that's why the letter hasn't yet appeared.'

Bef said very little. The stone floor was bitingly cold on the soles of her feet and she was finding it difficult to walk. She'd hardly ever taken her shoes off in all the centuries that she'd lived and had patched them when she'd needed to, rather than throwing them away. To think of them in the hands of a woman who had no taste in shoes at all, who chose shoes in the most garish styles and colours, was making Bef's head fizz. It would explode before much longer.

She drummed her fingers on the table, waiting and waiting and waiting for the letter to arrive. The post came and there was no letter within it. She stuck her head up the chimney, but there was nothing there. She looked inside every jar in the kitchen, but nothing was to be found. She even looked inside the huge sack of potatoes that she always kept in the kitchen for broom fuel and under the bucket of horse manure that she had to mix with them for a good tuber charge.

In the end, she became weary.

'I'm going to lie down for while,' she said. 'It's been emotionally draining over the last couple of days and I need some rest so that I can think straight.'

She trudged up the stairs, lifting her legs ridiculously high, as if still wearing her shoes. She laid her head on her pillow and rolled on to her side. The pillow felt lumpy and she bashed it with her fist, to get it into a different shape. It was still unbearable. She shook it hard and out fell a piece of card. It was the letter she'd been seeking all day, along with another riddle. This time, she had another letter A and a riddle, which read,

'The Bef woman was destined to lose,

Her footwear was like two canoes.

It's now with the stars,

But nowhere near Mars:

It's in concrete that she'll find her shoes!'

'What does this mean?' she cried. 'I haven't a clue where they are! She rushed down to the toilet to see if anything had come through the Flush Telegraph, but there was absolutely nothing. Natalia and Gaspar had got to their feet as she'd dashed down the stairs and straight past them. They blocked her way back.

'Whatever's the matter?' asked Gaspar.

'I've had another letter and a riddle,' she exclaimed, 'but it means absolutely nothing to me. It's gobbledygook! It's poppycock! In fact, it's double Dutch!'

'Let me see,' said Gaspar. He took the riddle out of Bef's hands and read it. 'You're right,' he said. 'I don't know what it means. We need to sit down and think about it.'

Sly stood up, leaving the small stool he'd been occupying by the fire.

'It sounds far too clever for Capriccia,' he commented. 'I can see her work in the first two lines, but think someone else has written the rest.'

'Hardly helpful,' said Natalia. 'Unless you have some light to cast on the whereabouts of Bef's shoes, perhaps it's better for you to keep quiet.'

Bef gave Natalia a look, which indicated that she should be a bit more pleasant to their guest.

'Sorry,' said Natalia. 'My nerves are on edge.'

Sly beamed. He wasn't used to people apologising to him, or treating him like a person with feelings. He took himself back to his stool and began to flick through some of Mel's magazines.

'We need to have a brainstorm,' said Gaspar. 'They must want us to know where the shoes are, so they can have a good laugh and hurt us, but we must be missing something here. Let's think about it.'

Natalia picked up the riddle. 'I think they must be on another planet,' she said, 'but not Mars. They make that clear.'

'I'm not sure they have concrete on other planets,' said Gaspar. 'It clearly says that the shoes are in concrete. That implies they must be on earth somewhere: in a place where humans can use concrete.'

'But there are zillions of places like that these days,' said Bef. 'Things were different in past centuries. We didn't have all this building work and mixers and cranes. We had men making houses with their bare hands. Those were the days.'

'But that's it,' said Gaspar. 'There are zillions of places with concrete, so this must be a famous place with concrete, or the clue is meaningless.'

'Are you sure they don't have concrete on other planets?' asked Natalia.

'Almost 100 per cent sure,' said Gaspar. 'We need to think about it.'

'I'm seeing stars, I'm so confused,' said Bef.

'Gaspar's a star, isn't he?' said a voice from the corner. The other three all turned to look at Sly.

'What do you mean?' asked Bef.

'Well, not all stars twinkle in the sky, do they,' explained Sly. 'Some stars are humans. That's all I'm saying.'

Gaspar stroked his stubbly chin. 'You're absolutely right, Sly,' he said. 'We've been looking at this too literally. We need to think in a broader way about the word stars. Capriccia would be very interested in human stars, wouldn't she? She likes the celebrity lifestyle.'

'Indeed, she does,' agreed Sly. 'She's never got her nose out of 'Gello' magazine reading about the Hollywood stars.'

The room fell silent. Sly continued to flick through his magazines. 'Concrete and stars,' he said. 'Stars and concrete. What's that expression … heroes with feet of clay. Or hands of clay, judging by this photo.'

'What photo?' asked Gaspar, with thoughts whirring around in his brain.

'This one, here,' said Sly. 'Stars putting their hands in …'

'Concrete!' said Gaspar, finishing his sentence for him. 'Stars putting their hands and feet in concrete. Film stars, in fact … putting their hands in concrete at Grauman's Chinese Theatre in Hollywood!'

'I've seen that!' said Bef. 'I've delivered presents to the children of quite a few Italian-American film stars and I've flown over that place a few times. Are you telling me that my shoes are stuck in concrete in the middle of Los Angeles?'

'They'll be statuefied shoes, I would imagine,' said Gaspar. 'They'll just be concrete-looking shoes stuck in concrete. Well done, Sly! You've cracked it!'

Bef looked pensive.

'Where is all this leading?' she said, almost trembling. 'I don't understand what their game is any more. I thought they just wanted to ruin Befland and take my broom away, but there seems to be another reason for all this: a deeper purpose.' She turned and looked at Sly. 'Do you have any idea what's going on?'

For a fleeting moment, Sly thought of mentioning the fact that they knew about Bef's deal with Old Father Time. In fact, his mouth was open and he was just about to reveal all. But in an instant, his mind went blank. He sat there with his mouth gaping.

'Well, do you know anything?' asked Natalia.

'Not a thing,' said Sly, his head wobbling from side to side in a very strange manner. 'They always kept me out of their discussions.'

Natalia stared at him accusingly, not believing a word he was saying.

'Do the wand test,' she said to Bef. Bef reached for her willow wand and pointed it at Sly.

'What on earth are you doing?' shrieked the elf. 'Take that thing away!'

The wand wavered a little, as if uncertain as whether to name him friend or foe. It moved back and forth of its own accord and then just stood bolt upright, not committing to anything.

'Strange,' said Bef. 'It's indecisive. It can't determine whether he's lying or not.' She racked her brains as to what this could mean before saying, 'Sly, does your head hurt?'

Sly was actually rubbing his forehead as she spoke. He was experiencing a terrible pain in it: a sharp, stabbing pain that was suddenly becoming all woolly and fuzzy. He looked at Bef like a forlorn puppy.

'Yes, it's killing me,' he said. 'It's just started out of the blue.'

'O Dio,' said Bef.

'What?' asked Gaspar, confused about the whole thing.

'I think his memory's been wiped. I think Fiery Tina must have performed a memory spell.'

'Can't you undo it?' asked Natalia bluntly.

'No. Unless I had a clue as to what it was he was about to tell us, I can't.'

'Should we give him some amethyst, to keep him safe?' asked Gaspar.

Bef thought deeply.

'Maybe,' she said. 'They won't snatch him, as they know he's not important to me, but they could steal him back, just to prevent him helping us. Prepare an elixir and give him a drink.'

Sly grovelled, in a very slimy manner.

'Thank you so much,' he mumbled. 'I could not face going back to those people.' He bowed down in front of Bef and then returned to rubbing his head.

'So what do we do now?' asked Natalia.

'I guess we sit and wait,' replied Bef.

In a castle on the hill, three vicious people were having a massive row.

'It's a good job you've got me to clean up your mess!' yelled Fiery Tina, directing her anger at Bernhardt and Capriccia. 'How stupid of you not to know the conditions attached to the 1020 wule. How widiculous of you, Capwiccia, to claim you'd snatched the bwoom, when you hadn't! Why am I suwwounded by imbeciles? Lucky I came round fast enough to perform a memory wipe on that cweepy elf! He could have given the whole game away!'

Capriccia was not amused.

'What difference does the broom thing make?' she said. 'I snatched her shoes and there are two of those, so just send her another letter.'

'It doesn't work like that, dumbo!' snapped Fiery Tina sarcastically. 'A pair of shoes is classed as one thing, not two. We are now missing a vital item for our conundwum! We now need to think of another thing the Bef woman loves – a ninth thing! Get your bwain cells working … if you've got any! What is it?'

Capriccia looked completely blank and flicked her hair back and forth in a most annoying fashion, as she tried to think, while fuming inside and wanting to explode. Bernhardt sat next to her doodling annoyingly on a piece of paper, sketching weird and wonderful designs all over the page.

'I don't actually know whether she is right about the 1020 rule, or not,' he said, trying to deflect attention away from Capriccia. As he spoke, he wrote two names on the paper, so that Capriccia could clearly see them. She glanced at the paper and saw he had scrawled down, 'Santa' and 'Lars'.

Fiery Tina bustled over to Bernhardt and rested her nose on his.

'I don't care a fig now!' she said. 'That bird, or should I say bwoom, has well and truly flown. What I need now is to know what the ninth thing is that the Bef woman loves most in the world.' She moved behind Capriccia and put her crooked neck next to Capriccia's face. 'So TELL ME!' she yelled, deafening Capriccia in her left ear.

Capriccia stared at the piece of paper and the words written inside Bernhardt's crazy doodles. She couldn't decide which to name. Bef had been engaged to her husband, but a long time ago. Bef had recently been helped by the Reindeer Whisperer, but it wasn't clear that she 'loved' him.

She stared into Bernhardt's eyes, pleading with him, with a truly desperate look, to help her.

Bernhardt hovered his pen over the name 'Santa'.

Much as she didn't want to, Capriccia said, 'She loves my husband. He's the ninth person or thing she loves most.'

'At last!' exclaimed Fiery Tina. 'We finally get an answer! Now sit there and work out how we can snatch him. This is, of course, very twicky, as he's not with her or anywhere near here. How are you going to manage this, Capwiccia?'

'We vill fly to Lapland,' said Bernhardt, coming to her rescue. 'Capriccia vill know where Santa is likely to be spending his time and she can carry out ze statuefication. It should be very easy. No need for you to come with us.'

Fiery Tina glared at him.

'So are we not planning to move him to somewhere that the Bef woman can see him every day?' she asked angrily.

Capriccia leapt in with jealousy rushing through her veins.

'NO!' she yelled. 'I will not have that woman anywhere near my husband, even if he is turned to stone! I shall set him in a snowstorm in the middle of the village, so all of Lapland can see the trouble that the Bef woman has brought him.'

Fiery Tina considered this plan for a few minutes.

'Not bad,' she conceded. 'Not bad at all. Get on with it!'

'No time like ze present!' shrieked Bernhardt. 'Let's get off and sort out ze Santa snatch.'

'I shall freeze to death,' replied Capriccia. 'I only have this flimsy dress. I need a new outfit.'

Fiery Tina looked at her with total disdain.

'All you think about is clothes, Capwiccia,' she moaned. 'But if it makes you any more effective, here you go.' She waved her wand and Capriccia found herself dressed in a grey woolly onesie with a thick blue jacket over the top that was inflated with hot air.

'I look like a puffer fish,' screamed Capriccia.

'Take it, or leave it,' answered Fiery Tina, sniggering to herself at the sight of her vain pupil now looking as glamorous as a fisherman who'd been out at sea in a tempest.

Capriccia gritted her teeth.

'Get me out of here, Bernhardt,' she yelled. 'If you don't, I will not be responsible for my actions.'

As the drama queen and Bernhardt rushed to the broom and took off for Lapland, Fiery Tina laughed insanely to herself.

'You never are, Capwiccia,' she said. 'You never are,' which is why I cannot possibly allow you to take back contwol of your pwecious Casa of Contentments, when it would be so much more fitting for me to live in it.'

A manic chortle could be heard echoing around

the ruined castle on the hill, which turned the milk of the cows in the fields below into curd and which sent a shiver down the spine of a distraught witch and VIPB sitting at her kitchen table without her beloved shoes. The skies above Bef's village turned a little blacker, as the pink trails left behind by Bernhardt's broom were replaced with charcoal clouds forming the pattern of a fairy's finest black tutu.

CHAPTER TWENTY

The toilet flushed loudly of its own accord while Bef and her friends were enjoying a bowl of warming carrot soup that the wily witch had rustled up on the stove, despite having virtually no ingredients to mention. None of them dared venture out to the village's shops, leaving them with bare store cupboards.

When she heard the water whooshing, Bef ran into the little WC just in time to catch the capsule that contained her enemies' message. She took it to the others, so all could see the latest upsetting scenario. Bef opened the capsule in dread. She prayed they hadn't snatched Lorenzo. She had done so much to try to keep him safe and under wraps.

Every one of them was stunned when the image turned out to be a picture of Santa, statuefied and within a snowstorm. Flakes of snow were swirling around his head, but he was motionless. Sly, who knew Santa's village better than the others, peered at it for a while.

'He's been placed outside his post office,' he said, 'right in the place where nobody can fail but see him. Even though he sacked me, I can only feel sorry for him. Poor, poor man.'

Bef felt upset, but was also partly relieved that Lorenzo was safe. She couldn't for the life of her work out why they had snatched Santa. It didn't seem to fit the pattern they had set. Nevertheless, what was true to form was the arrival of another letter. It was another A, along with a scribbled note to say this one replaced the previous A sent after the snatch of her broom.

'That makes three As now,' said Gaspar. Whatever this word is, it's got a lot of them in it.'

'There's no riddle with zis one,' said Natalia.

'They know we would instantly realise where he is,' said Bef dejectedly. 'The question is, what or who next?' She looked at Sly to see if any sign of knowledge passed over his face. It was clear this was not the case. His memory had been well and truly wiped.

The decision not to send a riddle had been made by Capriccia. She didn't see the need for them, not being as keen on games as her mad fairy tutor. Besides, it hurt her head to try to devise them and it took her hours. Right now, back here in Lapland, she had other things she would rather be doing.

The minute she had clapped sight on her Casa of Contentments again, there had been a huge tug at her heartstrings. At first, it had looked strange. She wasn't used to seeing her glorious, fuchsia pink building set against a bright red sky. There was a colour clash that she didn't appreciate and she stamped her foot hard.

'Who's turned the sky red?' she yelled in despair. 'The whole point of the Casa being pink is to provide a colour contrast! See what happens when I'm not here!'

'I think you'll find zat a red sky means bad things are in ze offing,' said Bernhardt. 'I seem to recall it being something to do with ze Arctic Fox.'

Capriccia scowled.

'Dratted animals,' she said. 'It's probably being helped by the pesky reindeer.' She looked at her Casa again. 'I'm going in!' she declared.

'Zat is really not a good idea,' said Bernhardt. 'Ze building is protected by elves. You will not get in without a fight.'

'I'll fly through a window,' answered Capriccia defiantly. I used to leave one window open on the third floor. Although I used to whack the temperature up as high as it would go so Santa wouldn't visit me, I used to get rather hot myself, so would sit in front of the seventh window from the back of the Casa just to cool down. Pesky elves won't have realised that. We'll go in that way.'

'What is all zis talk of 'we'!' shouted Bernhardt. 'I am advising you not to enter ze building until our work is done. You are jumping ze gun, as you people like to say!'

Capriccia wasn't listening. Her heart was set on seeing her precious belongings again, not to mention grabbing a fresh pair of shoes and a change of clothes. Nothing Bernhardt could have said to her would have stopped her from entering her beloved home. And that was what Bernhardt feared.

As she prepared to fly up to the window she'd mentioned. Bernhardt paced up and down muttering to himself.

'I cannot let her get in there!' he declared. 'She will never leave once she sees ze state of things. All of our plans will be ruined because she vill not complete ze conundrum. The Bef woman will never be made to pay in full for what she has done! I vill never become a VIPB!'

But before he could stop her, Capriccia was already in mid-air on his broom. He rushed after her, waving his arms in the air.

'Wait for me,' he roared. 'I forbid you to take my broom.'

Capriccia weighed the situation up. She found Bernhardt exceedingly tiresome, but she might need him. If elves did get in her way, at least she would have some backup. She lowered the broom to allow him to climb on board, before whooshing upwards towards the window that she prayed was still open.

Sure enough, it was. It was actually too high for the elves to close, but as it was, they hadn't even noticed that it was off the latch. All Capriccia had to do was wrap her long fingers around the frame and push. It opened wide and she jumped off the broom and went through. Bernhardt debated whether to circle the Casa on his broom, but decided he had better accompany her.

The moment Capriccia started to walk around her former home, she was like a child in a sweet shop. She started to stuff all manner of possessions in her small rucksack, before fingering her perfume collection and spraying scent madly all over her body. To her way of thinking, getting her Casa back was all that mattered and had she not already regained control of it? Santa was now out of the picture and here she was back inside. She simply could not bear to leave all of this again. What if she never got back in? What if the elves did close the window? What if the locks were changed? What if Lars the Reindeer Whisperer blocked her entry? Why not just stay put and never leave again?

Bernhardt could see these thoughts whirring around her head. He simply had to make her angry – angry enough to ensure she left the Casa and headed back to finish the Bef woman off. Unless she had fire in her belly, she would revert to her normal lazy self and sit here all day and every day filing her nails or brushing her Northern Highlights. He had to act swiftly.

'Come with me,' he said. 'We must assess ze most recent situation with regard to your shoes.'

Something clicked in Capriccia's brain, despite finding it hard to think of more than one thing at once and the current one being the perfume.

'My shoes,' she exclaimed. 'My lovely,

stupendous, unique shoes! Let me at 'em. I need to stroke them, caress them, walk up and down the room in each pair twice and admire every pair in the mirror in 360 degrees. I need my shoes and I need them NOW!"

She yelled so loudly that Bernhardt had to put his hands over his ears. Down on the first floor, the elves standing guard looked at each other.

'Did you hear that?' said one. "What the devil was it?'

Capriccia was heading up her elevator, even though the stairs would have been just as fast a route. The elevator doors opened and she witnessed a scene that tormented her soul from the moment her heavily skylashed eyes clapped sight on it. Hundreds of moths were hovering over her grotesque shoes, while hundreds more were resting on them, eating them away and making more holes in even those that were already designed to have holes.

Capriccia breathed in hard and then emitted the loudest scream Bernhardt had ever heard. The elf guards instantly ran up the stairs, knowing only one woman in the world had lungs powerful enough to create a scream such as this one. Capriccia began to hyperventilate, gasping for breath like a fish out of water. Finally, she wobbled and turned purple. At that point Bernhardt did the only thing he thought could possibly work and slapped her hard across the face.

'Pull yourself together,' he said menacingly. 'You have alerted ze guards. I can hear zem on ze stairs. We have to get out of here fast. More importantly, you have to return to Fiery Tina and complete your mission. Look around you. Look at ze horror scene zat has resulted from ze Bef woman's actions. If she hadn't shoved you down a parcel chute, zis would never have happened. You need to make her pay Capriccia. She must pay.' He grabbed her by the arms, jumped on a chair and looked her in the eye. 'Now tell me what you must do!'

'I must make her pay,' said Capriccia, as if in a trance. 'Pay she must. The Bef woman must pay. I will make her pay. She will even pay for more shoes by the time I'm finished with her. We need to pay her a visit!'

'Good girl,' said Bernhardt patronisingly. 'Now let's go. Ze elves are approaching.'

It was as if Capriccia were stuck to the ground with glue. Try as she might, she couldn't lift her feet or will herself to get back on the broom. Bernhardt tugged at her arm, but couldn't shift her. She stood facing the door and waiting for the elves to barge in. Within seconds, they came streaming through the door, grinding to a halt when they saw the angry look in the eyes of the woman they had feared for years.

'And you will pay too,' yelled Capriccia, picking up those of her shoes that were completely moth-eaten and hurling them across the room at the elves. The first pair clonked one elf on the head. The second completely knocked an elf out. The third hit the door as all the other elves fled in a terrified state, rushing off to find reinforcements.

'Wait till I come back here permanently,' shouted Capriccia. 'You will all pay for neglecting my shoes, for letting the moths eat them, for allowing the dust to settle on them and sully them. For being inattentive, useless, ignorant elves AS USUAL!' Her voice rose at the end of the sentence reaching a volume that made the whole of the Casa shake as if Lapland were experiencing an earthquake. The reindeer in the fields heard the terrible commotion and jumped in fright, startled by the angry tones of a woman who had made their lives a misery.

And not too far away, in his compact hut, Lars also heard it and sat bolt upright.

'Oh my word,' he mumbled to himself. 'That dreadful woman is back here. Why on earth is she here? Has the conundrum ended? Am I too late? Has she destroyed Bef?'

As questions ran through his mind, he rushed out of his home and ran in the direction of Santa's village. His feet pounded through the snow as he headed towards the post office. He had to find Santa and advise him of his wife's return. He had to let Santa know of the whole dreadful situation with regard to Bef. He had to warn Santa to take some amethyst.

But as he rounded the corner, he stopped dead

in his tracks. There, in front of him, sat Santa in a snowstorm bubble. There sat a Santa turned to stone.

As he felt dismay pass over his whole body, he heard the shrill shriek of elves exiting the Casa of Contentments. As he looked up into the sky, he saw a woman resembling a puffer fish flying away on a broom with a little man wearing red and white, stripy pyjama bottoms.

'I don't understand,' thought Lars. 'Why is she leaving the Casa? Why would she abandon all her precious belongings again, gross though they are?'

He fingered the bottle in his pocket and remembered the images that had meant nothing to him. First there was the place with the letters on a hill. Secondly, there was the image of the man with Bef's huge book of spells. How did Lars know him? Why did he seem so familiar?'

Lars felt helpless as he looked at Santa. Why did Fiery Tina think he was one of the people or things that Bef loved most, which seemed to be the pattern of other snatches? It was all completely baffling. As he looked back at the bottle, he realised there was only one thing he could now do.

In Bef's kitchen, that was also the thought passing through Gaspar's head. There'd been far too many hours in which he'd sat and thought about what was going on. Now, he'd been sitting here for a few more hours wondering why Santa had been snatched. He wanted Mel and Thaz back. The game had to be brought to an end and it seemed this could only happen if all the letters of the conundrum were received. How many more could there be? He could think of only one thing that was dear to Bef's heart that was left to snatch. That one thing had to be holding up the whole process of getting the victims released. That one thing was him.

He knew he had to do the right thing and had to do it fast. He had to broach the subject with Bef. He needed to make her see what was necessary.

Natalia looked at him quizzically across the table.

'You have thoughts whirring through your brain, young man,' she said. 'Perhaps they are the same ones that are rushing through mine.'

Gaspar looked her in the eye. He glanced around. Bef was busy cleaning the kitchen, doing the manic sweeping routine that she always employed after a snatch. Today was her way with dealing with the image of Santa.

'What are you thinking then?' he asked.

Natalia checked Bef was still occupied.

'I think the conundrum is coming to its conclusion, but key parts of the puzzle are missing.'

'Me too,' said Gaspar. 'and I think the key part is me.'

'Yes,' said Natalia, 'but I also think I am the other part.'

'What makes you think that?' asked Gaspar.

'It seems to be the things and people closest to

Bef that are being taken away. That list would definitely include you. I'm not sure whether it would include Lars and me. Now Santa's been snatched, the list could be longer than I thought.'

'She was engaged to Santa though,' said Gaspar. 'There is a kind of logic there. I don't mean to be rude, but I hadn't included you in the list. Not so long ago, you two were at loggerheads. Added to that, you only arrived after the conundrum had started, so you wouldn't have been on the list.'

'Perhaps you are right,' said Natalia. 'What do you think the answer is to our quandary?'

'I need to convince Bef to try to reverse the amethyst protection and then I must venture out on my own. It's the only way. I have to let them take me. If they do, we might end the conundrum. If that doesn't happen, you will have to decide whether to contact Lars and ask him for his advice. Maybe you or he, or both of you, will have to sacrifice yourselves as well. You will only be able to decide that after you see what happens when I am snatched. The important thing is to make that happen.'

Natalia nodded. 'You are very brave,' she said.

'Yes, indeed,' said a voice from the corner. The pair of them swung around. They'd almost forgotten that Sly was sitting on his stool in the corner.

'Have you remembered something, elf?' demanded Natalia, having never been convinced that his memory had been wiped.

Sly rubbed his tummy – something he liked to do when thinking.

'Yes, I have,' he said. 'And how it makes me laugh.'

Natalia rolled her eyes. Whatever it was, it was nothing to do with snatches and conundrums. She could already tell that by the grin that had broken out across his face.

Gaspar decided to humour him.

'What's that then?' he asked.

Sly began to roll around on his stool in hysterics.

'I've been wondering how all the moths got into the Casa to eat Capriccia's shoes,' he giggled. 'And now I know. Now I've worked it out and it serves her right.'

'So,' said Natalia, irritated by his frivolous attitude. 'How did they?'

'If I'm not mistaken,' said Sly, 'and it's as clear as a bell to me now … they got in through an open window on the third floor that Capriccia used to leave open when she got too hot in her ridiculously warm Casa. She let the moths in herself!'

Sly continued to roll around on his stool even more. Bef seemingly didn't hear or see him and carried on sweeping her floor vigorously. Natalia and Gaspar urged each other to bite the bullet and talk to Bef about the need for Gaspar to sacrifice himself. Over in Lapland, another thirty moths had entered the Casa through a window on the third floor.

Chapter Twenty-One

Lars hitched the reindeer up to a sleigh. He'd summoned them and his faithful friends had instantly realised that Lars the Reindeer Whisperer would not ask them to fly twice within a week unless absolutely necessary. Lars had whispered in the ear of the head of the herd and had asked him one important thing. 'Are you able to take me to the Know-it-All?' The head of the herd had nodded, much to Lars' relief.

The bottle was still safely in his pocket. He desperately needed to know to what the confusing images within it referred. What were the letters on the hillside? Where was the hillside? Who was the man? The only way he could possibly find out was with the help of a creature he had never encountered, but whose name was mumbled by Lapps in their village huts when they required knowledge. He had lost count of the times he had heard a Lapp say, 'I must ask the Know-it-All'. At first, he had thought this an imaginary being and a figure of speech. Then, one day, he was shown drawings that suggested the Know-it-All was far from imaginary.

The drawing had shown a strange creature, living in a dark cave, shining bright green like a luminous cross between a frog and a lizard. Some described it as a small dragon; others claimed it had hatched from an egg, but was actually a small man. A few were too in awe of it to relay any information about it at all.

Lars pulled warm blankets around his knees as the sleigh left its runway on the edge of Santa's village. They soared into the sky, flying high over the mountains and down into a valley. Rising up a little more, the reindeer circled a few times and then headed to a plateau, where they landed the sleigh, with no assistance from Lars. He looked around him and saw a cave.

'Head in there,' said the head of the herd. 'Take a lantern, but extinguish the light when you encounter the Know-it-All. He will cast enough light for you to see better. Your lantern will automatically light as you leave, thanks to the knowledge that you possess after meeting the creature.'

Lars took all of this in and nodded his head. There was fear in his belly. While he could control the minds of Lynx speakers and communicate with reindeer and birds, he was sure he would be very much under the thumb of the Know-it-All. The Lapp tales spoke of him as a creature who could be cantankerous, obstinate and unhelpful when in a mood. At other times, they hailed a being generous in its willingness to share its great intelligence and wisdom. Who knew what mood it would be in today?

Lars began to make his way through the cave. Ice water had melted on its uneven floor and made it extremely slippery. He gripped the rocks around him to help keep his balance and prevent a fall. He trod carefully, as the cave became darker and more foreboding with every footstep.

He could hear a noise: a noise that had not entered his ears previously. There was a humming and a buzzing, as if a source of energy was close at hand. He followed the noise and entered into a passage leading off the main cavern. At the end of the passage, he could see a small, bright green light flashing and almost signalling him to approach. He cautiously moved towards it, checking that the bottle was still in his pocket. He felt butterflies in his stomach. This was not usual behaviour for Lars the Reindeer Whisperer, but somehow he felt he was being judged and watched and observed by a superior being. He extinguished the lantern.

A shrill voice began to speak.

'Why do you come here, reindeer man? Why are you bringing me that which the Rock of Erik the Enraged gave you? Why did you consult the Rock first and myself second? Do you not think that an insult to the Know-it-All?'

'Are you the Know-it-All?' he asked, realising that the green luminous shape he had seen was hidden behind a thin white net curtain. Now he understood why those who had met it could not describe its appearance. At one moment it looked like an anemone in the sea: at others, like a creature with the head and chest of a man, but the tail of a chameleon.

'Of course I am the Know-it-All,' it said, in a real huff at not being instantly recognised. 'Do you think more than one creature lives in this dark, unwelcoming cave?'

Lars felt he was off to a bad start with the bad-tempered thing. That was the last thing he had wanted. He desperately needed its help. He had to make amends very quickly.

He breathed in deeply and said, 'I consulted the Rock of Erik the Enraged first, as I did not realise the huge complexity of the problem. I did not wish to waste the time of someone as learned as yourself with something that was trivial. Little did I know that there were many layers to my problem and things I could not possibly understand. As soon as I realised this, I remembered the tales I had heard of your profound knowledge: of your clever mind and sharp intellect. I then knew that only you could assist me.'

The creature seemed to like the praise, curling up behind the curtain as if feeling very content.

'How may I help you?' it asked in a stilted fashion, becoming almost an automated message that Lars was tapping in to, rather than a living creature with a changeable personality. It seemed it was now in response mode, rather than questioning his motives.

'I need to know what these images mean and who the people in them can be,' explained Lars. 'They are captured in this bottle, but mean nothing to me.'

'You will have to let them out,' replied the Know-it-All.

'But once I do, they will be lost forever,' said Lars in a nervous tone.

'Do you trust me, or not?' snapped the Know-it-All. 'Do you think I would let images escape without knowing exactly what they show? Do you want my help, or do you wish to slowly make your way back through my cave, clinging feebly to the walls, having achieved nothing? If you do not trust me, this is how it will be. If you question what I tell you in any way, you will not act correctly. It's up to you. Take it or leave it. Let the images out of the bottle, or do not let them out of the bottle: it's all the same to me.'

Lars felt sick. It was a big thing to do. The responsibility of looking after Bef was immense. If the images were lost, she would also be finished, of that he had no doubt. Nevertheless, he had to trust this creature. Without him, all he had were trapped images that meant nothing and which would continue to mean nothing, day after day. He had to place his trust in this strange thing behind the curtain.

He reached into his pocket and withdrew the bottle. He thought about it for another ten seconds and then pulled out the stopper. The images began to swirl around in the dark cave, being lit by the illumination coming from the Know-it-All's body. Round and round they twirled, right over Lars' head: first the letters on the hillside and then the man with Bef's book of spells.

'Let me separate the two thoughts,' said the Know-it-All, before starting to hum to itself. 'Do you want me to tell you where the letters are?' it asked, going back into a tone of an automatic answering machine.

'Yes, please do,' answered Lars.

'The hillside is in Hollywood,' said the Know-it-All. 'The letters are a trick. They spell out the name of a woman. A name by which she must never again name herself. She will be asked to resolve an anagram.' It paused, before resuming its automated voice. 'She will then become old and wart-ridden, as she once was.' He paused again. 'I am trying to resolve an issue.' It fell silent, before saying, 'She will break a promise she made to Old Father Time.

Lars was dumbstruck. It now started to make sense.

'How can I prevent this happening?' he asked.

The Know-it-All pondered.

'What other images did the Rock of Erik the Enraged give you, other than these two?' it asked.

'An image of Tomte and an image of the Gnomes of Zurich,' answered Lars truthfully.

'The Gnomes of Zurich are who you need to turn to,' answered the Know-it-All. 'They too control time.'

Lars opened his mouth, about to speak again, but was interrupted by the Know-it-All, who got in first.

'Now you wish to ask me about the man,' it said. 'You look at the man and think you know him, but you have never met him.'

'True,' said Lars.

'Of course it's true!' exclaimed the creature. 'I am the Know-it-All!'

Lars fell silent, not daring to upset it any more.

'You also know that he is reading the book of your friend, the friend you must help,' said the Know-it-All. 'What else do you note about this image?'

'That he looks like someone else,' replied Lars.

'Exactly!' said the Know-it-All. 'Who is the person he looks like?'

Lars thought deeply. He had been asking himself this question day after day, but could not think of the answer.

'Shall I give you a clue?' asked the Know-it-All sarcastically.

'Again, yes please,' replied Lars.

'Her name begins with B,' said the creature.

'Of course,' said Lars, feeling truly stupid. 'He has traits of Bef.'

'That is because it is her brother,' said the Know-it-All.

'She doesn't have a brother,' replied Lars, without thinking.

'Are you questioning me? Undermining my authority? Thinking you know best?' shrieked the highly-strung green entity behind the curtain. 'I am telling you that this is her brother. I even know his name. He lives in a house in her village with a golden door knocker shaped like a lion. She keeps him hidden for his own safety. She loves him dearly, but will not show it and he feels the same about her.'

'I did not mean to question you,' replied Lars humbly. 'I knew not of his existence. May I ask his name?'

'Lorenzo,' said the Know-it-All. 'But you have angered me now, so I will only give you one more bit of knowledge.'

Lars wanted to cry, angering the creature having been the last thing he had wanted to do. He knew, however, there was no point arguing.

'I shall be grateful for that last piece of information,' he said.

'Lorenzo will be her salvation,' said the Know-it-All. 'Now go. I will light your lantern to help you get out of my cave. Do not dilly-dally. I need my rest.'

For an instant, the creature's illuminated body

disappeared from view, but suddenly a bright light shot forth and re-lit Lars' lantern. He turned around and started to make his way out of the cave, treading as gingerly as he had on the way in. A stream of thoughts was babbling through his mind. He needed to get to Hollywood, he had to find the Gnomes of Zurich, perhaps he should seek out Lorenzo … but in what order?

A voice echoed down the cave.

'Listen to your inner feelings Lars. You know in which order to do these things.'

Lars turned, but could see nothing in the darkness behind him. He walked forwards, walking towards the light – the light of a red sky that beckoned to him and encouraged him to use his own knowledge to the full. As he stepped out of the cave, it was as if a weight was lifted off his shoulders. He knew exactly what he had to do.

Chapter Twenty-Two

Gaspar had waited his moment. Bef had eventually stopped sweeping and plopped herself down in an armchair by the fire. She kept pinging a bright, stripy pair of legwarmers that she was wearing over trendy leggings. 'Fiddlesticks and rhubarb,' she kept repeating over and over again. 'Fiddlesticks and rhubarb.'

Gaspar had pulled a chair up next to her. 'What's the matter?' he said caringly.

'I can't make matters right,' she answered. 'I'm a useless witch and not much of a VIPB at the moment. If I had any true witchiness about me, I'd be able to sort this mess out with just a quick spell or two. I should have listened better to my mother. I was always the third best.'

'Third best where?' asked Gaspar, not understanding.

A look passed over Bef's face that told Gaspar she had said too much and let something accidentally slip out. She paused for a few seconds.

'At school,' she finally answered. 'Always third best at school.'

Gaspar wondered what deeper thoughts were whizzing around her brain, but decided now was the time to act.

'I could help you sort the whole thing out,' said Gaspar. 'I know you could do that, if I did what I'm intending to do.'

'What's that?' asked Bef, not really concentrating too much on his words, being lost in thoughts of her own.

'I need to give myself up,' said Gaspar. 'I need to let them snatch me. Natalia agrees with me. I am a missing piece of the conundrum puzzle and I'm holding the process up. Our friends are suffering longer than they need to, because I should be suffering their fate. The amethyst protection was great for giving us more time to work out what to do, but it's now time for you to reverse it and let me wander outside alone. That will bring you another letter. If that's not the final one, Natalia is prepared to give herself up too. If necessary, you will have to ask Lars to do the same. There can't be anyone else left after that.'

Bef instantly knew differently. There was, of course, Lorenzo, but she was not going to reveal that here. She knew only too well that walls have ears. She would not risk her brother's welfare.

She looked Gaspar in the eye and held his hand between hers.

'I can't let you do it,' she said. 'You are too important to me.' Thinking she'd been overly soppy, she added, 'And Natalia and I could never cope on our own.'

'Yes, you can,' answered Gaspar. 'You've just lost your confidence. You need to get back to being that plucky witch who would take on anyone. You need to use the spells that you've used for centuries. Something in your repertoire must be useful. You need to be the Bef I first met, who clambered into my apartment through the window, having ridden up in a window cleaning crane! Where's the witch gone who sent Capriccia packing down the parcel chute?'

'Or the one who barged me out of the way with her coal truck!' said Natalia.

Bef looked thoughtful.

'You're right about that!' she said. 'I've become a bit of wimp and I know I have, but it's been deeply upsetting for me to lose my friends and then there was that complete disaster at Befland! I've never been so humiliated in my life.'

'Then get the better of your enemies and show them who's boss,' urged Gaspar. 'To do that, you need to let me go.'

Bef knew he was right, but didn't want to listen at first.

'I don't know how to reverse an amethyst elixir,' she said very honestly.

'But you made one,' said Gaspar. 'You knew how to do that.'

Bef almost gave the game away again by saying

that it was Lorenzo who had told her what to do, but stopped herself just in time.

'I'll consult my notes,' she said, holding her forehead, pointing her eyes at the ceiling without moving her head and letting ream after ream of paper flick through her mind.'

'Where's the Grandissimo Libro di Scongiuri?' asked Gaspar, suddenly noticing the gap on the shelf.

'I think I left it in the office,' lied Bef.

Gaspar looked at her oddly. She didn't sound too convincing.

'There's nothing about amethyst in it anyway,' she added, to try to avoid Gaspar suggesting they should go and look for it.

'Think hard. There must be some way of reversing the amethyst protection,' chipped in Natalia.

Bef knew she had no spells to use for this purpose. She just looked blank and lost for an answer.

'The Lapps use a lot of amethyst protection,' said a voice out of nowhere. Sly had sprung to life on his stool. 'One once told me they could reverse it by drinking three pints of very salty water and then uttering the word …'

Bef cut him off and completed the sentence for him.

'Contro minerale!' she exclaimed.

'I don't think that was it,' replied Sly. 'That doesn't sound like a Lapp word at all!'

'No, but there is a Contro Minerale spell that my

mother once taught us when ...' she halted, having almost uttered the words 'my brother'. She corrected herself quickly, 'when a child swallowed copper sulphate crystals one day.'

Gaspar looked at her oddly, wondering what cat she'd nearly let out of the bag. There was definitely something.

Bef continued. 'If Sly is right and salty water is the reversal elixir, we can let you drink three pints, distasteful though that will be, and I will then do the Contro Minerale spell for good measure. I have to say that I really don't know whether this will work. However, if you insist on sacrificing yourself, I can but try.'

'Go for it!' said Gaspar. 'Do we have salt?'

'Bags of it,' answered Natalia. 'I'll get the water mixture ready.'

Jugs of cloudy water were carried to the table with a drinking glass for Gaspar to use. Bef declared that she would cast the spell as the last gulps of water were being taken and Gaspar insisted that this would be very quickly, as he couldn't stand the taste of salty water. Bef nodded, agreeing strongly and reached for her wand. Gaspar picked up the first glass of water and tipped it down his throat, pulling a face as the taste of salt hit his tongue. Another glass and then another and another followed, until there was just an inch of water left in the jug.

'Ready?' he asked Bef.

'Assolutamente,' she replied, nodding.

Gaspar picked up the last glass of water and began to drink. Just as the last few drops were touching his lips, Bef yelled out 'Contro Minerale!' Gaspar put the glass back down.

'I don't feel any different,' he said.

'But we didn't feel any difference after taking the amethyst,' said Natalia. 'We won't know if this has worked unless you are snatched.'

'Let's get on with it then,' said Gaspar. 'I'm going outside now and may not be back. Take care of yourselves and remember to be that feisty witch that I first met. My Bef does NOT take things on the chin. She gets up and fights and sends candy balls bouncing down the street.'

A tear was rolling down Bef's cheek, so she turned away not wanting him to see. He knew full well what was happening, but didn't embarrass her. He said goodbye to Natalia and saluted Sly. Hopefully, his knowledge on amethyst reversal would prove spot on.

Gaspar opened the door and stepped out into the cobbled street. In his own mind, he'd already decided where he would go. He would stand in the piazza, close to Mr Passarella and in the shadow of the church tower in which Marianna still hung upside down like a bat. Their enemies would surely see him there very quickly and snatch him. He didn't wish to prolong the agony any longer. If he was going to be turned to stone, it might as well be sooner rather than later.

He winded his way through the town, as local people lifted their hat on seeing him, or tried to ask him how Bef was, as they hadn't seen her since the disastrous opening of Befland. Luckily, Gaspar didn't speak enough Italian to answer, so just smiled at each passer-by and tried to move on as fast as possible.

Every time he saw a figure approaching, he wondered if it was Fiery Tina, or Capriccia in disguise. He was pretty sure he'd spot Bernhardt in his pyjamas and there was no way of hiding his toilet brush hair. If Bernhardt were in the street, he would look like a walking cactus! That thought amused Gaspar and made him feel slightly less fearful.

He kept checking in the reflection of shop windows, to see if anyone was following him. He had no idea how snatches happened. Did someone physically grab him, or was he transported away by magic? He couldn't imagine how it would feel, or whether he would be in pain when turned to stone. He remembered the looks on the faces of the other victims and they didn't seem to be in pain. Most were just wearing a look of surprise. He could cope with surprise.

Where were their enemies? He looked up to the sky, but could see nothing up there. He gazed up at the balconies of the houses he passed. They could be there: he'd never know. They always seemed to have known every move Bef's friends made, so they must have some sort of lookout post, or so he believed.

Why was it that nobody from the town ever saw them? It was all baffling.

Right now, he wished he had the broom's invisibility shield. He hated all this waiting and walking. His mind was causing him torment. This was his last thought as he entered the piazza.

He looked up and saw Marianna still suspended in the bell tower. He walked past Mr Passarella's statue and was again almost sure he saw him move his clipboard. Perhaps they would make a statue of him too and let him sit next to Mr Passarella. He didn't fancy becoming a bat, however.

He lifted his sunglasses and popped them on his head. He wanted them to recognise him. He walked into the very centre of the square, making his way through the pecking pigeons. People bustled around and across the piazza, but Gaspar just stood there rooted to the spot. He stood in the sun and waited. Looking up at the sun without his sunglasses, he thought he saw a glistening and a sparkle, as if rays were reflecting off jewels. Suddenly he felt weightless, as his feet left the ground. After that, he remembered nothing.

Bef and Natalia sat at the kitchen table watching the hands of the clock move slowly round its face. The ticking was driving them mad, but they had to sit there clock watching. If Gaspar did not return, it was more than likely that he had been snatched. Three hours passed by and then a fourth. By that point, they concluded that Gaspar was not returning. Bef's eyes filled with tears and Natalia produced a white handkerchief for her to use. Sly kept quiet. There was no point irritating Natalia.

'Where is the letter?' said Bef. 'Why has nothing come through the Flush Telegraph?'

Natalia shrugged her shoulders.

'We must wait,' she said. 'Maybe there's a reason for the delay.'

Indeed there was. Up in the ruined castle on the hillside, a row had broken out. Capriccia had been determined to snatch Gaspar, viewing him as the most handsome member of the boy band, but Fiery Tina's jealousy had seen her deciding to get in first. She had told Capriccia to think of a place to which to transport him and, while Capriccia was racking the very few brain cells that she seemingly possessed, had fluttered down into the piazza and carried out the steal. Fiery Tina already knew exactly where Gaspar was going to be placed. He was such a lovely boy and sang so nicely. He deserved to be put there.

Rather than instantly turning him to stone, she had decided that he could provide a lot of amusement back at the castle. Secretly, she wanted to make Capriccia even angrier, so delighted in bringing him back with her and landing him in the middle of the ruined walls.

'Look what I've got,' she declared triumphantly.

'How could you?' seethed Capriccia. 'I'd been looking forward to snatching him for days.'

'Oops,' said Fiery Tina. 'I didn't we-alise that

Capwiccia. Why didn't you say?' She laughed to herself, leaving Capriccia in no doubt that she'd done the snatch on purpose, just to make her mad.

'Right,' she shouted in Fiery Tina's face. 'I'm doing the statuefication!'

Fiery Tina couldn't care less now. She was walking around Gaspar saying, 'What a nice boy. What a very lovely boy.'

Gaspar looked at the pair of them, coming out of the shock of being snatched and flown up into the ether.

'You're all mad,' he said. 'What's this sick game all about anyway?'

Bernhardt had been asleep in the corner, but the row between Fiery Tina and Capriccia had awoken him.

'This sick game, as you call it, is to pay zat Bef woman back for all ze harm she has caused us,' he said.

Gaspar spoke up.

'She's done nothing except protect her VIPB patch and make sure Italian children had someone decent to look up to: someone with principles, not nasty, vile people like you three. None of you are fit to be a VIPB!'

He wasn't sure where this sudden streak of bravery had come from, but he was absolutely certain that his words were true. He was greeted by three angry glares from the three wannabe VIPBs.

'Turn him into a statue now!' yelled Fiery Tina. 'Then I'll twansport him.'

'You don't know where I'm going to put him!' shouted Capriccia.

'Not intewested,' said Fiery Tina. 'I know exactly where he's going.'

'WHAT!' yelled Capriccia. 'I'm supposed to decide. I'm the engineer of the conundrum!'

'Hardly!' replied Fiery Tina. 'I've done it all and just made you think you were playing a part. You couldn't twansport a loaf of bwead from the bakerwee to your house without dwopping it!'

Capriccia was ready to spin, until Bernhardt stepped in.

'Ladies, ladies!' he yelled. 'I cannot take much more of zis! For goodness sake, just transport him and let him sit in stone!'

Capriccia danced over to Gaspar, turning pirouettes in her tutu until she came up to his chest. He looked her in the eye defiantly.

'My apologies,' she said. 'Nothing personal!' With that, she pointed her wand, but felt the sparks of another wand cut across it. Gaspar was turned to stone, but not by Fiery Tina.

'Oops,' said Capriccia, cruelly imitating Fiery Tina. 'I seem to have statuefied him first!'

With that, Fiery Tina pointed her wand again and the stony-faced Gaspar, with a steely look in his eye, disappeared from view.'

'Where has he gone?' shouted Capriccia.

'Next to the Bef woman's shoes,' replied her tutor. 'He's a star and now he's with the stars … so app-wo-pwiate!'

'That's a stupid place!' said Capriccia. 'Now I suppose I've got to make up a riddle about a spot that was hard enough to put in a riddle the last time! Thanks a bunch!'

Fiery Tina was very pleased with herself. Capriccia had no idea what was happening next. Even Bernhardt didn't know what Fiery Tina had got lined up – quite literally. The pair of them would change their tune when they saw how clever she was. More fool them for not realising before.

She twitched her wings and began to hop.

'I'll send the invitation to the Bef woman,' she said.

Capriccia dug Bernhardt in the ribs.

'What invitation?' she hissed. Bernhardt shook his head.

Fiery Tina was already composing it. Within seconds she had come up with it. Having scribbled it down, she wrapped the piece of parchment around a lump of coal and flew off, leaving Capriccia and Bernhardt open-mouthed.

Back at Bef's home, the clock kept ticking. It was the only thing breaking the silence until … a big lump of coal with a parchment message attached to it came down the chimney and frightened poor Sly to death.

Bef picked up the piece of coal and unwrapped the message. It carried a letter E and read:

Gaspar was really a catch,

Until he fell prey to a snatch.

So will you repent,

Now he too's in cement?

Go to find him and you'll meet your match.

Bef was fuming when she read the last line. As if Fiery Tina was any match for her! Who was it that had won the battle of Florence all those centuries ago? Who was it that was still the VIPB of Florence long after Fiery Tina's uprising? Who had a theme park and who didn't? As her blood boiled, she remembered Gaspar's words about being the feisty witch he had first met. As she steamed, her candy balls began to bounce out of sacks in her cupboards and roll under the door and down the street. As she turned bright red, her broom leapt up a few inches in delight at the return of the mistress he adored.

'Grab your belongings, Natalia!' she ordered in the voice of an army officer. 'The conundrum is set and the gauntlet has been laid down. It's time for us to fly to Los Angeles, the city of angels, but not of evil fairies, unless I'm very much mistaken! It's time to try to win the game!'

Chapter Twenty-Three

Natalia was as nervous as a Russian VIPB could be. She had never flown as far as the USA on her broom, so was quick to take up Bef's offer and jump on board with her as a passenger. Bef had flown to Italian families in America many times before and was familiar with the different, swirling winds that they would encounter en route. Her broom was also accustomed to the long flight. After its tuber charge – the careful mix of potatoes and horse manure that Bef always used – it was more than capable of tackling the many miles ahead.

Bef got all her gadgets and broom features ready: her night vision spectacles, her radar fogging device and the Broom Barrier, which allowed her to fly within six feet of a jet at any one time, without hitting it. All of this was essential when flying trans-Atlantic.

Natalia packed both of their wands tightly in a long leather pouch strapped to her thigh and packaged some more amethyst in a bag attached to her hip. She had quickly made another elixir and popped that in there too. She wound her lasso around her waist and made sure her warmest Russian clothing wrapped tight around her body.

Bef wore the warm outfit Jeremiah had made for her, knowing they would need to fly across the Atlantic and, although it wasn't as cold as the ice caps and Northern Canada, it could still feel very chilly indeed.

Both wondered whether they would even be allowed to land in California, or whether Fiery Tina would cut across them before then, though both felt the game entailed them landing in Los Angeles and dealing with whatever they found when they got there.

This was not a joy-filled flight, so there were no broomies or loops, or even mouth shapes in the sky. Bef and Natalia wore looks of grim determination on their faces. This was all about getting their friends back and ending the game, one way or another. There was no time for tricks.

The cold air whipped around their legs as they flew on and on, praying they'd fuelled up with enough potatoes and manure. They eventually spotted the bright lights of New York and the Statue of Liberty, before noticing land beneath them and knowing that a very long crossing of America lay ahead before they could reach the west coast and the Pacific coastline.

Natalia was mesmerised by some of the sights she saw, having never ventured out of Europe. She was enthralled by skyscrapers and the vast expanse of sea that they crossed together. She could feel how the broom responded to Bef's commands and was in awe of Bef's navigational skills. It was all an adventure that the Russian VIPB had never imagined having.

Many many hours passed by before they started to see an ocean ahead of them once more and realised that they were now approaching California.

'Head for Los Angeles now broom,' instructed Bef, as they took a slight turn to the right and headed a little bit north.

The broom remembered visits here to the homes of great Italian actors who had made it big in Hollywood. It rather liked the glitz and glamour of the place and loved flying over the mansions of movie stars to see if they were sunbathing by their pool, or sitting on their glamorous terraces.

Bef began to notice features and the many long rows of houses that looked as if they were buildings in a miniature village. These were the homes of the ordinary residents of Los Angeles, but they needed to head to Hollywood, where life was very different indeed. Within half an hour, Bef spotted the unmistakable roof of Grauman's Chinese Theatre. She leaned down and stroked her broom.

'Down now, my faithful friend,' she said. 'I promise to keep you safe.'

Her plan was to land behind the building and not where she thought her enemies would be waiting. She would then place her broom under its invisibility shield and, if asked, tell Bernhardt that they had flown on Natalia's broom.

This is how it unfolded. Bef and Natalia parked the broom, having seen nothing and nobody malicious. They walked carefully, almost on tiptoes round to where the actors and actresses placed their hands and feet in cement, to record their contribution to movie history. This was the location where she thought she would find both her shoes and Gaspar, unless it was all a big joke and they had been forced to fly all this way for nothing.

They trod cautiously, keeping close to the wall and peering around every corner to check what was ahead of them, before moving on. Sometimes Bef led the way and, at others, Natalia took the lead. It felt as though danger was all around them.

They turned the final corner and surveyed the scene. There was nobody there, but Bef's shoes certainly were, cast in stone and looking as if they could never be shifted from the concrete. They cautiously walked up to the concrete slab in which they had been placed. Bef had hoped it might carry a message saying that the shoes were those of the famous Italian VIPB, Bef. She was horrified to see it actually said that they belonged to a woman totally lacking in style and grace, who was a laughing stock in her little village in Italy.

Before Gaspar's pep talk, this might have left her in tears, but it now just made her blood boil.

However, her mind was on other things and she was distracted. Where was her beloved Gaspar?

She walked slowly down the row of concrete slabs carrying the names of the rich and famous – past Johnny Depp, Marilyn Monroe and more. That's when she spotted him: standing helpless with his feet in the concrete and turned to stone, but looking every inch the star that he was. Leaning on one of his arms was Fiery Tina. On another sprawled Capriccia. Bernhardt was sitting cross-legged in front of him.

'Well, well, well, here she comes,' said Fiery Tina. 'Oops, we seem to have her fwend in cement. What a shame! What a twagedy for the Bef woman.'

Capriccia smirked.

'And her horrendous shoes are just down there, looking as ghastly as ever,' she remarked.

'And her broom will soon be back with me,' added Bernhardt.

'My broom is thousands of miles away and in a safe place,' lied Bef. 'Now tell us what this sick game is really about. I know it's not about taking my broom back into your dreadful care. What is your purpose?'

'Let's think about that, shall we?' said Fiery Tina in her usual deranged manner and holding her neck as straight as she could. 'What could it be about? Why would we want to bwing you here and why have we taken all of your fwends? Any ideas Capwiccia?'

'Could it be about the conundrum?' asked Capriccia, as if she herself wasn't quite sure of the answer.

'Ah, yes,' replied Fiery Tina. 'That's it … the conundwum. Should we unveil the conundwum now, do you think? Should we give the Bef woman the chance to get all her fwends and possessions out of stone? Should we give her the opportunity to show that she thinks more of others than she does of herself? Should we let her think carefully about giving other people the chance to become VIPBs?'

Natalia laughed out loud.

'You three could never be a VIPB!' she declared. 'To be a VIPB, you need to care about children. You need to receive joy in your heart when you leave them presents. You need to have a heart – somezing that none of you have. All you have is an ego. You, you silly little man, zink you are important, but you run around in your pyjamas. You, Capriccia, zink you are beautiful, but anything of beauty zat you have is man-made and not natural in the slightest. And you, you deranged fairy, you have a heart, but it is a black heart. Not a child in the world could ever love you.'

'Oops,' said Fiery Tina. 'Someone thinks that words can hurt us. How wong can they be!' She wafted her wand at Natalia to turn her into a statue, but failed. Natalia was still protected by the amethyst.

'Oops,' said Bef. 'You seem to have failed to turn

Natalia to stone. Could your magic be failing you by any chance, just like it did the day you lay in an alley and had your tutu ripped to shreds by a stray cat?'

Fiery Tina turned completely orange as she remembered that terrible day.

Capriccia turned to her.

'Don't listen to them. Unveil the conundrum.'

Fiery Tina pulled herself to her senses and wafted her wand to reveal the famous hill above Hollywood, on which letters spelling out Hollywood were one of the city's most well-known sights. Suddenly, the H O L L Y W O O and D disappeared to reveal another set of letters, which read: B A N A F L E A.

Bef screwed up her eyes and stared at the scene. There was a man standing next to them: a man with a candy tie and giant candy spectacles and a candy walking stick, which he used to point out each letter in turn.

'The letters are made from candy,' exclaimed Bef.

'Oh yes,' said Fiery Tina. 'Candy made by a special fwend of ours, who also doesn't like you very much. Do you know who that is, or is the Bef woman too stupid to we-member?'

'Rocky Candymeister,' said Bef. 'It's Rocky Candymeister.'

'Quite wight!' said Fiery Tina in a patronising tone. 'Now, Bef woman, let's see how clever you are when it comes to what Wocky's made for you. If you wish to free your fwends from their stone impwisonment, you need to answer the question that I give you. The answer can be found by unscwambling the letters. Are you good at unscwambling?' She looked up at Bef in her usual crooked way, having danced over and crouched in front of her.

Bef looked at the letters. "It says Ban A Flea,' she said.

'Now unscwamble those and answer this question,' said the horrid fairy. 'Who am I?'

'Well, you are Fiery Tina,' said Bef, 'but I don't get that by unscrambling your stupid candy letters.'

'I don't want to know who I am!' exclaimed the deranged hopscotch addict. 'I want you to tell me who you are. Unscwamble the letters and tell us all who you are!'

Bef looked at the letters but could only see Ban A Flea. She was Bef, but that was just three letters. She couldn't fathom it, but others had.

'Stop this!' Natalia said to Fiery Tina. 'What purpose can it serve?'

Bef still didn't get it and was sorting the letters in many ways. Eventually, she got as far as starting the word with La and that's when the penny dropped. She realised that the letters actually spelt out La Befana. She found herself tongue-tied, torn between what to do to save her friends and what to do to prevent herself being turned back into a centuries old witch with bad legs, acne, warts, wrinkles and not enough energy to look after her VIPB patch and retain the hearts of her Italian children. She had made a pact with Old Father Time and she knew that, if she broke it, there would be no more life as Bef: there would be no more Befland or mass popularity. Fiery Tina would be able to take over Florence and who knew which part of her patch Capriccia and Bernhardt might fancy. She stood open-mouthed, much to the amusement of Bernhardt and Capriccia.

'For once you seem to have nothing to say, witch,' said Capriccia.

'Your broom vill want to return to me when it sees what an ancient wreck you are?' laughed Bernhardt. 'You see, our silly little game is actually very clever. Now answer ze question!'

Suddenly, images of all the people and things cast in stone started floating in front of Bef's eyes. First came Marianna, hanging like a bat, but seemingly pleading with Bef to answer the question. Next came Mr Passarella, moving his spectacles down his nose, as if to tell Bef to speak. Then Thaz appeared, drumming angrily, perhaps to tell her to free him.

Bef breathed in deeply as Jeremiah sat hopelessly in his prison cell, with a tear rolling down his cheek. Mel appeared, waving his arms to tell her to free him from his bungee rope. Then there were her shoes, looking desolate, before Santa emerged surrounded by snowflakes that spelt out the word

'HELP'. She didn't need to see an image of Gaspar. He was right in front of her.

She opened her mouthed wider. She only had one choice. "I am La…'

Just as she was about to utter the rest of her name, and as Natalia was holding her head in her hands in despair, something totally unexpected happened. Gaspar, began to move and jumped out of the cement, screaming at the top of this voice,

'NO'.

Everyone leapt out of their skin, with only Natalia and Bef realising that some amethyst had to still be providing him with some protection.

'Get back, pretty boy,' said Fiery Tina angrily.

Capriccia pointed her wand menacingly, to try to turn him into a statue, but failed. The curse instead bounced off his body and bounded outwards and up the hill, bumping on the land as it went, finally reaching Rocky, who was still standing triumphantly by his gigantic candy letters. Within an instant, he was turned to stone.

'Oops,' said Fiery Tina. 'No more gummy bears for us!' She giggled insanely, seemingly forgetting what was happening to her game.

'I have to say my name,' said Bef, looking Gaspar in the eye. 'I have to set them all free.'

'We will find a way,' said Gaspar. 'Please don't do it. It will ruin your life. You will no longer be an important VIPB. You might not be a VIPB at all. You will let these awful people take over from you, because you will be too old to fight them. I beg you not to say your name.'

Bef took his hand in hers and took Natalia's hand in the other.

'Our friends are coming back to us and that is what matters,' she said. 'I don't know what will happen to me next, so make sure they are all well and do what you can to help them. Tell them that I am sorry that they suffered because of me. I had no idea what this game was about and would have willingly said my former name, if I had known that was what these three vile people wanted.'

Before either Bef or Gaspar could say anything in response to this, she took a step forwards to Fiery Tina.

'I am La Befana,' she declared.

The valley was filled with an agonising shout from Gaspar, a shout of 'NO-oooooooo' that echoed around for a full minute. Natalia burst into tears, as Fiery Tina cackled and Capriccia and Bernhardt danced around in celebration.

'Now you will become the haggard old woman that you were,' shrieked Fiery Tina, waiting for the ageing process to begin.

She stood and stared at Bef, waiting for wrinkles to start appearing and her skin to start sagging, but nothing was happening. She poked Bef to see if she was flesh and bone and her skin felt firm and plump and young. She tilted her crooked head to one side and stared even more closely.

'What's happening?' shrieked Capriccia. 'Why isn't she ageing?'

'Shut up,' yelled Fiery Tina. 'I don't know what's going on.'

'I think zat sly elf fed us a lie,' said Bernhardt. 'It was his tale about Old Father Time, after all. We only had his word for it. He obviously got it wrong.'

They all stopped speaking, crying and shouting. There was a strange rumbling on the breeze. The air was swirling in a weird manner, as if a gale had sprung up. They all put their hands on their ears as the wind whistled. Suddenly, clearing the Grauman's roof by just inches, there appeared a team of reindeer, pulling a sleigh driven by the best reindeer whisperer the world had ever known.

'No,' he roared. 'It is you who got it wrong! Your evil conundrum is flawed. You have made a schoolgirl or schoolboy error.'

Bef looked around her. The suspended images of all her friends were changing. All were coming back to their normal state, free of their stone imprisonment. Jeremiah was moving his knitting needles, Santa was brushing snow off his nose, Marianna was beginning to roll back up from her bat position. Every one of them had been freed!

Fiery Tina marched over to Lars.

'What do you mean I got it wong? Of course I didn't!' She stared at Lars in her usual scary way.

She received no answer, so turned and yelled at Capriccia.

'You got it wong, Capwiccia. You absolute dunce.'

As a catfight broke out between the two spiteful women and Bernhardt tried to tear them apart, Lars signalled to Bef, Natalia and Gaspar to jump on board. Natalia and Gaspar jumped in, but Bef started to run.

'I've got to get my shoes and then pick up Jeremiah on the way.'

'And her broom,' whispered Natalia.

Lars gestured to her to get into the sleigh. She did as she was told and he started to let the reindeer run. They approached Bef's shoes and she leaned out to sweep them into the sleigh. She then whistled hard and her broom suddenly appeared, hovering above the sleigh before dropping into it.

'Don't forget Jeremiah,' she urged.

'And I'll ring Mel and tell him to board a plane,' added Gaspar, 'but where are we going?'

'Back to Bef's village,' said Lars. 'Bef isn't out of the woods yet, but luckily they got the conundrum wrong. They thought they'd snatched the eight people or things that Bef loves the most, but they hadn't, had they?'

Bef looked him in the eye.

'No,' she said. 'They got one wrong.'

'And that's given us a lifeline,' replied Lars. 'We just have to hope that they don't suddenly discover what they missed. Bef will start to age, because she has broken her pact with Old Father Time, but we have to try to counteract that, with a little help from our friends. It's literally a race against time and we need to race as fast as we can.'

With that, he geed up the reindeer, urging them to fly just a little faster, knowing that every second counted. They had to return to the village and carry out his plans before the other three could possibly guess the missing link in the conundrum.

Lars seemed to know exactly what he was doing and was very much in charge. That was just as well, because sitting in the sleigh with him, Bef, Natalia and Gaspar didn't have a clue what he was talking about.

Chapter Twenty-Four

The aftermath of the failed conundrum was truly dreadful. Fiery Tina and Capriccia fought for hours, pulling each other's hair, screaming, stamping their feet and doing even more childish things. Capriccia messed up a hopscotch court that Fiery Tina had created by scuffing and blurring all the markings in the ground with Bernhardt's broom, while Fiery Tina spitefully pulled the liquorice laces off Capriccia's shoes.

Bernhardt tried to keep the peace for about an hour, but then gave up and sat and sulked in a shady spot. Rocky Candymeister had the best of it. He was still set in stone on the hillside, as he had not been one of the snatches that made up the conundrum and had been statuefied by chance. Fiery Tina decided he looked impressive standing on the hillside above Hollywood and so made no move to try to free him. He would be her lasting legacy in Los Angeles.

After all the screaming subsided, Capriccia collapsed in a heap.

'What are we going to do now? What's plan B?' she asked.

Fiery Tina was also exhausted.

'We must decide which part went wong,' said Fiery Tina 'and then try to put it wight.'

'What do you think was wrong?' asked Bernhardt. 'Surely there is nothing she loves more than ze things we chose?'

Capriccia twiddled her Northern Highlight-streaked hair around her long stick insect fingers.

'Maybe she didn't love my husband after all,' she said finally. 'There's no doubt she loves her awful shoes, those boys and her Befland friends. If only we hadn't lost the broom!' She looked accusingly at Bernhardt.

'Don't blame me!' he ranted. 'You should know whether she loves your husband.'

'We must get back to her village and think hard,' dictated Fiery Tina. 'We will be allowed thwee guesses as to who or what is missing from the conundwum. If we get it wight, there is nothing they will be able to do. She will definitely become an old woman again for-wever more. I can't see how that weindeer man thinks he can beat us. He can't possibly save her, even if we get it wong. What can his plan be? What is in his head?'

Capriccia sighed deeply, having had enough of Fiery Tina not being able to pronounce the letter r. Fiery Tina, on the other hand, paced up and down, debating this point over and over again. Bernhardt and Capriccia began to pack up their things and then waited for instructions. Eventually she snapped out of her own thought bubble and snapped her fingers.

'We must fly,' she said. 'Back to the castle we go. Get your bwoom charged and fly us all there immediately.'

Bef and her friends were already well on their way home. Lars was tempted to suggest not picking up Jeremiah, to save them a lot of time, but knew that Bef would have none of that. He asked for directions and she began to draw up maps in the sky, working out their position according to the stars and charting a course for Jeremiah's prison cell in Siberia.

Jeremiah could not believe his eyes when he saw a fancy sleigh approaching in the sky, silhouetted against the moon. He stood with the snow coming up to his knees and waved his arms madly, hoping they would stop. He needn't have worried and, when he saw it was Bef, his heart filled with joy. He grabbed his knitting needles and wool and a few other bits and bobs and jumped on board as fast as he could.

'We have to rush,' explained Bef, 'but I don't quite know why. Don't worry, however, because Lars seems very much in charge.'

Indeed he was. He had never driven the reindeer faster and each and every one of the team knew that they had to fly at top speed, because Lars the Reindeer Whisperer needed their help. They dashed through the night skies, saw dawn rise and then eventually began to make out the outline of Bef's village, with a little help from Bef's broom, which took over the navigation once they flew above Italy.

'We must land near the biggest clock in the village,' said Lars. 'Where will we find that?'

'In the main piazza,' said Bef, 'in front of the church. Why do we need a clock?'

'Quite simply,' replied Lars, 'we must turn back time. We have a small window of opportunity and that will be lost if Fiery Tina and Capriccia manage to get the conundrum right. Is there any reason that they should?' He looked at Bef questioningly, remembering the pictures of her brother that he had seen in the image generated by the Rock of Erik the Enraged.

Bef thought carefully. She was pretty sure she had kept Lorenzo a secret. There was no reason they should know about him. As long as he didn't do something stupid and reveal his identity to anyone.

'I see no reason,' she replied.

Gaspar listened to this, but couldn't figure out what the missing link could be. He asked Natalia if she could guess and she shook her head. Gaspar racked his brains, but came up with nothing. If he didn't know, how could their enemies possibly guess?

They saw the piazza below them and carefully descended into the square, causing quite a stir among those townsfolk who saw them dropping from the sky. Lars got his bearings, scouring the town buildings looking for something, or rather some people, he couldn't see.

'Oh my word,' he gasped. 'I hope they got the message.'

The others looked at him completely baffled as to what he meant, but he didn't give them time to query it.

'Right everyone,' he yelled, looking up at the medieval clock tower. 'Run up the tower's stairs as fast as you can. I want every woman and man up there now please!'

They all rushed to the bottom of the tower without even asking why. As they headed up the ancient stone steps, they met Marianna and Mr Passarella coming down, with Luigi having gone up to help Marianna recover from her many days spent as a bat.

'Great! More hands to help!' said Lars. 'Turn around. We need you back at the top!'

They all headed up the spiral staircase and arrived in the bell tower, in which the clock was housed. Lars surveyed the scene and drew out a shiny, golden watch from his embroidered waistcoat pocket. He cleared his throat.

'I estimate that we have to turn the clock back 16 hours and we need to do that within the next hour,' he said.

All gasped, looking at the clock with its very heavy hands and ancient mechanics. How could they possibly turn it back 16 hours? They began to grasp the massive metal hands, but they hardly moved. This was going to be an impossible task and, as that thought entered the brain of each and every one of them, it was also troubling Lars greatly. Was his plan going to fail at the last hurdle?

Their thoughts were broken by a commotion that broke out in the piazza. Fiery Tina, Capriccia and Bernhardt had descended at a super speed and given passers-by their second amazing sight of the day.

'It's all been happening around here lately,' said one man.

'Yes, this is rapidly becoming the place to be,' said another, sitting at a café table and sipping a small espresso coffee.

Fiery Tina hopped off the broom and walked right into the middle of the piazza. She tilted her skewed neck backwards, to stare at the gang in the clock tower.

'By the Fair-wee Law welating to conundwums,' she said, 'we can have thwee more guesses to get the conundwum cowwect.'

Lars' heart sank. He had half hoped she wouldn't realise this.

'So,' continued Fiery Tina, 'we will start to make our guesses as you twy to complete that simply hopeless task in which you are engaging wight now. You'll never manage to turn the clock back in time, so it will give us gweat pleasure to see you fail, despite all your efforts, weindeer man.'

She looked up at the time on the clock.

'Oops! You haven't got very far have you!' she giggled. 'You would need an army of helpers to win this game!' She began to dance around the piazza. 'Well, Capwiccia, what's your first guess,' she asked, feeling very confident that they'd finally get this right.

Capwiccia straightened her spine, drew herself up to her full height and looked up at the tower.

'The Bef woman loves the Reindeer Whisperer,' she shouted, looking up at the sky.

Clouds above the piazza began to reshape. Gaspar was holding his breath, thinking in his own mind that they must have got this right. Lars had helped Bef so much during her last mission to save her VIPB patch. He looked up at the strange movements in the sky and to his relief saw that they had formed a big black cross. Somehow, the enemies had got it wrong and Lars wasn't the correct eighth thing.

'Push harder,' instructed Lars, 'we must get the hands moving back.' He hadn't been slightly concerned about Capriccia's guess, as he knew he wasn't the missing thing. He was, however, panicking like mad. He had expected help to be here, but it wasn't. At the rate they were going, they could never turn the clock back sixteen hours. He could see Bef beginning to age and she herself could feel her skin changing. He scanned the square. There was still no help to be seen.

Fiery Tina was not at all happy on seeing the big black cross. She hated getting things wrong and Lars had been their best guess. She bustled over to Capriccia and hissed in her ear.

'What's your next guess?'

Capriccia spat it out and Fiery Tina nodded. It was possible, even though she hadn't thought the Bef woman and this person had enjoyed the best of relationships in the past. She began to pirouette.

Capriccia ignored her strange behaviour and filled her lungs with air again before belting out her next guess.

'The Bef woman loves Natalia Lebedev,' she shouted.

Everyone in the clock tower held their breath, praying this wasn't accurate, but something else was demanding their attention. At the far end of the piazza a lot of commotion was arising, accompanied by a sound they could all swear was that of marching feet.

'What is it?' asked Mr Passarella. 'It's as if the ground is shaking.'

They all strained their eyes, other than Lars, who already knew what the noise was. His heart leapt with joy and he clasped his hands together in delight.

'My friends,' he said, 'may I present the Gnomes of Zurich.'

Sure enough, a long, snaking chain of little green gnomes was marching into the square and walking right past an aghast Fiery Tina.

'Can't we statuefy them?' asked Capriccia, realising that these little men were enemies, though she had no idea why.

'No!' shrieked Fiery Tina. 'Their diet consists of quartz, so they are immune to statuefication! Why are they here?'

She was horrified to see them marching up the steps of the clock tower and was so distracted by this that she almost failed to notice that another big black cross had formed in the sky.

'I knew that it wouldn't be me,' declared Natalia, though she had secretly hoped it might be her, just from the point of view of flattering her ego.

'Ladies and gentlemen,' said Lars, 'move aside and let the Gnomes of Zurich deal with our little issue up here.' The first Gnomes to arrive in the clock tower brushed past them and instantly grabbed hold of the clock hands.

'How many hours?' asked the Gnomes' leader.

'Now, another 15 hours and 27 minutes,' said Lars.

Each Gnome of Zurich grabbed the waist of the one in front of them and the Gnomes at the head of the chain began to turn the heavy hands of the clock back, as the rest of the chain transferred their powers to their chosen hand movers through the very special Gnome energising method that they used.

The hands of the clock started to whiz at a real old pace, compared to what had happened previously, as Fiery Tina looked on in horror, seeing time being moved back in front of her very eyes.

She put her hands on her head and screamed.

'We need to think hard, Capwiccia,', she said. 'We now only have one guess and they are turning back time so fast now. If we don't work it out before they finish, we will have lost. All our plans will be in tatters. You have to clear that little blonde head of stupid thoughts and think carefully about who or what the Bef woman loves most. We seem to be missing something obvious, or else missing something we just don't know about!'

'How long have I got?' asked Capriccia, shaking at the thought of not ruining Bef once and for all.

'Judging by ze speed of their work so far,' said Bernhardt, who had been observing the clock face ever since the arrival of the Gnomes of Zurich, 'I would say we have a maximum of three-quarters of an hour. We must tread carefully and consider what ze last person or thing could be. Let's not rush in this time, Capriccia. We still have 45 minutes in which to get it spot on. There must be something staring us in the face zat we are not seeing!'

At that precise moment, there was a strange sequence of knocks on Bef's door at home. A man with long, grey curly hair and a sweeping and dramatic robe was standing outside in a very nervous fashion, hovering on the cobbles with a massive book of spells tucked under his arm. He got no responses, so repeated the sequence of knocks.

From a stool in the kitchen, there leapt up a little man – a little man who had once hated Bef with a passion and loved Capriccia with all his heart. Sly jumped to his feet, a little bit terrified by the knocking and wondering who on earth it was. He seemed to have been on his own in the house for an age and he had no idea when Bef and Natalia might return, if at all. He wondered what on earth to do about the knocking, being a little bit fearful for his own safety.

He decided to not open the door, but to speak to try to discover the identity of the caller. For some other unknown reason, he attempted to imitate Bef's voice.

'Who is it?' he said firmly, adopting the tone he thought Bef would use if a little irritated by knocking.

There came no reply, just another sequence of knocking, identical to that which he had now heard twice.

'I said, who is it?' he said boldly. 'Who on earth would trouble me with such infernal knocking?'

This time a voice answered.

'You know who it is,' it muttered in an irritated tone – exactly the sort of tone that Bef would use. 'I have come to return the book.'

Sly looked puzzled. Who on earth could this be? What book was he talking about? Why did he assume Bef would know who it was? He glanced at the shelves behind him. There was an enormous gap on there. That must be where this book usually sat. Perhaps he ought to let the man in and take the book from him.

He tentatively lifted the latch and saw the man for the first time.

'Who are you?' said the man, in a most anxious tone and ready to turn and flee. 'Where is the owner of this house?'

Sly looked at him closely. He seemed terribly familiar, but he couldn't put his finger on it.

'Not at home,' he answered. 'If you wish to leave the book, I will pass it on to her.'

Lorenzo eyed him up and down.

'Have you permission to live here?' he asked.

'Oh yes. Bef insisted, because I was so helpful to her.'

'Very well,' said Lorenzo. 'Pass the book on to her.'

Sly bowed slightly.

'Certainly. Who should I say returned it?'

'She will know,' replied the stranger. He hesitated. 'What's that accent I detect in your speech?' he asked nosily.

Sly tried to be friendly.

'I don't speak the Lynx type of Elf that most elves speak,' he explained. 'My Elf is more akin to the tongue of owls.'

'As I thought,' said Lorenzo, before turning and heading out of the door as fast as he could. Sly was a little perplexed and left alone in the house once more, with an enormous book of what appeared to be spells. He looked at the shelves. Bef would probably be pleased with him if he put it back in place. He stretched his arms as wide as he could, to try to pick up the huge book. It was almost as tall as he was, so he struggled greatly, staggering as he tried to carry it to the shelf on which he was sure it should sit.

As he wobbled across the floor with this unexpected delivery, something fell out – a piece of paper. He rested the book against the table and picked it up. It was blank on one side, so he turned it over, just to see if it was anything important. It carried a message which said, 'Take care, sister. Your loving brother, Lorenzo.'

The sugar lump read the message again and again. He slumped back on to his stool, without bothering to complete his mission with the book. Then suddenly, something took him over. He felt compelled to leave the house, to run out of the door, to belt down the cobbled streets and take himself off to the main piazza. Something told him that this was where he needed to be, though he knew not why and he scarpered so fast that he left the front door wide open. As the wind gusted through it, the sugar bowl on the table blew over. One solitary sugar lump fell to the floor.

The clock ticked loudly, but there was nobody at home to hear it. Sly was already approaching the small town's main piazza as fast as his legs would carry him and the dark clouds that had formed an X in the sky after Capriccia's first and second guesses, were slowly reshaping and moving apart. Sly felt his heartbeat race and excitement pour through his veins. Something inside told him he was finally going to play an important part in the whole dramatic saga that he'd been largely watching from the sidelines.

Chapter Twenty-Five

The picture froze as Sly rushed into the square shouting, 'Wait. Wait for me!' There was an eerie stillness and everyone's eyes turned and focused on the strange little elf, once more wearing his jumper with 81 knitted into the pattern. Those in the tower held their breath, wondering what on earth Sly knew. Capriccia stared at him as if she didn't quite recognise who he was. Fiery Tina glowered, wondering why he was trying to steal the limelight. Bernhardt just saw him as a complete pain and tutted loudly.

Sly himself didn't know what was happening. It was as if he had been possessed by a strange force and wasn't in control of his movements. He didn't even know what was unfolding in the piazza and was amazed by what he encountered. Firstly, there were the three evil ones, who he had never expected to find here. Then, he noticed that Mr Passarella was no longer standing there as a statue. He looked up at the bell tower and, instead of seeing Marianna hanging like a bat, saw a lot of little green faces and

Lars the Reindeer Whisperer. He could also just about make out Bef, peering over Lars' shoulder.

He tried to make sense of all of this, but couldn't. He noticed the hands of the ancient clock moving backwards, but didn't have a clue what that meant. It was as if he was in a weird and wonderful dream. He pinched himself, just to check.

'What are you doing here?' said the haughty Capriccia, towering above him and looking down her nose at the elf who had once been her spy in Santa's Post Office. 'I thought you were long gone,' she said, almost disappointed to see him again.

'I don't know,' said Sly. 'It was as if a voice was telling me I had to come to the square. Maybe I am here to help solve a problem. I really don't know what it is, but it feels as if I am important. As if I am the last piece in a puzzle.'

'Hardly,' said Capriccia. 'I seem to remember you jumping ship and joining the Bef woman. You thought you were better off on that side of the fence, so what possible help can you be now?'

Fiery Tina had been eavesdropping. She hopped over and butted in.

'What did you say?' she demanded. 'Did you say that you felt something was telling you that it was important that you came here?'

'Yes,' said Sly. 'But I don't know why. What's going on?'

Capriccia yawned.

'I really don't have time to tell you,' she said.

'See that clock up there, the hands are moving backwards, or are you too dumb to see that?'

'No, I can see,' he said, 'and I can see Bef. I hope she'll be pleased with me.'

'Why should she be?' yawned Capriccia again. 'Just because you chose her over us, that hardly makes you a hero.'

'I opened the door,' said Sly truthfully.

Capriccia laughed loudly.

'She's hardly going to reward you for that!' she said scornfully.

'I allowed a book to be returned to her,' explained Sly.

Capriccia smirked.

'Oh, well that makes you very important then, doesn't it!' she said in her usual sarcastic way.

Fiery Tina was taking things a little more seriously, however.

'Do you like doing nice things for the Bef woman?' she asked sweetly. 'And does she do nice things for you?'

'She let me stay in her house,' answered Sly honestly. 'I actually solved the riddle about the cement. Bef and Gaspar were very pleased with me.' He puffed his chest out with pride.

Fiery Tina looked thoughtful. She remembered her own words. She'd told Capriccia they'd perhaps been missing something: that maybe Bef loved someone that they had been over-looking or not seeing in their picture. This elf had proved very useful to her. Was it beyond the realms of possibility that he could be the final thing? Maybe she'd always secretly liked him, even when she worked with him in Santa's Post Office. She was so carried away with this idea, that it overtook her mind and drove out any rational thinking about where in the plot Sly had been when the conundrum had first been created.

She moved over to Capriccia and whispered in her ear.

'I think Sly is the we-placement eighth thing. Let's face it, there's nobody left. What do you think?'

Capriccia looked almost incredulous. Surely this annoying, jumped up elf couldn't be loved by anyone? She shook her head.

'No, she said. I can't possibly agree. There's no way she'd love this elf.'

Fiery Tina didn't like to be contradicted. She tried to force the point.

'Look awound you,' she said. 'Who or what else could it be?'

Capriccia tried to think. Bernhardt came to her rescue.

'Befland,' he said, 'or ze Coaler Coaster, or maybe her special postbox. It could also be candy balls, or even dirty, horrible coal, or maybe ze town itself.'

Fiery Tina scoffed.

'We can dismiss coal, candy and the town – they couldn't be easily statuefied. I simply we-fuse to believe she loves a postbox that much and Befland's too we-cent a development. Her shoes and bwoom have been with her for centu-wees. No, listen to what the elf said. He felt something was telling him that he had to come here today. He's been forced to come here to give us the clue. Seeing him is supposed to tell us that he is the we-placement eighth thing in the conundwum.'

Capriccia tossed her locks.

'I absolutely refuse to believe it. If we get this wrong, I shall never forgive you. I think you are sadly mistaken.'

Movement in the crowd was accompanied by whispers. A man had appeared in their midst, who they had not seen for years: a man with long, grey curly hair and a voluminous robe. He was moving between them, which was strange, as he hardly ever left his home – a house with a golden knocker shaped like a lion. Even odder was the fact that he was not alone. A Tawny Owl sat on his arm and did not blink an eye as he moved through the bodies of people observing what was happening in the piazza.

Up in the bell tower, Bef spotted her brother and gasped.

'O Dio,' she exclaimed, 'tell the Gnomes to work faster! They must turn time back very quickly. I think this is all turning sour for us. Something has happened of which we are unaware.' She looked down at Sly and wondered why he was here too.

Were the two appearances connected? She hoped not.

'There are ten more minutes to go,' advised Lars. 'Energise!' he shouted to the chain of Gnomes. We need to move time back faster.' The Gnomes responded and the hands began to spin very quickly indeed.

Fiery Tina noticed.

'Look Capwiccia,' she said. 'They have speeded up because they know we now have the answer. I command you to declare what it is that the Bef woman loves most.'

'May I say something,' said Sly, suddenly realising his importance to this whole situation. The sugar lump in him began to surface. Could he possibly get back in favour with Capriccia, if he revealed the existence of Bef's brother? He looked around and spotted Lorenzo in the crowd. Was he here to try to silence him?

Then he looked up at the bell tower and remembered how Bef had taken him in when the others had treated him in such a vile way. Why should he help Capriccia? What had she ever done for him? She'd poured bilberry juice on his head and had spent years sneering at him, using him and regarding him as a slave. Even her spinning-top act didn't amuse him any more.

He was torn. Where did his future lay? Who should he side with? What was the right thing to do and what was the wrong thing? In the end, it all became crystal clear. A voice was speaking to him, though not a soul could hear it. The voice was saying, 'Do the right thing.' Strangely, in the middle of the day, an owl hooted.

Sly opened his mouth and began to speak in a very loud voice.

'I know very well, that the final thing that the Bef woman loves is …'

In the bell tower, Bef closed her eyes and knew that it was over. The Gnomes still had to turn time back by another two minutes. She had just run out of it.

But something else happened. Capriccia had grabbed Sly by the neck of his woolly jumper and lifted him up to her shoulder height.

'What do you think you are doing elf?' she hissed. 'This is my moment of glory, not yours. What on earth do you imagine an elf like you could say that anyone would take seriously.'

Sly moved his creepy, slits of eyes from side to side, to avoid looking at her and seeing all the venom in her face.

'I was just going to tell you,' he said, 'that the final thing the Bef woman loves is me. She told me so, just before she flew to Hollywood.'

Capriccia dropped him to the ground.

'Ouch,' he shouted as he hurt his knees and nearly got kicked by her horrendous platform shoes.

She tilted back her head, looked skywards and

yelled with all her might, as she saw that only 20 seconds remained on the clock.

'The correct eighth thing the Bef woman loves is the 81st elf, who now goes by the name of Sly!'

Everyone stared at the clouds, with Capriccia, Fiery Tina and Bernhardt fully expecting to see a tick form. But instead, the clouds drew close together, darkened and formed a big, black cross. At that moment, a shrill scream shattered everyone's eardrums as Fiery Tina agonised at the failure of her marvellous conundrum.

The hands of the clock had just a few more turns to make. The Gnomes pushed with all their might and reached their goal. Time had been turned back 16 hours.

An image appeared hovering over the square. It was an image of the scene in Hollywood.

'Unscwamble the letters and tell us all who you are!' demanded a demented fairy, as a bewildered Bef looked at letters on the Hollywood hillside.

The Bef image answered slowly but clearly.

'My name is Bef and will remain Bef forever more. The letters you have up there mean nothing to me.'

A cheer went up in the clock tower.

'We've done it!' yelled Lars. 'We've turned back time and changed it. How do you feel?'

Bef, who had started to age, felt her body rejuvenating again.

'Fine,' she said. 'Everything's just fine.' She

looked down into the piazza. Lorenzo was no longer there. Keeping him secret had saved her, but why on earth had he appeared and why had be brought his treasured owl?

Fiery Tina, Capriccia and Bernhardt were now in a complete panic. Fiery Tina was a nervous wreck and more eccentric than ever. Bernhardt had no idea what to do. Surprisingly, Capriccia took the lead.

'Fly me to the Casa of Contentments,' she demanded, pushing Bernhardt hard in the back and towards his broom.

'I'm coming too,' said Fiery Tina, 'let me hop on.'

Rather than arguing about that, Capriccia put up no fight and simply smirked as they took off and escaped the angry group of people who had been in the clock tower, but who were now chasing down the steps hot in pursuit of their three, heartless enemies. Only Bef failed to move. She knew that revenge would have to wait until another day: re-launching Befland needed her attention for now.

The three evil plotters flew north, heading for Lapland and Santa's village, where they thought they would find some refuge in the Casa. The journey took several hours, but eventually Capriccia's heart leapt when she saw the pink monstrosity of a building that she called home.

'Head for the open window,' demanded Capriccia, knowing the doors would be guarded by elves. Bernhardt obliged and flew the broom to the third floor, depositing his passengers on the window ledge, so they could clamber in. Last but not least, he swivelled into the building, dragging his broom through behind him.

'We need a plan,' said Capriccia, having thought of nothing other than getting back to the safety of her Casa.

'I have a plan,' said Fiery Tina, who had come back to her senses. 'We need to set up a VIPB patch of our own. There's nothing to stop us. We can't do that here, because we can never beat Santa. I want to move the Casa to Flo-wence. We will take over the patch that I wanted to contwol all those centu-wees ago and we can wun it together, as a team. We will make the Casa a fortwess. What do you think?'

Capriccia's eyes lit up. Much as she loved her Casa, she didn't love life in Lapland. Her favourite place to shop – which she had done precious little of in recent months – was Italy. Fiery Tina's plan was genius. Being VIPB of Florence could not have suited her more. Images began to whir in her brain and, for once, she had an idea.

'It's a perfect plan,' she said, beaming at Fiery Tina. 'We can even give you a hopscotch court inside the Casa. Just take us there now, as fast as possible and make sure we don't transport any pesky elves with us!'

Fiery Tina began to murmur something, gripping her wand with both her hands. Gradually, Capriccia and Bernhardt felt the Casa lift and heard the yells of elves dropping out of the ground floor doors as it did so. Fiery Tina was in a trance, as she used all her energy to move the Casa, lock, stock and barrel, through the skies and on to Florence. Her companions were mesmerised as they saw the scenery through the windows change from the red sky of Lapland, to the golden fields around the Tuscan city. When they suddenly felt a bump and a jolt, they knew the Casa had landed.

Capriccia looked out of the window with deep satisfaction. Fiery Tina was in her element, applauding herself on the Transloco Manoeuvre, which she had just successfully completed.

'May I just say something?' said Capriccia, observing her tutor's joy.

'What's that then Capwiccia?' replied Fiery Tina, expecting a lot of praise and compliments.

'I never want to hear you mis-pronounce my name again,' said Capriccia. 'Added to that, you forced me to choose Sly as the final thing that the Bef woman loves and you got that wrong, ruining all our plans to put an end to her once and for all. Finally, I cannot put up with your ridiculous, demented behaviour any longer, which is why I have to do this.'

'What?' asked Fiery Tina. 'I doubt whether you can do anything without being told what to do.'

'That's where you are 'wong' as you would say,' sneered Capriccia. She lifted the silver wand that Fiery Tina had given to her, pointed it at Fiery Tina and uttered the word 'Combustione.'

Before her eyes, Fiery Tina began to burn, seemingly exploding into a fireball that engulfed her black tutu in black smoke and fiery red flames. Capriccia then lifted the wand again and blasted her through the window.

'What are you doing?' said Bernhardt in total shock at what he had seen.

'What I should have done ages ago.' said Capriccia. 'Just as I should have done this.' She twirled her wand in her hand and pointed it at Bernhardt.

'I always thought you'd make a perfect statue,' she said in an evil fashion. 'I'll be able to hang my necklaces round your toilet brush hair.'

One second later, she turned him to stone – the best broom artisan in the world was left in the centre of her Casa, without his broom and pointing a finger at her in anger at her actions.

Capriccia laughed in a most insane manner and flicked her hair around with glee as she envisaged life as the VIPB of Florence, delivering presents on Bernhardt's broom. All of a sudden, as she began to spin in delight, a juicy globular spider fell out of her locks and scurried down her dress and across the floor. Capriccia screamed in horror and tried to squash it with her big platform shoe, but missed. It scuttled away into her perfume collection and disappeared from view, as Capriccia freaked out and sobbed when she realised nobody could possibly help.

Bernhardt managed to open his mouth a fraction, just before the final part of his body turned to stone.

'Two of zem there always are,' he laughed maniacally.

29333463R00193

Made in the USA
Charleston, SC
09 May 2014